WAHKAN CORRIDOR

by

Stephen T. Gerdel

Wahkan Corridor

By Stephen T. Gerdel

Published by
Strategic Partners Group, LLC
705 Windy Ridge Dr.
Washington, MO 63090
www.thestrategicpub.com

Edited by Beth Swoboda

Cover design by Katy Tapley

ISBN 978-0-9978118-0-3

WAHKAN CORRIDOR

The Story Continues

by

Stephen T. Gerdel

List of Main Characters

Mike Trapper	Special Agent to the President
Angela Crain	Dept of Homeland Security, Washington DC
David Carapella	Presidential transition team leader
Alex Hodson	FBI, Washington DC
Ray Jergins	Department of Justice, Washington DC
Matt Kreiter	White House Secret Service
Capt. Steven Granger	Special Agent & Mike's best friend
August White	Central Intelligence Agency
Ronald Hunter	President-elect of the United States
Al Makin	President of the United States
Col. Aaron Stevens	MidWest Office of Counter Terrorism (OCT)
Keith Dillon	OCT technician
Robert Hitchens	Retired Special Forces
Yolanda Hitchens	Former Dallas hotel maid & Robert's wife
Failak Jahnangir	OIC MISC Communications compound
Elli Trapper	Mike Trapper's wife
Samantha Granger	Steve Granger's wife
Daniel Sim	Singapore Deputy Commissioner
Susan Hunter	President Hunter's wife
Wang Zhu	Chinese Ambassador to the United States
Perry Hitchens	Sheriff, Norman, OK, Robert's father
Kouzen, Mick Kohen	International spy, double-agent
Dmitri Fyodorovych	Russian lobbyist assigned to Washington DC
Brad Gentry	Hijack leader

This book is dedicated to

Leandra Lewis

For her plot creativity
and inspiration

chapter 1

Wahkan Corridor – 3:15 PM AFT
18,549 Elevation - 37°14'06.68"N 74°39'23.80"E

The two Marines moved quickly to pack the sensitive gear that had guided the highly-sophisticated drone to the mountain target. The mission had been a success, so far.

"Sergeant, are they still coming?" the captain said while he placed the collapsible antenna into its carrying case. He looked across the surrounding peaks. Snowcapped summits cluttered the landscape for as far as he could see. *How can such desolation even exist?*

The chopper had struggled with the high altitude carrying the two-man team to the drop-off point at fourteen thousand feet. It had taken two days to climb the last five thousand feet to their present position. Their return would be much quicker, only a matter of hours on skis, and all down hill. The HH-60W Black Hawk helicopter, dubbed the 60-Whiskey, would meet them at the extraction point.

The sergeant positioned himself and pointed his Oberwerk 25/40x100mm binoculars toward the smoldering wreckage of the secret communications hub. He focused on the craggy south face of mount Qala-e Mufushad just over seven miles away.

"Cap, they're still coming."

"How many?"

"Hard to tell. Twenty, maybe thirty."

"Let me see." The captain slid on his belly in the snow beside the sergeant and took the binoculars. The huge boulders of the mountain face appeared as rocks that could be held in one's hand. The men moving toward their position were little more than specks from such a distance. But the line was moving along a ridge and coming toward them.

"Damn."

"How'd they know we were here?" the sergeant asked.

"Well, until an hour ago they had some pretty sophisticated equipment. Maybe they had something that sensed our transmissions to the drone. Maybe they saw us. I don't know. The problem is, they're coming, and we need to go."

The sergeant stowed the binoculars and finished packing the transponder unit. The captain carefully placed the control box in its container. That piece of equipment had allowed him to pilot the stealthy drone between the peaks and along the mountain valleys using undetectable short-burst wave transmissions.

The drone had delivered a counter-electronics high-powered microwave advanced missile projectile device in a precision strike on the compound. The weapon killed the electronics without injuring human beings. However, injuries could never be totally avoided. Anyone sitting near a computer monitor could receive burns or be temporarily blinded by the electronic flash.

The captain stood and glanced eastward to the smoking mountain top. *Maybe if they had strapped some C-4 to that warhead the Daesh wouldn't be coming after us.* He snickered at his personal joke.

"What's that, cap?"

"Nothing, sergeant. Just wishful thinking."

He helped the sergeant shoulder the transponder unit, and then swung the lighter pack to his back. The two soldiers stomped hard into their ski bindings. The captain took one more look to the east. He didn't like what was coming after them.

"Let's do this." They began their descent along the face of the snow packed mountain.

White House – 7:55 AM EST

"Mike. Do you have a minute?"

"Yes, Mr. President. What's up?" Mike Trapper stopped and turned toward the president, Al Makin. He had served President Makin as his chief of staff for more than three years, and the two men had become close friends.

"Would you come by my office after the briefing? I'm somewhat out of the loop these days. The transition is more of a chore than I had imagined. Do you mind?"

Mike nodded. "No, not at all. I think I would enjoy a little time chit-chatting with the president of the United States."

"Not for too much longer, though," the president said tossing his hands in the air and spinning a whimsical grin. Al Makin had chosen not to run for a second term after the assassination of President Harriet Marshall. The horror and weight of the first week of his presidency had never left him. Most of the country had been busy rebuilding from the damage of the invasion. Few noticed how the experience had weakened President Makin. Mike had seen the full effect.

"You will always be Mr. President to me, and to anyone who loves this country. You know that."

"I do. I look forward to talking with you."

"Me, too, Mr. President." Mike smiled as he turned and continued down the hall. These corridors held a special significance to him. He would never forget seeing Chinese soldiers lining the halls of the White House. The surreal events of that week only three years in the past seemed as vivid as last night's nightmare. *Maybe it took a toll on me too.* He felt a silent shudder deep inside.

The transition team for the newly-elected president had been setting up in the Cabinet Room since two weeks after the election. The team consisted of individuals from both administrations whose job was to confer with representatives of every major department of government. Mike knew all of them.

Mike entered the Cabinet room and walked straight to the coffee bar. He had left Elli asleep earlier in the morning and skipped breakfast. He was glad to see rolls and fresh fruit had already arrived.

Angela Crain, with the Department of Homeland Security, smiled as she greeted him. "Mike, it's been a while. Where have you been keeping yourself?"

He looked up at her and smiled. "Just here. But I'm always glad to see a happy face. How have you been, Angela?" Mike poured her a cup of steaming coffee, then one for himself.

"You know, just keeping the country safe. How are Elli and the kids?"

Mike was pleasantly surprised. Angela had not always been so affable. "They are all fine. Kids are getting big though." Mike excused himself to greet the members of the president-elect's team.

As the representative of the sitting president, Mike held the responsibility of making sure the transition team had every bit of information they required, as well as every creature comfort possible. He felt more like a butler than a presidential representative.

"Good morning, David," he said extending his hand to the new team leader, David Carapella. A flood of faces, most of them new to Mike, flowed into the room behind him.

"Hi, Mike. I think President-elect Hunter will be joining us this morning. Just thought you should know."

"That's fine. I'll notify President Makin."

It had become a matter of protocol since the Chinese incident that the president and president-elect would not meet face-to-face in the White House. The risk of losing both men at once had become a concern. It was an extreme measure and probably unnecessary, but precaution had taken on a new value. Mike spoke to an aide who hurried off to advise President Makin.

"Do you know when President-elect Hunter will arrive?" Mike asked.

"I expect him momentarily."

Men and women crowded into the room, each representing their various departments of government. Each was followed by more associates and aides. Mike acknowledged Alex Hodson, Federal Bureau of Investigation; Ray Jergins, Department of Justice; Matt Kreiter, Secret Service; and Steven Granger, special agent to the president, which was Mike's old job. Last to enter the room was August White from the Central Intelligence Agency. Mike had met him only once, and it wasn't under the best of circumstances.

As time had passed and the events of the battle at Oak Mountain Power Plant had slipped into memory, suspicious reports surfaced casting doubt regarding the incidents. Much of what had occurred around the country, and even in the White House, had been brought into question, posing that the reports were exaggerated, or that the event had never happened at all. A quiet investigation lacked the proof of who spread the fabrications, but every indication pointed to none other than August White. Mike had very good reasons to not trust him.

Everyone was just settling into their seats when David Carapella spoke loudly to the group. "Ladies and gentlemen, the president of the United States!"

The president-elect's entire team immediately stood to their feet.

Well, yeah, but like . . . tomorrow, Mike thought. *We still have a sitting president, and the Inauguration isn't until tomorrow! What's going on?*

Those who had served with President Makin glanced at each other and slowly stood to their feet. It was unprecedented for a president-elect to command the pomp and ceremony of a sitting president. It would be fine after the Inauguration. Mike was half expecting someone to play a recording of *Hail to the Chief* as he entered.

President-elect Ronald Hunter swept into the room wearing a perfectly cultivated candidate's smile, lots of teeth, ear-to-ear. He was fifty-eight years old, moderately athletic, and overall a very impressive man. He beamed with approval at the adulation his team members lavished on him.

Ray Jergins caught Mike's eye. His face registered an unspoken *WTF?* Matt Kreiter sat perfectly still, reflecting no emotion or surprise. Mike realized his own mouth was hanging open.

President-elect Hunter made his way around the room shaking hands and making individual comments to each person. He knew a little about everyone. *That's pretty impressive*, Mike thought, his neck stiffened by reflex.

The room grew quiet as everyone settled into their seats. Mike's primary function was to facilitate the meeting. *Master of ceremonies and butler.* He shook it off.

"I'd like to welcome you all again. We have made significant progress this last week and are pleased that President-elect Hunter could be with us today."

A smattering of applause moved around the room. Everyone smiled. Ray Jergins moved his gaze to the floor.

"The first order of business—"

"Uh, excuse me Mr. Trapper. I'm sorry to interrupt, but there is a very important matter of national security we must discuss," August White, CIA, said, standing at his chair.

"I'm sorry, Mr. White, but the agenda that was agreed upon by both administrations—"

"I know this is irregular, but we just received some very important information about which President Hunter must be advised."

"Is this information classified?"

"Special Access Protocol. Higher than Top Secret."

Mike stood. "Everyone who does not have Special Access clearance will need to leave right now. Thank you." Nearly the entire room stood and made their way to one of the doors leading to the hallway. Those who remained were mostly from the sitting administration. The room quieted and the doors closed.

"Mr. White?"

"Thank you, Mr. Trapper, and again I apologize for the interruption to the agenda. The information I am going to share is regarding a mission that is currently underway. It is highly classified and must not leave this room. A high value MISC target has been destroyed. For years we have sought to eliminate the communication hub used by terrorist groups around the world. We could never locate it. But recently, we did."

"When was the target hit?" Steven Granger asked.

"Within the last thirty minutes. We—"

"Wait," Mike interrupted. "Are you telling us this is happening right now?"

"Yes. The equipment that was used in the attack is Special Access classified. Our men on the ground flew the drone to the site in very tight quarters. They also provided visual confirmation of the strike."

"We have troops on the ground?" Mike asked.

"Yes. We have a team in the Wahkan Corridor."

"Hold on," Angela broke in again. "The Wah-kan what?"

"The Wahkan Corridor is in the panhandle of northeast Afghanistan. It's a stretch of land left as a buffer between Tajikstan and Pakistan after World War II. On the far eastern end, it borders China. It's believed Marco Polo actually traveled through the valley, the Wahkan Corridor, and returned to his homeland with silk from China. For centuries it's been called the Silk Road."

"But we have soldiers up there *right now*?" Mike insisted. Public outcry against American troops on the ground in Iraq and Afghanistan had been intense. A military presence was acknowledged but little was ever said about what the troops were actually doing in the Middle East.

"Yes. We sent in a small commando team to do the fly-in and confirm the kill on the target."

"Fly-in . . . *exactly* what do you mean by that?" Alex Hodson asked.

"The compound was built on top of a mountain more than sixteen thousand feet above sea level. Navigating a multi-million-dollar drone to a close proximity strike with sophisticated ordnance sometimes requires special forces."

"I don't see the problem," Angela said, sitting upright and raising her hand to make the point. "Why can't we just send in a cruise missile and blow it up?"

"Collateral damage, for one. The higher ups didn't want to risk the lives of possible innocents. Secondly, the drone flew into an area of Afghanistan that's only five miles wide. Pakistan is a few hundred yards to the south, and China is about the same on the east. A fighter would not be able to drop the ordnance, effectively reverse course, and return without a potential airspace violation of a sovereign nation, much less a hostile one. A cruise missile could destroy everything, but a malfunction, or some sort of jamming device might send it off course. We didn't want to risk that."

"What ordnance was used? Wouldn't collateral damage happen anyway?"

"Mike, I can call you Mike, right?" Mike nodded. "The drone carried a counter-electronic high-powered microwave advanced missile projectile, called CHAMPS, with the capacity to destroy all of the electronic equipment in the compound."

Mike could not believe what he was hearing. "But—"

"An EMP bomb?" Granger asked.

"Even more effective." August White looked around the table at the blank faces of people who were left speechless by what he was saying.

"But help me here," Angela pressed. "What makes this communication facility, way up in the mountains, such a valuable target?"

"We believe it is the primary source of terrorist communication. Destroying it shuts down their entire network. The attack leaves every terrorist in Iraq and Syria blind. Terrorist groups across the Middle East and around the world will find themselves without orders. Hopefully it forces them to use less covert means of communication. At least, that's what we're hoping for. For a short period of time, we have the advantage. They no longer have a secret method of communication. We hope the confusion will draw many terrorist groups out into the open, so to speak.

"You are all aware of the recruiting efforts we have seen in the expanding operations of different terrorist organizations around the world. First, we saw Al Qaeda, then ISIL, or ISIS, whichever you prefer, and most recently MISC. I know there has been a lot of confusion regarding this group, especially their name. It is *not* MISC-ellaneous. The acronym stands for the Mahdi Islamic State Caliphate. It is pronounced *misk*, the 'C' is a hard 'K' sound.

"*Misk* is an ancient name. It's actually mentioned in the Qur'an. That gives it special meaning to Muslims. Literally, the name means 'musk' or a perfume. It's implied in their teaching that the shedding of the blood of infidels is a sweet aroma to Allah. Thus, *MISC* brings death to sinners, and that pleases Allah."

"Well, good for us. Never wanted to piss off Allah," Ray Jergins interjected sarcastically. "Who, or what is this Mahdi?"

"Mahdi is the savior for Islam. According to legend, this guy is going to remove all sin from the world. Jesus Christ is supposed to help him at the Second Coming. It's all legend, and as far as I'm concerned it's hokum. But these guys believe it."

"You mean someone like the Twelfth Imam, right?" Steve asked, leaning forward and putting his elbows on the table

"Yes. They are convinced that the Second Coming is just around the corner and Allah has given them the task of cleaning up as much sin as they possibly can. Of course, the biggest sinner on the planet is the Great Satan . . . the United States.

"So, they've been recruiting like mad all over the world, telling young men how they can serve Allah and bring on the Second Coming. That's been the problem. They operate on the dark side of the Web through a grouping of sub-channels that are neither licensed nor regulated. They use them constantly. We've known that for months. What we haven't known until very recently is where it all comes from."

"How can you confirm this was a secret communications hub? Or better yet, how did you find it?" Mike asked.

"Shortly before the election we stumbled across it, and I mean totally by accident. We captured a light-beam transmission on a digital image that pinpointed the origin. Had to be by chance, but an image was taken at the very instant a transmission was sent.

"While doing routine satellite mapping, a technician at NOAA detected an aberration in the digital signal. The VizLab system is used primarily to detect climate variation to help project weather patterns. The data picked up by the satellite is very sensitive to temperatures. As they measured the temperature of the mountains, mostly frozen rock, ice, and snow, a beam was detected registering a temperature common to communication lasers. We use them to communicate with satellites all the time. The heat signature ran in a straight line from the very tip of the panhandle in Afghanistan, to a point high in the mountains, one hundred miles south of Tehran. That led us to begin satellite surveillance of the compound in the Hindu Kush Mountains."

"So, their base up in the mountains is destroyed?" Granger asked.

"We believe so. At least the recruitment and propaganda part is."

"How much of a window do we have to further degrade their capabilities?"

"It's hard to say, Mr. Granger. We've already sent alerts to our Offices of Counter Terrorism in Little Rock, Zurich, Hong Kong, Singapore, and Johannesburg to watch for increased chatter. We expect terrorist cells all over the world to react to their network's failing. I'd say everyone should be very watchful over the next thirty-six hours."

Steve Granger sat back in his seat. "If this is the hub, how are plans and information distributed worldwide?"

"That's the million-dollar question," White replied. "We know the folks in Iran have duplicated a silent distribution system much like the WhisperNet program used to dispatch books to individual Kindle appliances. Transmitting several hundred pages of data to a certain terrorist cell anywhere in the world can be done in an instant.

We only suspect that's the method, but we have no idea where that hub is."

"And this is a CIA operation?" Angela asked.

"Yes, supported by the United States military."

"And we have men up there right now, right?" Mike asked.

"Yes, sir, we do. And we need to get them out."

"Before anyone leaves . . ." President-elect Hunter had been silent. He raised his hand and leaned forward in his seat. "I want this kept secret. Not a word of this gets out. Not . . . one . . . word. Am I clear?"

Several "*Yes, Mr. President*" comments were muttered around the room. Those of the old guard, those with experience, shot quick glances back and forth.

Mike caught Ray Jergins's eye. This time Ray mouthed the words "*What the. . .*"

chapter 2

Wahkan Corridor – 4:25 PM AFT

Olympic downhill racers can reach speeds in excess of ninety-five miles per hour. The captain felt they were close to that speed, even though he knew they were not.

It has to be the pressure of being pursued. He signaled the sergeant to come to a stop. They dug their skis into the snow pack sideways, spraying crystals of ice and snow across the shimmering surface.

"In a minute we're going to move behind that ridge, and we won't be able to see if they are still coming toward us."

"I'll check," the sergeant replied, pulling his binoculars from the case strapped to his chest. He focused on the mountain face below the still smoldering compound. "Yep. The bastards are hot-footin' it in our direction."

"I figure we have another mile before we need to ditch the skis and go on foot. What I don't know is if those guys are the only ones coming. We need to keep watch ahead as well."

The sergeant swung his glasses down into the canyon below them. A little more than a mile downrange the snow gave way to the rocky landscape. It might as well have been Mars. He stood perfectly still, slowly scanning the mountainsides.

"I don't see nuthin', Cap."

"Let's keep moving. We still have four hours until the chopper arrives."

The two men, loaded with heavy equipment, poled themselves to a fast speed for the last stretch of snow.

If we can reach the rocks in the next forty-five minutes, we might have a chance. The captain knew how quickly the enemy was able to run up steep, rocky grades. He'd seen the Mujahideen scamper up mountains and nimbly run along narrow ledges with dizzying skill. They were like machines, and he didn't expect those following them were any less skilled.

The soldiers' packs were heavy and cumbersome. Trudging through the rocky gorge would be slow going compared to that their pursuers.

We need more time.

White House, Oval Office – 8:35 AM EST

"Mr. President," Mike said as he entered.

"Good. Finally someone I can talk to." He stood and walked around his desk to greet Mike. President Makin looked tired. Every president ages while in office. It's part of the job. Al Makin had been ill prepared for his ascent to the presidency. The events that brought him to the office still weighed on him. "Mike, what's going on? I can't get anyone to talk to me. It's like I left office last month or something."

"Sir, I'm afraid that attitude is all around us. It was very strange in the briefing. President-elect Hunter was acting like a president, being treated like the president, and obeyed as if he already holds the reins of power."

"He just about does, Mike."

"I know, Mr. President. It just seems to me the sort of swagger I saw in the Cabinet Room would be more appropriate after the Inauguration."

"Listen, it is a much better atmosphere for the change of administrations than the last one. I think the country needs that confidence. Maybe it will help everything remain calm a while longer. Maybe it's a good thing."

"Mr. President, I hope you're right."

"What was all the secrecy about? I mean everybody out in the hall? You can tell me. I'm the commander-in-chief." He smiled. He had never been a commander. He still wasn't. He could delegate well, he could approve ideas that someone had presented, but he wasn't a commander.

"We've hit a major hub that has shut down the MISC communication network." Mike told the president the details that had been shared in the closed session with the CIA chief. A serious scowl crossed the president's face.

"They actually *used* a CHAMPS device?"

"That's what he told us. Is there a problem there?"

"Could be," the president said. "From what I've been told, the CHAMPS system is very finicky. I imagine that's why those poor boys had to fly it in. It's effective, but difficult to deploy."

"And that's why we needed men on the ground."

"Yes. But they need to get *out*." Al Makin's eyes widened. "It is very important we get those boys out of there as soon as possible."

"I believe that's going on right now. From what White said, the compound was hit about an hour ago, then the soldiers needed to get back down the mountain to an altitude the chopper can fly in. He didn't give us the extraction time."

"Let's hope the rest of the mission goes well. That control box in the wrong hands could be a serious problem." President Makin seemed detached for the moment. As if he was imagining himself on that mountain, making his escape. Concern was etched deep in his expression.

"Mr. President?"

"Oh . . . sorry. Sometimes the reality that I will walk away from all this tomorrow gets mixed up with how serious things are today. Tough thing to sort out, Mike."

"Sir, I can only imagine."

"Right. Well, you need to get your personal stuff together, same as I. Is everything all set at NSA?"

"Yeah, I think it's a go. I'm getting a little bit of a pay hike and my own department."

"International intelligence, right?"

"Yes, sir. And they promise it's a nine-to-five job." Mike smiled.

The president returned a grin and said, "And of course anything promised in Washington D.C. is ironclad."

Mike snickered. Deep inside he knew the promise of regular hours would never be kept.

Mid West Office of Counter Terrorism (OCT), Little Rock, AR 7:45 AM CST

Colonel Aaron Stevens folded open the pages of the Democrat-Gazette and grunted at the headline, "I-30 Corridor construction through downtown snares traffic."

"Tell me something I don't know," he muttered, reflecting on his morning commute. Colonel Stevens was looking forward to retirement. The hassle of maintaining the daily grind was beginning to be more apparent to him. He was crabby.

The nightmare of the assassination and invasion of the United States borders haunted him. His job was to know what was going to happen before it happened, not as it happened, and never *after* the fact. The heavy traffic on his commute in had made him cranky before his day began.

"Colonel, got a minute?" asked Keith Dillon, a top OCT technician, as he entered.

Stevens crumpled his paper in his lap and peered over his readers with a distasteful scowl. "What?"

"Traffic," Keith replied curtly.

"Yeah, I know all about it." The paper was returned to its former position blocking out the rest of the world. "Really pisses me off."

"No. *Internet* traffic. Super heavy. We haven't seen anything like this since 9/11."

Stevens bolted from his chair, crumpling the paper, and moved quickly around his desk. "Are you sure? What kind of traffic? Where's it coming from? Have you been able to determine who's sending it? What's it about—"

"Hold on! Come over here." Keith's lanky strides required Stevens to nearly jog to keep up. Stevens would have muttered under his breath about a slower pace, but he sensed this was important.

"Colonel, about twenty minutes ago we received a DHS notice regarding a step-up in Internet traffic. I didn't think much about it. You know, stuff like that might happen anytime, or not. No sooner than I set the memo aside, the whole thing blew up like crazy."

They turned the corner and entered the Grid Room.

"When you say *blew up*, what do you—ho-lee crap!" Stevens stopped in his tracks.

One entire wall of the Grid Room held a massive screen that displayed worldwide Internet usage. Corporations employed similar programs to purchase unused bandwidth, maintain communications links with international accounts, and transfer of information of sales or production requirements around the world. Google used the same information to place ads in social network sites to drive up business for advertisers.

The OTC used the data transfers to monitor and locate potential security threats and terrorist activity. Normal corporate communications and business transfers were color coded in soft pastels and light shades of blue. Suspected terrorist Internet usage was coded in oranges and reds.

The entire room glowed in a soft orange luminosity, casting a tinge of alarm over the twenty-two men and women at their consoles. The center of the world map along the Equator was a blaze of orange. Shimmering strands of red and orange stretched from Central America, across northern Africa covering the entire Middle East, and reaching as far as Indonesia.

"When did this start?" Stevens demanded.

"No more than three minutes ago. Everything was normal, and then *boom*, it went nuts."

"Okay, I want every point of origin noted. I want to know where *and* who. Now! I want end points identified as well." Stevens was barking orders that even he knew were not necessary. "Let's get on this, people!"

They were on it. The team members were furiously tagging and tracing hundreds of transmissions. *Something has happened. Something is going on!* Stevens turned to Keith and said, "Ride these transmissions like your life depends on it. I'm going to call Trapper."

Colonel Aaron Stevens and Mike had never met face to face, but they had a history. The events following the assassination of President Harriet Marshall nearly three years earlier had bound the two men together with an unbreakable trust. Stevens knew that if Mike was in the White House he would have his finger on the pulse of whatever had transpired in the last few minutes.

Stevens rounded the corner into his office and grabbed his phone as he sat at his desk. Mike's number was still on his auto dial. As he sat in his desk chair he heard Mike's voice.

"Trapper."

"Mike, Aaron Stevens at OCT in Little Rock."

"I had a feeling you'd be calling."

"Well, you know more than I do. We have experienced a huge increase in underground traffic in the last few minutes. I've never seen anything like it. What the hell is going on?"

"Already?" Mike's tone gave away his surprise.

"You were expecting something? I'm in the dark here. What's happening?"

"We hit their communications hub, or at least we think it's a hub."

"Damn straight, you hit something huge. We haven't seen an up-tick in traffic like this in . . . well, ever!"

Mike brought Colonel Stevens up to speed on the attack.

"This sounds exactly like the outcome the CIA was hoping for when they ordered the strike," Mike said. "I think they were hoping we might rediscover a lot of people who have gone dark in the last six or seven years."

"No question about that. Our boards have gone crazy."

"As soon as you compile the data, get it to me. We're going to move on this very quickly."

"Already putting it together. I should have the first batch of confirmed locations to you in the next ten minutes. Is that soon enough?"

"Perfect. I imagine we'll be getting similar information from Hong Kong, Zurich, Singapore, and Johannesburg very soon. Thanks Aaron. We have to chase this thing down fast."

"Will do, Mike." Colonel Stevens lowered his phone to its cradle. "Ho-lee crap."

Shangri-La Tanjung Aru Resort, Koto Kinabalu, Malaysia
8:55 PM BNT

"Okay, Dad," Robert said into his phone. "We'll see you tomorrow night in Oklahoma City. Love you. See you then." When he talked to his father Oklahoma seemed much closer than half a world away.

"Robert! Come look at the sunset." Yolanda beamed with excitement as she stood at the edge of the balcony. Their two-week honeymoon was drawing to a close. She treasured every moment. She made sure Robert didn't miss a thing.

"Sweetheart, the sun goes down every night, just like back home. What's the big deal?" He walked up behind her and wrapped his arms around her.

"My goodness, have you ever seen such a wonderful view?" An amber sun flooded the horizon silhouetting Mamutik Island. The golden rays of waning sunlight melted into crimson, finally dropping into purplish-blue darkness high overhead.

"I have to admit, this was worth the wait," he said softly.

Robert Hitchens and Yolanda Vasquez had met on Interstate 35 just outside Norman, Oklahoma, at a citizens' barricade established to stop an advancing army of insurgents who had invaded through the southern border. Robert and Yolanda had been together ever since. They had waited nearly three years and finished their degrees before planning a wedding. Robert had completed his Masters in Criminal Justice and Yolanda, a degree in business. Their friendship had blossomed, and they had married just before the new year.

Yolanda was fun-loving but had a will of tempered steel. In Robert's arms she discovered she was soft and pliable. Melting. She laid her head on his chest and pulled his muscular arms tightly around her.

"You're right," Robert said softly into her ear. "Nothing compares to a tropical sunset."

"Not even sunsets in Oklahoma?" She grinned, turning her face toward his.

"Not even Oklahoma sunsets."

"Not even sunsets in Wichita?" Her grin broadened as she teased him.

"Nope. Not even Wichita sunsets." He was smiling.

Yolanda looked at her husband. She felt as if she was about to explode with happiness. "Not even . . . me?" She began to laugh.

"You just went over the line, lady." Robert swept her into his arms, and she squealed with delight. He took two steps into their room and stopped. His face was very close to hers. He spoke softly his warm breath caressed her cheek. "Nothing on this planet is as beautiful as you."

She kissed him as he lowered her gently onto their bed. "Robert, do we have to go home? I don't want this to end."

"This . . . this, right here, it doesn't matter where we are. *This* will never end." Passion flooded over them as darkness claimed the tropical night.

Wahkan Corridor – 5:05 PM AFT

"Can you see them?"

"No, sir. They've moved behind the ridge."

Failak Jahnangir had served with the Mujahideen since he was twelve. First, as a goat-herding spy for the real fighting men, then as one of the thousands of holy warriors who scampered up mountainsides tormenting Russian troops. After the Russians had invaded his homeland, he trusted no one. He hated the pasty white Europeans and Americans as much as any Russian.

"We must move faster." Failak's slight frame enabled him to leap from boulder to boulder like a coiled spring. Even at age fifty-three he could outpace the younger soldiers. He was proud of the strength Allah had given him to wage jihad, but humble enough to recognize the source of that strength. Himself, Allah, and pure hate.

Those who had left the burning compound by truck took the long way around on the road, or what served as a road. He felt sad for them. Real warriors for Allah ran through the mountains with the grace of a mountain goat at alarming speed. Running through seven miles of rugged terrain was nothing.

chapter 3

White House – 9:20 AM EST

Mike left the Oval Office and turned down the hall toward the Cabinet Room. He was hoping August White would still be around. He had a few questions he wanted answered.

Mike opened the door to the Cabinet Room and immediately realized he had interrupted a serious conversation. President-elect Hunter, David Carapella, and August White were huddled at the far end of the conference table speaking in hushed voices. They all turned toward Mike as he entered.

"Sorry, didn't mean to interrupt," he said as he backed toward the door.

"No, Mike. Come in, please," Ronald Hunter said stepping toward him. "We can all use some of your expertise."

"Okay." *Be careful here, buster. You are going to get schmoozed or set up for something.* "As long as I'm not interrupting." Mike closed the door and walked toward the three men.

"David, what were those items we were going to ask Mr. Trapper about? Do you have that list with you?"

"Yes, Mr. President." David Carapella immediately began shuffling through a stack of yellow note pads. "I saw it here . . . just a bit . . . Here it is."

He turned to Mike with a smile on his face, but Mike could see the blank look in his eyes. He *had* interrupted something. Mike glanced at August White who kept his eyes averted.

"Are you sure this is okay?" Mike asked again.

"No problem," President-elect Hunter said. "David, pick Mike's brain a bit and I'll step across the hall with Mr. White for a few minutes." Across the hall meant they were going into the Roosevelt Room. A nagging feeling told Mike something was underway. He didn't feel good about it.

Ronald Hunter and Mr. White left the room.

"All right. I think I have everything here." David Carapella stopped fumbling with papers, smiled, and squared himself off, facing Mike with a hundred transition questions.

Mike smiled faintly. *This is not what I had in mind . . .*

Wahkan Corridor – 5:35 PM AFT

The captain and sergeant slowed to a stop. They hadn't made great time coming down the mountain. The lower elevation was warmer and the snow pack less suitable for a rapid descent.

"Check both behind us and down into the canyon."

The sergeant focused his glasses back up the mountain, straining to catch any movement no matter how small.

He turned and peered down into the canyon. "Still nothin' that way, cap." The steep slopes were littered with boulders, jagged rocks, and baseball-sized gravel. No life, no vegetation, nothing but broken, grey rock. He looked behind them. "It's clear up there, too . . . so far."

The young sergeant returned his binoculars to their case and faced the captain. "It's your call. Do we go on or set up an ambush?"

"Do you mean a surprise attack of two against twenty . . . or thirty Mujahideen?"

"Makes it about even, right?" The young sergeant broke a smile and began removing his skis.

"Leave the skis. They know we're here, and they probably know we're going down the mountain, so it's not like we're giving them any clues. We just need to get the hell out of here."

The skis clattered on the rocks as the two soldiers discarded them, tossing them it different directions.

"Who knows, maybe they won't see 'em."

"Fat chance, sergeant. We've gotta cover eight klicks as fast as we can. Lace up tight." Both men checked their boot lacings, shouldered their packs and headed into the canyon. From their starting point they had skied down three thousand feet in elevation. The ridges on either side of the canyon were serrated rock blades, separated by a mile and a half of empty space. The canyon floor lay two thousand feet below, between the mountain ridges.

Rocks clattered down the slope under the heavy weight of the soldiers and their equipment. When the steep mountainside slipped from under them, they rode the small avalanche until they could gain their footing. Down, and down quickly was the goal, and hopefully in one piece.

The two men ran and leaped down the jagged face. Their pursuers were behind them, probably gaining ground. Stopping was not an option.

White House, Oval Office – 9:50 AM EST

Mike tapped gently on the Oval Office door standing in the secretary's office. He heard the president's voice from the other side.

"Come in."

"Excuse me, Mr. President. Do you have a minute?"

"It seems that is all I have. In a few minutes I'm sure someone is going to come along and boot me out of this place."

"I doubt that will happen, sir."

He could tell Al Makin was collecting his mementoes and personal items. Many were already gone, but the things the president had treasured most were left until last to pack. His secretary and two aides were assisting him with loading the boxes.

"Do you mind if we speak privately?" Mike asked.

"Let's go into the study."

The president's private study was through the door in the west wall of the Oval Office. It was the private office where a former president had entertained private sessions with White House interns. That fact caused Mike to shudder every time he had entered the room. President Makin seemed to be fine with the history of the room.

"Okay, Mike, what's going on?"

"Shortly after I left you, I got a call from Aaron Stevens at OCT in Little Rock. Moments before he called they had experienced a huge up-tick in Internet chatter. I think that's the proof that we hit a nerve at that compound up in the mountains."

"Have you discussed this with President-elect Hunter?"

"No. I tried to bring it up but he brushed me off with some admin BS with David Carapella. We can go to my office and check what OCT sent. It's probably just sitting there waiting for me."

"Let's go. A little adventure might do me some good about now."

Mike and the president left the study through the dining room and into the hallway to Mike's office. The West Wing was buzzing as men and women, all fresh faces to government, busied themselves with becoming acquainted with the building. Those who would not be retained by the new administration were quietly sorting their belongings and packing.

"Molly, has anything come in from OCT?" Mike asked upon entering his outer office. Molly had worked at the State Department before the events at Oak Mountain Nuclear Power Plant. Mike had sought her out and brought her in as his personal secretary.

"Yes, Mr. Trapper," she said turning from the box she was packing. "Oh! Mr. President. I didn't realize—"

"Hi, Molly. You can almost just call me Al. I'm almost unemployed." He smiled like a high school student ready for summer break.

"No, sir. It's always Mr. President." She smiled back. "Mr. Trapper, the pages should be in your machine tray."

"Thanks, Molly." Mike walked past her and into his office. "Yes, they're right here." Mike hurriedly scanned the pages from Little Rock. "Wow. They're turning up a ton of leads. Mr. President, we are seeing email from subjects we lost track of four years ago. Some from Central America, New Zealand, and—" He looked up sharply at the president.

"What is it, Mike?"

"Some here in the States," he said flatly. The color drained from his face as memories flooded his mind. He had felt the same after his second tour in Iraq. They called it battle fatigue. For a brief moment the feeling swept over him, but then faded.

"Are you all right, Mike?" The president came to his side, putting his hand on Mike's shoulder. "Do you need to sit?"

"No . . . no, thank you, sir. I'm fine." He looked at his friend, and smiled slightly as the color returned to his face.

"That was certainly unusual for you."

"I know. I guess it proves that none of us are unaffected by events, or even trauma. Sometimes it just pops up. It just now . . . well, popped."

"Who else is getting this information from OCT?"

"At the moment, I don't really know. I can call Aaron and ask him."

"Do that. In the meantime, I'm contacting some people who can put the big picture together for me. After all, I *am* the president of the United States." He turned and quickly left the room.

White House, Roosevelt Room – 10:05 AM

"So, we're good with all that, right?" President-elect Hunter asked.

"I don't see a problem with any of it. I think everyone expects some celebration. And personally, I think this town has been down in the dumps for too long. I mean, for God's sake, three years of depressing leadership is more than enough." August White had never been a fan of President Makin. His departure from office was a reason for celebration, even a personal celebration.

"Okay, I just don't want to overdo it."

"I don't think it can be overdone. At least half the country is ready to put this terrible time behind us and get back to normal. Let's have some fun for a change."

"I couldn't agree more, Mr. White." Ronald Hunter smiled and firmly slapped August White's shoulder.

Mr. White turned and began gathering his papers from the conference table.

"Oh, and one more thing," the president-elect said stopping short of the door. "This little operation in Afghanistan. I want to hold on to it for a couple of days. You know, keep it under wraps. Can we do that?"

"Certainly, Mr. President. That's no problem at all." Mr. White was curious. *Why does he want to hold it back?* He decided to risk it. "Do you mind my asking why you want me to sit on it? In reality, it never has to be made public at all."

"No, I want it out there. I just want . . . well, you know, I want it to look like it was my idea. Sorta puts me out front, on top of my game, as it were. Like in the first couple of days of my first term I'm really takin' it to the bad guys. Know what I mean?"

"Absolutely, chief. I can make that happen."

"Good." Ronald Hunter flashed a winning smile and left the room.

We can make it look like anything you want, Mr. President. August White stuffed his papers into his valise, all the while looking at the closing door with his own style of grin on his face.

White House – 10:45 AM EST

Mike busied himself in his outer office packing his personal items with Molly's help. The entire time he kept an eye on the hallway outside his door. August White walked passed.

"Mr. White," Mike called after him. White reappeared in the doorway. "Do you have a minute?"

"Sure, Mike. But please call me August."

"Okay, if you insist. Let's step in my office." Mike ushered him in and closed the door softly. "Have a seat, please." The two men took the chairs in front of Mike's desk, facing each other.

"What's on your mind, Mike?" White asked. He shifted and crossed his legs.

"I wanted to talk with you privately about the mission in the Wahkan Corridor."

"Sure, but you know it's classified."

"I have the clearance, August. Now and tomorrow after the Inauguration as well." Mike noticed a twinge of disgust flash in the man's eyes.

"What is it you need to know?" White brought his fingertips together.

"You made it clear that a Top Secret ordnance was used to kill the communication compound, and that two soldiers pulled it off while they sat within feet of the Chinese border."

"Yeah . . . and?" White touched his index fingers to his lips.

"You said nothing about the equipment they used to do the fly-in and deliver the explosive."

"No. That was on purpose. That program is also Special Access."

"You mean, USURP?"

"Yeah. How'd you know?" White moved his hands to the arms of the chair.

"August, the president of the United States is the commander in chief. It's something he knew about. I didn't, but he did."

"You mean Makin, right?"

"Yes, I mean *President* Makin." Mike felt an edge in his voice he regretted.

"Well, yeah, you're right. Mostly a technicality though. Election's over."

"It's a small matter of taking the oath of office, August." The knot that tightened in Mike's gut confirmed to him he felt more than aggravation toward this man. "The point is that the CIA has initiated an extremely delicate operation at a serious time between administrations. The CIA has put our men in harm's way and some very valuable equipment at risk in the process. You do realize that a CHAMP device would incapacitate a very small number of the enemy troops stationed at the compound, and they might be just a little upset the facility has been destroyed."

"Of course, we—"

"Most of the enemy would be fit and able to pursue our soldiers. What sort of risk assessment was made about getting those men and the equipment out of enemy territory? Was the size of the enemy force taken into consideration? Was the compound heavily armed? Did they indicate any defensive capabilities whatsoever?"

"We are using standard extraction procedures similar to every—"

"And what if the events in the field are *not* standard? What's the backup plan? What happens if things don't unfold according to normal procedures?" Mike strained to maintain his calm.

"That has to be up to the command on the ground. We don't control everything from Langley; it just can't be done."

"But you can watch how things go down, right?"

"Well . . . yes."

"Are they monitoring the mission right now?"

"I assume . . . it would be common practice to do so. But I don't know for sure."

"Mr. White, perhaps it would be best for you to get to Langley and confirm they *are* watching, just to protect our men and property. Then, I would recommend you inform President Makin as soon as possible."

Tension flashed between the two men. White clenched his jaw, eyes glaring at Mike. Both his feet were now firmly planted on the floor.

"I think I'm going to leave now." Mr. White stood. Mike followed suit. "Please inform the president I will have an update for him within the hour."

The two men stood face to face. *Go ahead, White, throw a punch. Please!* Mike thought.

"That would be greatly appreciated, Mr. White."

August White strode briskly from Mike's office.

This may be the last day of President Makin's administration, but I'm still going to be here, Mr. White. I'm still here.

chapter 4

Wahkan Corridor – 6:55 PM AFT

The two soldiers scrambled down the rocky face. Their legs ached from the strain. They had maintained a near dead-run, downhill pace for over an hour, covering more than a third of the distance to the extraction point.

Keeping balanced was the most difficult part of the run. Although most of their equipment was disposable and left at the top of the mountain, the packs on their backs still weighed more than sixty pounds. That equipment was not disposable. They had to get it out safely.

The captain came to a stop. The sergeant slid down beside him.

"What is it, Cap?"

"It's getting dark. Can you see anyone in the canyon behind us?"

The sergeant removed his binoculars from their case and focused back the way they had passed. His heart sank. "Sir, there are quite a few of them. We need to go!" The enemy was coming.

The captain turned downhill, bounding in long strides. The younger sergeant followed with equally reckless leaps. A twisted ankle, or worse, a broken bone would mean certain capture and probable death.

Capture and interrogation of prisoners was a thing of the past for American troops. The limits placed on enhanced interrogation techniques left little choice for gaining new information from enemy soldiers. The field protocol had evolved from capture to kill. It didn't take long for the enemy to adopt similar practices. There were no prisoner swaps.

The sergeant followed as closely as possible, trying to prevent falling and landing on top of the captain. Their pace was frantic. Stones clattered all around them. Sharp edges tore at their boots.

Over the noise of their retreat, the sergeant heard voices. *They're getting closer!* he thought. He pressed harder down the graveled slope. The voices grew louder. *No! That's not behind us. Those voices are ahead of us!*

"Captain!" he shouted. "We've got Daesh below!"

The captain slid to a stop sitting on the rock. "Check how far."

The sergeant focused his glasses into the lower floor of the canyon. The shadowed shapes of dozens of armed men charged toward them. A shiver ran through his body. "Cap, there's more comin' up at us than behind us."

"Damn." The captain ripped open his pack and pulled an emergency transponder from its case and activated it. The transponder was to be used only in life or death situations. The signal would alert supporting American forces that they were in trouble.

The sergeant strained to see the approaching enemy through the darkening shadows. "Sir, I think they've seen us." A darkened figure stood from behind a rock. *"On your left!"*

"All right, we need to take cov—"

Thup. Thup. The captain pitched forward and slowly slipped a few feet down the graveled hillside.

"Oh, Jesus. . ." The sergeant slipped beside his fallen officer. "Cap! Cap!" No response. "Captain!" He pulled his own rifle from his shoulder and took aim.

Zing. Zwesh. Bullets ricocheted and buzzed close enough he could feel the disturbance in the air around him. He fired.

Pop. Pop. Two Daesh soldiers toppled over. The men on the left were closer than those he had seen in his binoculars. *Pop.* Another man fell to the ground.

Zing. Zing. More bullets bounced off the surrounding rocks.

"Oh, baby. I'm sorry to put you through this." *Pop. Pop. Pop.*

More enemy soldiers appeared directly below the sergeant. Frantically, he fired, first at those on his left, then at the men below, striking each target.

"Sweetheart, I'm sorry," he screamed to his young wife half a world away. "I love yo—"

Thup.

White House, Oval Office – 11:20 AM EST

Mike was sitting across from President Makin as he scanned reports on the action in Afghanistan. A half dozen files lay scattered and open on the Resolute Desk. The president's face was dour. The two men's voices were hushed.

"Mike, the CIA did this entire operation on their own. None of the joint chiefs were advised or consulted. *I* was not consulted on this." President Makin scanned another folder. "I don't like it, Mike"

"Me neither, Mr. President." Mike had been required to make decisions of national security without being able to ask permission. Those times were very difficult. But he had never considered creating the situation that challenged national security. That was exactly what someone at the CIA had done.

"You said White was going to bring me up to speed on this, right?"

"I hope we will hear from him soon."

Sharon Fair, the president's secretary opened the door from her office. "Please excuse me, Mr. President."

"Of course, what is it Sharon?"

"They're asking for you and Mr. Trapper to come to the NSA office. It's urgent."

The president left his desk and exited through his private study. Mike was close behind. The National Security Agency Office was moved to the West Wing shortly after September 11, 2001. It was in this room earlier presidents had watched important military missions since that time.

The two men rounded the corner beside Mike's office at almost a jog. Mike could see down the hall and into the NSA office. Others were already in the room watching events unfold. They entered the room.

"Mr. President," Ray Jergins said loudly. The four people in the room with him stood to their feet. The group was comprised of the "old guard," those who had been around since the Southwest Invasion and the incident with the Chinese. Mike was instantly grateful no one on the president-elect's team was present.

"What's happening?" the president asked.

"Sir, we just received this live feed from the CIA. August White called me moments ago and provided the link. This is an infrared image of the mission that was launched in the Wahkan Corridor a couple of hours ago." Jergins stopped and glanced at Steve Granger who leaned against the far wall. "I'm sorry, sir, but it's not good news."

The president stepped forward to get a clear view of the screen.

"We'll roll it from the beginning of what was sent to us."

The screen showed ghostly white images of two men scurrying down a mountain side. The view was from overhead and the men looked distorted and squat.

"These are American soldiers in the mountains of eastern Afghanistan. We know who they are because of the markers they carry. The computer sees them and colors them in bright white." Jergins turned again to the screen.

"Here we see them stop. You'll notice it appears one is looking through some field glasses. See here, it looks like his elbows are up, like this." Jergins held his arms up as if he were looking through binoculars.

"I see."

"Then, here . . ." The man who had looked through the field glasses pointed down range from where they stood. ". . . and, this." The other man pitched forward to a prone position. He did not move again.

The second soldier moved to the side of the fallen man and raised his rifle aiming downhill. The muzzle flashes were clear. He shot in one direction, then another. Back and forth in what could only be described as a furious battle. He suddenly jerked to the right and remained still.

"Oh, my God." President Makin stood in shock. The room around him was silent.

"It takes a moment, but watch."

After nearly a full minute, more men swarmed the screen. One or two bent over each man lying on the rock floor of the canyon.

"These are probably Mujahideen soldiers from the communication compound," Jergins said. "They weren't injured in the CHAMPs attack earlier. We think they're going through the soldiers' pockets. They'd be looking for maps, orders, communication devices, anything like that." Jergins turned back to the screen. "Here's where it gets a little disturbing."

The images on the screen seemed to huddle around the man who had been shot first. They removed the pack he had been carrying and began to examine it. An item roughly the size of a small suitcase was removed from the backpack. Three small bright lights became clearly visible.

"What's that?" the president asked.

"It's the USURP device, Mr. President." August White stood in the doorway. His presence surprised everyone in the room.

"But you were. . ." Jergins began.

"When I got to Langley I learned this was not going well. I instructed them to send you the feed immediately, and I came back."

White was noticeably uncomfortable. "Everyone in this room needs to understand, this is top, and I mean *top* secret."

Besides Jergins and Steve Granger, Alex Hodson, Angela Crain, and Matt Kreiter had lingered after the meeting with president-elect Hunter. Their discussion had been muted, but each shared their concerns about the display they had witnessed.

When the feed came in from the CIA, no advance notice had been given regarding the sensitive nature of the video. But now they had all seen what had happened. Mr. White had some explaining to do.

"In the rush of it all, security protocol was violated. I apologize for that. You cannot speak to anyone else about what you have seen. Do you understand?"

"We understand, Mr. White," Mike said. "But we need a lot more explanation about what we just witnessed. For example, exactly what are the three little lights?"

White sighed heavily and cast his gaze to the floor. He then looked at Mike. "Mr. Trapper, those are markers. Normally the USURP device is manipulated without being removed from its protective case, the backpack. When we can see the markers, we know the device is out of the pack."

"So, the enemy just took possession of one of our most secret weapons systems."

"Yes, Mike."

"But we can track the device by following the transmissions of the markers."

"Yes. Just as we could see our men, we will be able to see whoever is carrying the backpack. A separate marker, one that is intended to identify our soldier, is in the harness of the pack. The computer sees that individual's movement and tags them electronically."

"And when they examine *the device* and find these markers, can they not remove and destroy them?" Mike felt the venom rising gain.

"Yes," White said as he shuffled a bit, "but the markers are not obvious. They don't have little blinking lights on them or anything.

The markers are infused into the casing that holds the device. They are activated when the device is removed from the casing."

"The backpack." Mike strained to control the temper of his voice.

"Yes. But the mission was a success."

"And two men died." Mike's eyes burned with anger.

"Yes," White said in a whisper.

"Where is the extraction team right now?" Granger asked.

"En route. They are being told what has happened. They will go in with guns blazing, kill everyone they can, and hopefully retrieve the device."

"Hopefully," Mike echoed dryly.

August White was silent.

"Do you know what kind of force they are up against?" the president asked.

"Do the guys in the chopper know?" Granger took a step toward White.

"Doesn't matter. We don't leave any of the enemy alive. And we will bring our boys home." Mr. White flushed slightly.

"*Mr.* White, I'm directing you to bring a live feed into this office, *immediately.*" President Makin's anger was uncharacteristic of his quiet demeanor. "I want an *exact* count of the enemy force at the scene, and if any more are coming. Mr. White, I want that information right *now.* Alex give notice to your people at the FBI that we have a situation underway and instruct them to step up monitoring on all channels. Angela, same thing at DHS. Ray, I know you're here just in case one of our guys accidentally breaks some stupid regulation, and we need to get around it somehow, but please stick around. Steve, come with me to my office. Mike, you stay here and make sure Mr. White completes the job." President Makin glared at August White and stormed out of the room.

Mike watched him leave. He had never seen him so angry. *His last day in office and he acts like a real president.* He turned back into the room. At his glance, August White quickly began dialing his subordinates at Langley.

Wahkan Corridor – 7:45 PM AFT

"What is it?" Failak Jahnangir was not highly educated, but he had seen enough communication equipment to know this device was something unique.

"I cannot be certain, Failak, until I can examine it very closely. We need to take it back with us to the compound."

"I trust your knowledge and skill, my friend. Put it in the backpack. You will be responsible to carry this to your workshop." Failak's casual gaze struck terror in the heart of every man who served him. The mission was everything. Total, unquestioning obedience was demanded. Failak knew the power he held over the soldiers. He also knew how to use their fear to motivate them.

"Yes, sir. I will," the young soldier replied. He carefully lifted the small box into the protective backpack.

Failak turned away from him and stepped down the rocky slope. "Listen to me," he called to the small army around him. "You are to finish cleaning up here. Say prayers for our fallen warriors and bury them before you leave. Do not worry about the Americans. Let them collect their own garbage."

No one laughed. Death was held in high regard by these men. They had seen a lot of it. These brothers, their fallen comrades, were in Paradise and their remains would not be disrespected. The dead were honored and revered as long as they were Muslim. They would not touch a dead infidel.

"When you are through here, return to our base by the high pass. Their helicopters cannot fly at that altitude. You will run like the wind over the mountains, above where the infidels can fly."

A cheer rose up from the soldiers. They would have victory over their enemy, and they would do it on foot.

Failak turned to the young soldier who hoisted the pack containing the device onto his back. "You will come with me. We will take the truck back to the compound where you can begin your work."

"Yes, sir."

The two men trudged down the rock covered incline. The man carrying the backpack stumbled, nearly falling on top of the device. "Come," Failak said. "Let's carry this bundle between us. Your clumsy fall might damage it." The technician removed the pack and each man grabbed a shoulder strap with his hand.

They were only a mile from where the truck had stopped and deployed the soldiers two hours earlier. The road would carry them around the mountains before beginning the climb to the outpost. The hour-long drive was slow, and the road was rough. It would be dark long before they arrived.

chapter 5

"Those have got to be the bad guys, right?" Ray Jergins leaned forward to see the ghostly grey images on the screen. More than fifty shadowed figures moved across the field of view.

"Our guys would be colored a soft white. They have the markers," Mike added. "Well, they did. The markers are sensitive to body heat, and without it they shut down."

"Right. That's why our two guys—"

"Yeah. They're . . . cooling off." He felt sick, helpless.

Steve Granger entered the room. He had gone to the Oval Office to tell President Makin that the video feed was finally working. It had only taken twenty minutes.

"What's up?" he asked.

"It looks like they're preparing to leave," Jergins said.

"Where's the backpack?" The three men searched the screen. The image of a man wearing the pack was not visible.

"We saw a guy put it on and walk out of the frame."

Mike grabbed his phone and dialed the number at Langley from where the feed originated. "Hey, can you guys adjust the range of the feed? We think the Daesh who was carrying the pack left. Can you track him?"

He held the phone away from his ear momentarily. The scene on the live feed jerked awkwardly back to cover a greater area. Granger and Jergins strained to see movement on the left side of the screen.

"There," Jergins said, "on the left almost to the edge."

Two shadowy figures lumbered down the rocky slope. Something dangled between them. It was the backpack.

"And the marker isn't working because they're carrying it between them. No body heat to activate it."

"We got it," Mike said into his phone. "Do you see those two? We need to follow them. They have the device."

He listened as the voice on the other end spun a long line of excuses explaining why the satellite needed to stay with the larger group of Mujahedeen.

"It's your call," Mike said. "If you're sure we can pick it up later, fine. Do what you need to do." He turned off his phone.

"They aren't going to follow the backpack, are they?" Jergins asked.

"Nope. They want to clean this up first."

"And they can find the device later?"

"They believe they can. We're not in charge of this operation." Mike sat in the large office chair behind the desk. A familiar voice spoke from behind him.

"No, Mike, we aren't." Mike turned to see President Makin standing in the doorway. "Sometimes we need to leave stuff like this in the hands of the guy who's really in charge."

Corner Bakery Café, Washington DC – 12:20 PM EST

"Not too bad. What do you think?" Ronald Hunter asked as he and David Carapella entered the small café.

"I think it will do nicely." Carapella smiled, perusing the decor. "Sort of an away-from-home, home office." The walls were decorated with antique bicycles, old band instruments, playbills, and pictures. Lots of pictures of very well-known politicians, all smiling, enjoying a meal, hobnobbing with the people. Of course, most of the people had been paid to be there and to be happy, but the pictures were great.

"Exactly." Hunter pulled a chair back from the table in the center of the room and sat. "This guy was a great supporter during the campaign. Now, all I gotta do is make a phone call, slip him a grand or two, and the place is mine, all afternoon long." Hunter smiled, stretching his feet in front of him. He was aware of the constraints of the formal office of the president. The White House would be his residence and primary place of business, but if he wanted privacy, the small café was his preference.

"And you don't even need a pair of fake glasses with a big nose attached." Carapella laughed at his own joke, but stopped abruptly when he noticed Hunter was not laughing. The smile was still on the president-elect's face, but his thoughts were elsewhere.

"David, exactly how much political capital do you estimate we have at this point?"

"Well, a lot. I mean, you just won a landslide election. I think you can do pretty much whatever you want, and with the proper explanation everyone will think it's just wonderful."

"That's the way I feel about it. Sort of like Camelot reborn, isn't it?" Hunter smiled broadly. He leaned forward, placing his elbows on the table. "You know you won't be here most of the time, don't you?"

Surprise registered on David Carapella's face. "Oh, well, whatever you want, sir . . . I'm here to serve in whatever manner you see fit."

"That's the spirit." President-elect Hunter leaned back in his chair and swung his long legs toward the spool-backed chair to his right. "Of course, it all depends on who I'm meeting, and the time of day. You understand, right?"

"I do. It's not my job to be at the center of everything. I just want to make things go smoothly for you." Carapella nodded, affirming his loyalty to the new president.

Hunter had noted the hesitation when he told Carapella of his limited role, especially regarding the café. He knew he would have to watch him. *Keep your friends close and your enemies closer*, he thought as he smiled back at Carapella.

"That's all I can ask, David. Let's get back and do a run-through for tomorrow." The president-elect hopped to his feet and headed toward the door. David Carapella was right on his heels.

1004 19th Street NW, 3rd Floor, Washington DC – 12:35 PM EST

"Did we get that?"

"Of course."

"No, I mean all of it. I know we got the voices. What about the video?"

"Got it."

"Have you checked it to be sure?"

"I don't need to. I set the damn stuff up. We got it."

"So *you* say."

"Relax, it worked."

"Until I see it, I can't be sure. Show me."

The two men leaned over the screen. The one seated at the computer typed his instructions smoothly into the system. The results would take a few seconds to assimilate the data, but he knew the results would be more than satisfactory.

The darkened room overlooked the busy intersection between the Staples store three floors below, and cater-corner from the Corner Bakery Café. The equipment was set to view the exterior of the café from two directions: looking west down L Street NW, and north on 19th. The view of anyone entering or exiting the café was perfect.

Inside the café an array of sophisticated cameras provided a continual three-hundred-sixty-degree view of everyone in the room.

The clarity of the sound would seemingly place the viewer inside the room. But the program that combined the data was the magic.

"Here we go," said the man at the computer. He continued to type as the video started to play on the screen. "Now . . . watch this."

The picture on the screen *flew* across the room and centered on the face of the president-elect. Ronald Hunter's smiling face filled the entire screen.

"Ho-ly sh—"

"Hold on." A few key strokes and the image rotated one hundred eighty degrees focusing on the face of David Carapella seated across from Hunter.

"Man, it's like the camera is in the middle of the table. How the hell—"

"Science, man. Science." The view quickly slipped up to the ceiling providing an overhead shot of the two men at the table. "It's all in the program. The cameras see everything, the mikes pick up and collect the sound, and the system weaves them all together in a flawless all-around, everything-all-the-time record of what goes down. Cool, huh?"

"Amazing. I've never seen anything—"

"Watch this." His fingers danced over the keyboard, barely touching the surface. The program responded presenting Hunter and Carapella as they entered the café. The view swam around them again and again in a dizzying swirl. The video showed the two men walking to the center of the room where they sat. The spin followed every move as the men talked.

"Slow it down. You're making me sick."

"Weird, isn't it? It's like we're in a little helicopter right there in the room." He tapped the keyboard and the churning motion slowed, but not to a stop.

"You mean, we can do this anytime someone is in the café?"

"Well, anytime we need to have a record of anyone in the café. What are you thinking?"

"Chicks! I mean, holy cow, what a great way to check 'em out."

"You are one sick son-of-a-bitch, you know that?" He typed two keys and the screen went black. "This is not a toy for your demented proclivities. This is a very expensive and highly technical surveillance system. Show some respect."

"No, I only meant if we needed to run a check on the system—"

"No."

"No, what?"

"No, it isn't going to happen. Got it?"

The second man muttered something and turned away.

White House, NSA Office – 12:50 PM EST

Mike's phone buzzed in his pocket. "Trapper."

"Hi, it's me." Elli's voice always softly overwhelmed the stress in Mike's day. He loved her, and from the day they had met, her voice had calmed him.

"Hey. Not really a good time, honey."

"I won't be long. I was talking to Sam about their coming for dinner tonight. Is it gonna work for you guys?"

"Hard to say. Stuff going on right now."

"Well, I'll have her come over, and you bring Steve when, and if, you can. Okay?"

"Yeah. That's good."

"Love you."

"Yeah, I love you, too." Mike turned off his phone before he realized how distant he must have sounded. He didn't like that. He never wanted to be short or distant with Elli. He thought about calling her back, but the tension in the room drew him back in. This was about to go down hard and heavy.

Office of Counter Terrorism, Little Rock – 12:05 PM CST

Colonel Aaron Stevens and Keith Dillon hunched over the lighted table screen in back of the OCT Grid Room. The massive screen behind them tracked Internet activity of known terrorists: where they were and to whom they were sending messages. The technicians in the room electronically tagged each contact as fast as they could. The computer caught all of them, stored them, and then plotted the contact on the big board.

The sixty-inch table top allowed single threads of contact to be identified, located, marked, and, if needed, pursued. The locations of more than seven hundred forty-five known terrorists and their affiliated groups had been identified in eleven countries in just a few hours.

"Wow." Keith Dillon stood up and bent backward with his hands in the small of his back. After hours of leaning over the table he needed the stretch. "I knew we had ISIS in Mexico, but Kansas?"

"That's where the link took us. Contact the FBI in Wichita and have a team go talk to this guy," Stevens replied.

"Colonel?" a young lieutenant called to him.

"Yes, lieutenant."

"You have a call from a Daniel Sim. Some guy from Singapore. Do you know him?"

"Oh, my gosh, yes. He's a deputy commissioner with their police. Where is it?"

"Line two, sir."

Daniel Sim had been the officer who arrested the gunrunner Rene Broussard after the assassination of President Marshall. He had also been a friend of the late Phil Stearns who had been killed in the Oak Mountain incident. In the few years that had passed since the incident, Sim had been promoted to Deputy Commissioner of Investigations and Intelligence in the Singapore Police Department.

Stevens picked up the phone and pressed the button to open the line.

"Stevens, here."

"Aaron, Daniel Sim in Singapore. How are you doing?"

"Busy as hell, commissioner. It's good to hear your voice. How can I help you Daniel?"

"Good to talk with you as well." The two men had become well acquainted in the aftermath of the assassination of President

Marshall and the Chinese incident in Washington DC. They had shared information for months in an effort to clean up what had become a world-wide conspiracy. "We've been following the data on the Internet traffic, as you have, and we see many ties throughout Southeast Asia, Indonesia, and Malaysia. Can you tell me how we can work together?"

Stevens halted for a moment. *Was this an international concern, or only one for the security of the United States?* He knew he could trust Commissioner Sim. He was also aware that any assistance or collaboration from another nation required clearance.

"Aaron?"

"Oh, yes. I'm sorry Daniel. Brain fart, you know.

"Brain fart?"

"Yeah, well, never mind that. I need to run this through DC before we start swapping information. You understand, don't you?"

"Of course. And I know all about your stations in Hong Kong and Johannesburg as well as here in Singapore. I also understand your limitations."

"Thanks, Daniel. Let me—"

"And because we are not hindered by those limitations, we have some information you might find interesting."

Again, Colonel Stevens paused.

"Oh . . . I'll get right on it, Daniel. Can I give you a call in the next hour or so?"

"Sure. You do know it's the middle of the night here. But when it comes to visiting with you, I don't mind. I have arranged to have a very comfortable sofa in my office. I will be here."

"Thanks, commissioner. I'll call as soon as I can." He walked away from the table.

"Somethin' big?" Dillon asked.

"Probably," Stevens said over his shoulder. He needed to talk to Mike Trapper.

chapter 6

Wahkan Corridor – 8:20 PM AFT

The 60-Whisky Black Hawk is a marvel of military aviation. Bolstered by a KEVLAR all-composite monocoque exterior skin, the new choppers have a ballistic resiliency that is ten times stronger than aluminum on earlier versions. A maximum speed of one hundred seventy-five miles per hour allows for effective rapid deployments, but the flight ceiling of fifteen thousand feet limits any helicopter's effectiveness.

"Condor base, this is Whiskey Fire Six, over."

"Condor base. Bring it Whiskey, over."

"Final approach in three klicks. Confirm new heading to one thirty-four point thirty-two degrees southeast, over."

"Roger that, Whiskey Fire Six. Execute wash suppression and prepare for course change in thirty-nine seconds, over."

"Wash suppression, up. LAAT hot, NITE-sight on, over."

"Roger that, Whiskey."

New rotor designs had muted the normal loud slapping sounds helicopters make in flight. Although air speed is reduced, the quieted approach further enabled the effect of surprise on a busy enemy. The Laser-augmented Airborn Telescopic Unit (LAAT) provides gunners clear vision of a target from more than a mile away. With the assistance of Night Imaging Thermal Equipment (NITE,)

American soldiers are identified with electronic markers and thereby digitally removed from the target list. The enemy remains unmarked and designated as a target.

"Whiskey Fire Six, this is Condor base, over."

"Bring it, Condor, over."

"Commence course change in ten, nine, eight . . ."

The three-man crew and four Marines sat frozen in anticipation of the assault. Pilot and co-pilot managed the operational systems and flight, while the gunner sat at a twenty-four inch flat screen waiting to acquire targets. He would not be sighting individual enemy soldiers through crosshairs on this night. That was the job of the armament system.

The BRITE Star II Turret and Targeting System employed data from the LAAT and NITE-sight units to electronically identify and target the enemy. Up to one hundred individual targets could be selected in less than two seconds. The computer then marked each target and assigned them to one of the four GAU-18.A lightweight .50 caliber machine guns mounted across the belly and on either side of the Black Hawk. If the team encountered a vehicle, the tri-barrel 20mm turret cannon on the belly would eliminate it with a single shot.

". . . three, two, one, *execute*."

The giant chopper leaned sharply to the right and swung into the ravine opening two hundred feet above the canyon floor.

"Condor base, conversion complete. Zero-three-three-one, paint it. Mark."

"Roger," the gunner replied. He flipped a switch that instantly illuminated the screen before him with the images of forty-eight enemy soldiers scattered across the rock slope ahead of them. He pushed a second key on the keyboard and each target was marked. Deep in the bowels of the electronic wizardry, the targets were assigned to the four GAU-18.A lightweights on the front of the ship.

"Targets acquired, over."

The Black Hawk sped up the gorge covering the distance from the opening to the optimal firing range of five hundred meters in less than ten seconds.

"Zero-three-three-one, commence firing."

The response was instantaneous. The muzzles of the four .50 lightweights erupted in a blinding blaze as more than two hundred rounds burned through the night air. The recoil of the blast brought the Black Hawk to near stop in mid-flight.

Seconds of time hung suspended.

"We need a target scan, zero-three-three-one, over."

"Roger." The gunner entered new commands and the computer scanned the fallen targets. Sensing lasers measured each enemy soldier for even the slightest movement, any sign of life. After fifteen seconds the scan was complete. None were alive.

"We're good to go, sir." The gunner had completed his work. The three-second blast had accomplished the task. The enemy had been eliminated.

"Condor base, this is Whiskey Fire Six, over."

"Whiskey Fire Six this is Condor base. Bring it."

"Condor base, forty-eight enemy targets neutralized, over."

"Bravo zulu, Whiskey Fire. Go get our boys, dustup, and bring them home. Condor, out."

The massive helicopter slowly approached the bodies of the two fallen American Marines, and hovered just above the broken stones of the canyon floor. The four Marines dropped to the ground and gently lifted the two men into the chopper.

"Sorry we were late, captain," a young Marine said softly as he gently strapped the body of the fallen officer to the floor of the chopper.

The mood in the chopper was somber. They had been sent to extract their fellow Marines from danger. They had failed to arrive in time.

"Yeah," another Marine replied checking the harness that held the sergeant. "We'll let the Daesh collect their own garbage."

White House - 1:35 PM EST

Mike's phone vibrated in his pocket. "Trapper."

"Mike, Aaron at OCT."

"What do you have for me?"

"I just got a call from Commissioner Daniel Sim in Singapore."

"Considering the events of the day I will assume it was not a social call."

"Nothing of the sort, Mike. Their intelligence picked up the increase of chatter on the Internet just like we did."

"It would be a little hard to miss, wouldn't it?" Mike regretted his acrid tone but he justified it in his feeling that the day was beginning to slip out of control.

"Not if you're watching."

"So, what did Commissioner Sim want?"

"It's not so much what he wants, but something he felt we might need to know."

"What would lead him to think that?"

"Mike, they know everything we do, everything we are planning, and where and how we're going to do it. They know about our units in Johannesburg and Zurich, and they even know about our teams in Singapore."

"Well, that says a lot for our level of security, doesn't it?"

"Don't beat yourself up, Mike. The way they do things is unparalleled. Better than the Israelis . . . and better than us. It's just what is."

"Okay, what did he say?"

"He said he had turned up something we might want to know about. Up until then, I thought this was on our plate. I had no idea anyone else was watching, or even gave a rip. I asked Sim to hold onto his info until I spoke to you and made sure we had clearance to talk about this to someone outside our government."

"You're asking me permission to hear what he has to say?"

"Basically, yes."

Mike felt he was surrounded by secret meetings and discussions that had been growing to near conspiracy level all day. He felt they was skirting the edge of doing something illegal. But hadn't the president-elect himself said he wanted no mention of the mission until after the Inauguration? Didn't he say he wanted this covert assault to appear as if it was his idea? Wasn't that bending the truth just a bit too much?

"Aaron, sometime tomorrow afternoon I'll have that authority, but let's just say, between you and me, I didn't have a problem with your getting a phone call from an old friend in Singapore. Isn't it already tomorrow in Singapore?"

"Mike, I think you are correct. I'll give Commissioner Sim a call and see what he has in mind. And thank you for your help here. . . tomorrow."

He didn't like the feeling, but Mike had felt uncomfortable all day. He wasn't about to keep this to himself. A brief meeting was in order. He put his phone in his pocket and headed toward the Oval Office.

MISC Intelligence Compound – 9:40 PM AFT

The electronics in the main building at the compound on mount Qala-e Mufushad had been completely destroyed by the CHAMPS device delivered by the drone. The building had been slightly damaged by shattered glass and a half dozen small electrical fires.

The barracks for the troops was untouched by the explosion. The electricity was on, and the building was warm. Most of the soldiers who remained to clean up and secure the compound had huddled there for a late evening meal and to establish shifts to patrol the area until the full force returned.

The arrival of Failak Jahnangir and one young fighter took them by surprise. Everyone scurried to a trivial task, anything they could think to do that would make them look busy for their commanding officer. It didn't matter to Failak. He knew it was a show.

"Be careful. You are a very bad driver. Now, see if you can find out what this is without damaging it further."

The young fighter who arrived with him carefully lifted the backpack from the truck and carried it into the barracks kitchen. A crowd of curious onlookers gathered in the shadowed corners of the room, keeping a safe distance from their commander.

The young warrior carefully examined the backpack in the glaring light of the bare bulbs hanging from the ceiling. He lifted every strap and flap, checked every outside pocket of the backpack looking for any clue that might explain the strange device.

He grasped the shoulder strap and lifted the pack upright, then opened the top to remove the unit inside. Unknown to him, the warmth of his hand triggered a signal that was noticed on the other side of the globe.

He gently slid the metal-framed unit from the pack to the tabletop. Everyone in the room strained to get a good look at the strange piece of equipment.

Failak furrowed his brow and leaned over the table. "Any idea of what it might be?" No sound came from the component, no lights flickered to indicate transmissions or if the power was on.

"No sir. I have never seen anything like this before. We have some tools here but nothing survived the blast that would enable me to scan the circuitry inside."

"Then take it apart and figure it out. We've wasted enough time already. I need to make a phone call."

The soldier nodded to affirm that he would begin deconstructing the piece until he could find some explanation for his commander. Failure meant death. He had seen it before. They had all seen it. The others kept their distance and stepped back as Failak left the table.

"Out of my way. Let me know when you discover something. Anything. Wake me if I'm asleep. And that's an order!" Failak paused. "I have to make a phone call."

The soldiers cringed at the thought of being the one to awaken their commander. Everyone feared he might shoot anyone surprising him.

The young man hunched over the unit, turned on his flashlight, and began a serious inch-by-inch examination of the mysterious box.

White House NSA Office – 1:50 PM EST

"Look! Did you see that?"

"See what?" Granger asked, sitting at Mike's desk. "What did you see, Matt?"

Matt Kreiter had left the St. Louis Regional Office of the Secret Service and joined the DC Bureau during the Chinese crisis three years earlier. He had proven his worth to the team and was under consideration for chief operating officer with the new administration. His fluency in Mandarin weighed in his favor.

"I saw a light on the screen."

"You mean like a flash or something?"

"No, it was more like the markers we saw on our guys before the deash showed up. Someone might have picked the backpack up by the shoulder strap and momentarily activated the tracker." The image on the screen was from Langley and had shown the brief battle on the snowy mountain. The satellite picture had pulled back from the battle scene and was in the process of being reassigned to another point of surveillance. "But it wasn't located where our guys bought it."

Granger stood and walked from behind the desk toward the live satellite feed. "Show me where."

"It was right over here somewhere. It was just a second."

"What some five or six miles east?"

"Yeah, depending on how far they have expanded the image."

"We need to call Langley. I doubt they are paying much attention to what's going on over there. I'm gonna go get Mike."

"Wait," Krieter said leaning into the screen. "The device markers just came on." He turned to face Steve. "They have the device out of the backpack. And it is definitely at the compound we hit this morning."

Steve Granger turned and almost ran toward the Oval Office.

chapter 7

OCT Little Rock – 1:05 PM CST

Aaron Stevens waited for the call to connect to the office of Daniel Sim in Singapore. Two rings were the only delay.

"Commissioner Sim speaking."

"Daniel, it's Aaron in Little Rock. We're good to go. Whatcha got?"

"Good to hear your voice too, and no, I wasn't sleeping." Daniel chuckled softly at his tease. He had never been one to be overly serious. Life was serious enough.

"Very funny, my friend."

"Aaron, I know your country has hit something very big to stir up this much activity on the Internet. We usually have to track these criminals on the dark web, and that is difficult. Suddenly, they're all over Twitter and Facebook. What did you do?"

"A few hours ago a small team of commandos took out what we believe was a main communications hub for the world-wide terrorist network. I'll assume you've come to a similar conclusion, right?"

"Yes, but we didn't know about the compound in Afghanistan you took out. Congratulations."

"You know where the site is?"

"Of course, but only after you hit it. We knew something like that site existed but we didn't know exactly where it was. All of those orders had to come from somewhere, from some common source for MISC to be as effective as it has been around the world."

"If it makes you feel any better, we found it by accident."

"Oh good. I thought you might have found a method of improving your spying techniques," Daniel chided.

"Nope. Our espionage efforts are still as clumsy as ever. But you mentioned something that might be important. What can you tell me?"

"We intercepted a call from a sat-phone. It came from someone high in the Hindu Kush mountains near the border with Afghanistan and Pakistan."

"The Wahkan corridor, right?"

"Yes, only a few miles from where you attacked."

"And . . ."

"The caller contacted a person here in Singapore we have been watching. Sometimes I think these criminals are truly stupid. Why in the world would anyone consider Singapore a safe location for clandestine activity?"

"You got me, Daniel. As I understand it, you keep your town pretty much on lock-down."

"And that's why we are so friendly," Daniel said. "The man he contacted is a double agent. We have no reason to welcome him to our city. He is ruthless and very cunning, which is probably why he is still alive."

"You say he's a double. Who is he trying to play both ways?" Aaron asked.

"I hope you're ready for this."

"If I wasn't ready, I wouldn't have asked, Daniel."

"He works for both the United States and Russia."

"You've got to be kidding." Visions of a re-emerging Cold War swam through Aaron's memories.

"See, I knew you weren't ready."

"No, I'm just . . . I mean, Russia?"

"Ever since their move into Crimea and the Middle East they have presented an increasing threat. Certainly you've been watching them."

"Yes, but not as a major focus. Congress has pretty much focused on things at home, and let *that* business be *their* business. Not ours. Know what I mean?"

"Of course. Turn a blind eye, and what you don't see isn't really happening."

"It's a little more complicated. But you know what's been going on for the last three years. We pretty much dropped the international ball, and then we intentionally took a backseat on the world stage. I can't blame the politicians. But at the same time, there's trouble on the horizon. The sad thing is I don't think we can do anything about it."

"I know, my friend. I've kept my eyes open for you."

"Do you have a name, photo, or some kind of identification on this double agent?"

"Not really. We think it's a code name. We have only heard the word *kouzen*."

"Two O's?"

"K-O-U-Z-E-N, we think. Don't know if it's a last name, or . . . well, a word in any of the nearly seven thousand languages and dialects spoken on this planet. Your guess is a good as mine. You could Google it."

"Some techno-nerd probably will." Aaron preferred data he could track. A single word, or name, without something else to track it down with was a path to frustration and probably a lot of wasted time.

"Oh, one more thing. As of about three hours ago we lost track of him. He vanished."

"So you have no idea where he went?"

"We know where he's been for the last week, but this morning . . . *poof!* And he was gone. You know I'll send you anything else that turns up, don't you?"

"Yes, I know you will. So far, we have a man with no description who received a sat-phone call from Afghanistan, and has used the name, or been called *Kouzen* somewhere by somebody, and suddenly he vanished."

"That's about it, Aaron."

"I'll put it into the mix. Thanks, Daniel." Aaron hung up the phone and leaned back in his chair. "It's like I have a single puzzle piece, and I have to find the puzzle where the piece fits."

Black Hawk HH-60W, Wahkan Corridor – 10:10 PM AFT

The thump of the massive blades piercing the night air was remarkably quiet. The chopper was designed for emergency medical rescue, almost a flying surgery. As the flight crew managed to maintain aloft on the thin air outside the cabin, the four Marines who had lifted their comrades into the Black Hawk sat in silence.

Their mission was to rescue, and they had arrived too late. The fact weighed heavily on them as a team. Failure was potentially a part of any mission. But that didn't mean they were satisfied.

The young Marine who had apologized to the captain for their late arrival while strapping him to the floor seemed deeply affected. He stared at the two men lying at his feet feeling a deep personal responsibility. Then he saw it.

He didn't believe his eyes at first. There it was again.

"He moved."

"What?" asked the Marine next to him.

"He moved. The sergeant. He moved."

"You're jacked-up. We loaded them. They bought it."

"No, I saw him move, twice!"

"Kid, it happens. When you've recovered as many guys as I have you'll understand it. It's in your head."

"No, I—"

"WAHHA!" the sergeant screamed as he sat bolt upright.

All four Marines jumped.

"I'm hit! I'm hit! Captain!"

The young Marine was out of his safety harness in seconds. He rushed to the sergeant's side. "We've gotcha, buddy. Thought you were KIA. We gotcha." The others joined him immediately and began cutting away the sergeant's blood-stained clothing.

"Lieutenant, throw some juice in this bird and get us home. We got one that just woke up. Repeat, we got a live one back here."

"What? Who woke up?" the pilot asked.

"The sergeant. He's not dead."

"Roger. Copy that."

The medical team of four Marines worked fast to stabilize the sergeant's vital signs. The pilot trimmed the chopper for maximum speed at high altitude, and the engines roared in response. They were headed home. The mission was a rescue after all.

MISC Intelligence Compound – 10:25 PM AFT

The young soldier had examined the strange piece of equipment for over an hour. He had been schooled in electronics in Tehran for three years before joining the effort against the American-led war in Afghanistan. His father had fought the Russians and the Iraqis on the border. The Iranians had never lost, at least from their perspective.

Since leaving his home in northern Iran he had been trained in communications and the special equipment required to make it all possible. Lasers were common, yet laser communication devices were proclaimed as the next great step for space communication. And since the Hindu Kush Mountains were almost in outer space, it made sense. The compound at the top of the world was the perfect spot to coordinate and broadcast clandestine warfare.

Laser Communications Relay Demonstration (LCRD) was first tested by NASA as a system for spaceflights to the moon and Mars. The expansion of the Internet introduced commercial interests for an error-free data upload rate of twenty megabytes per second, and a downlink speed of nearly seven hundred megabytes per second. If commercial endeavors could be interested in the concept, then why not terrorists?

The lasers had worked well for over two years. The silent distribution of information around the world brought a new level of coordination to those seeking to terrorize on a larger scale. The advantage had come to an end with the destruction of the sophisticated electronics in the compound.

Once the device was out of the backpack, the casing was not difficult to remove. He had worked slowly, half expecting an explosive device to have been incorporated in the design. His greatest fear was that anyone taking it apart could be blown to bits. He had designed many such devices.

The young soldier hunched over the exposed wires and circuit boards. Very little of the design was familiar to him. He felt pressured by the threats Failak had made. If the device exploded, he would probably die. If he failed to discover what work the device actually performed, Failak would certainly kill him. Better to die making the effort.

The device was mounted in smooth metal tubing much like the frame of a bicycle. It was very light and highly polished. The joints of the tubing were solid and even. Much stronger and cleaner than any welded joints he had seen. Even the bracings at the corners blended into the tubing.

He carefully rotated the device to inspect the bottom of the unit. There were four padded feet separated from the frame by a metal washer. He examined the feet closely. One washer was slightly thicker than the other three. *Why is one washer thicker than the others?*

Slowly he removed the screw that held the pad and washer in place against the frame. He held the washer under a magnifying glass that was normally used for soldering fine wires on a circuit board. He gasped quietly when he saw the edge, an opening along one side of the washer.

He pried gently along the edge with a very small screwdriver and began separating the washer into two halves. Inside the washer casing he discovered the smallest and most intricate system of circuits he had ever seen. Even under the magnifying glass the circuitry was tiny.

"It has to be for something," he said out loud.

"What has to be for something?" Failak's voice boomed behind him.

The interruption startled the young soldier. The small piece of electronics lurched from his grasp and fell to the table top.

"I am sorry, sir. You frightened me."

"It is I who should be sorry. I have been watching you and did not mean to disturb you. What did you find?"

The young soldier retrieved the small washer-like object. His hands trembled as he replaced it under the magnifying glass.

"Sir, this is what I thought was a washer, but upon examination, it isn't."

Failak leaned over the glass and looked closely at the miniature circuitry. "What do you think it is?"

"I don't know for certain. It does not seem to have any connection to the operation of the device, so . . . I can only imagine it is some sort of tracking module."

Failak turned to him, his face only inches away. "So, the evil American magic knows we have their device and even *where* we have their device."

"Sir, how can they possibly know? We are miles away from everything. How could they find us here?"

"The same way they found us this morning. They watch us from the heavens. Their black sorcery is all around us wherever we are. Never forget that."

"What should we do? How can we escape them?"

Failak stood to his full height. The young soldier stepped back.

"We must separate this tracking module, as you call it, from the device. You will take it far to the north, as far as you can go, and throw it into a deep ravine. I will take the device into Pakistan on the south road. We must go at once."

The young soldier hurriedly gathered the small washer-like piece of electronics and his heavy winter gear. He would travel north all night, and with any luck, he would be fifteen or twenty miles away by morning. In the back of his mind a new fear rose. *What if they can track me?*

White House, NSA Office – 2:50 PM EST

Mike and Steve entered the office followed by President Makin.

"That took long enough," Kreiter said in a mocking tone. The tone changed when he saw the president. "Mr. President," he said as he stood.

"Relax," the president said with a smile. "This time tomorrow I'm out of a job."

"Matt, we just got word that one of the soldiers survived the shootout we watched a couple of hours ago."

"Good news, Mike. He's earned his ticket home."

"Seen anything on the feed that will help us get the device back?" Steve asked.

"Other than the light an hour ago, no." Kreiter leaned back in his chair and rubbed his eyes. "Oh, and thank you, Mr. President, for instructing Langley to leave the satellite focused on the attack site."

"You're welcome, but I never got them on the phone. All this Inauguration prep. People packing up their personal items, others ramping up to new careers. Whoever is supposed to be there wasn't."

"In other words, there's no one minding the store at the moment," Kreiter said.

"That's about it."

"I hope the Chinese don't know that," Steve added.

"Wait. What's that?" President Makin interrupted.

"What's what?" Kreiter asked.

"Right here." The president leaned forward and pointed at a single tiny light inching its way across the screen.

"I don't know." Kreiter sat up to the keyboard and tapped in some instructions. In essence, he rewound the tape a little. As they watched, the tiny light that had caught the president's eye moved back to the compound and into one of the buildings. The tiny light joined the tracker light on what they believed to be the device.

"They found one of the tracking modules," Kreiter said.

"Where do you think they're taking the one they found?"

"I imagine they don't realize there is more than one tracker and they want to get the one they found as far away as possible." Kreiter returned the feed to real time. "We'll keep an eye on the device as long as we can."

"At least we know they're trying to get away with the device and not just tossing it on a scrap pile somewhere," the president said.

chapter 8

The activity around the White House was beginning to settle down. Those whose time was ending had said their goodbyes and left. The staffers who were moving in were out getting an early start on the celebration that would continue for at least another thirty hours through the Inauguration.

President-elect Ronald Hunter stood at the far end of the conference table. Papers and files were spread out before him. Many of them providing information that any president, and especially new presidents, must know.

To his left, August White, CIA, lounged unceremoniously in one of the plush chairs. The look of boredom on his face was as pronounced as was the steady glare on the new president's face.

"Ron, you need to walk away from all this for a while. You can't be sworn in as president wearing that scowl on your face."

"It's nothing for you to worry about, Augie. I have my own methods of relaxing. In the morning I will reflect the fresh start this country needs. Especially after four years of Morose Makin and his gang of neophytes. What an embarrassment."

"You have to admit they were dealt a pretty tough hand—"

"Only in the papers," Hunter sneered through a smile. "Only in the papers."

The events following the assassination of President Marshall had been tremendously difficult for the White House crew to face. Over time, questions had been raised and doubt cast over the seriousness of it all. The media played down the invasion as civil unrest. Politicians agreed the death of a sitting president was tragic, but tended to gloss over the battles fought by citizen soldiers to regain the homeland. Revising the history of those days was not difficult and by repeating the new stories enough, they became the new reality.

White turned the discussion away from the events of the past.

"Have you decided what your day will be like tomorrow?"

Hunter turned toward him with a surprised look on his face. "Augie, I would think you know already. The day is planned. I just need to follow other people around and go to several parties. It's what they expect, right?"

"Well, yeah. Don't you think you need to disappear for a few minutes to make it look official?"

"Oh, you mean the attack thing." Hunter stopped to consider White's words. "It would look very presidential if I slipped out of the spotlight for a few minutes. Maybe even a couple of times during the day. You might be right. I could show up late to a couple of functions, and no one would know where I am. Then, in a day or two, we could leak to the press, you know, that I was on top of things from the first minutes of my presidency. I like it."

"Thought you might," White quipped dryly.

"I just need to review the schedule and select three or four periods of blank time. Think four is too many?"

"I'd stick with three. Don't overdo."

"You are right again. I like the way this is shaping up."

"You'll need to keep a tight lip on this, Mr. President. Need to know only. Not for general consumption. Do you understand?"

"Of course, I do. It wasn't my handlers who got me elected."

"Absolutely not, sir. I didn't mean to imply—"

"No, you didn't. It was a tough-fought battle of ideas over ideals. We won because of the vision I have for the future of this country. Nobody wants to live in the past. Especially our past. What a grim period. The fact that Makin overplayed his hand wasn't my fault. He had no grasp of actually leading the people out of the mess he allowed."

"But, Mr. President—"

"You just can't fool everybody for very long in this business. He didn't understand that. I know how to lead, and I plan on doing that very thing."

"Yes, Mr. President."

"Where is the agenda for tomorrow? Have you seen it?"

"Sir, I have a copy on my tablet—"

"No, I need it on paper. Can't change paper, you know. Wait, here it is." Hunter paused and scrutinized the schedule.

August White stood silently.

"The Inauguration is at noon. Don't want to do anything before then. But I could be late for the luncheon. Not much, just enough to say I was attending to business." The president-elect scanned through the daily schedule. "Okay, then I could be whisked away just after the parade. Don't know why we do that anyway. Would it be too much to have me requested to get back in the limo and then hurry to the White House?"

"Might be a little too dramatic, sir."

"Right." Hunter hooked his index finger over his chin. "Yeah, let's just get me back in the car and continue as if nothing was going on."

"That should be convincing."

"Yeah." Hunter continued reviewing the schedule. He scanned down the list with his finger, moved again to the top and repeated the operation. "There, that one. I'll be late to the party at DHS. Someday, they will appreciate that I picked them."

President-elect Hunter stood to his full height and beamed a winning smile. "See? This is gonna be a snap."

OCT Little Rock – 2:15 PM CST

"No physical description. No name. No previous ID of any kind. That about cover it?" Keith asked.

"Pretty much," Aaron Stevens replied bleakly. "Do you have any questions that I *can* answer?"

"Where do you want to start?"

"What makes you think I can answer *that*?"

"You're the head cheese, ya know, and I thought that might be in your wheelhouse. Am I wrong?"

"No." Stevens loved the pursuit of information. He hated getting started. "Did you run *kouzen* through the Cray?"

"You asked me to, didn't you?"

"Yes."

"Then perhaps you should be asking me what I found."

"Okay. What did you find?

"Nothing."

"That's concise. To the point. What else?"

"Nothing . . . other than . . ."

"Other than what?"

Keith looked at his boss with feigned boredom. "Other than *kouzen* is very similar to the English word *cousin* in Polish, Turkish, and Haitian Creole."

"Well then, there you have it."

"Have what?"

"A starting point," Stevens leaned back in his desk chair and folded his hands together.

"And how exactly should I proceed with this starting point, if you don't mind my asking?"

"Keith, you know I never mind answering your questions. Please proceed."

"Would you like me to scan phone directories in each of those countries, every city and town, or should I hit the baptism records first?"

"That might work, but let's do something more direct. Check airline passenger manifests with flights departing from each of those nations and arriving in Singapore over the last two months. Enter a phonetic name search and see if anything turns up."

"So I'm lookin' for someone with a name sorta like *cousin* flying to Singapore from Poland, Turkey, or Haiti. . .over the last two months."

"I think you've got it."

"And then when that doesn't pan out, where to next?"

"Keith, we have the entire world at our feet. Who knows, Russia, China, maybe even the good ole US of A." Stevens smiled and folded his hands behind his head.

"Okay. Sounds like a plan." Keith slowly turned away from his boss, nodding his head in agreement. "Sounds like a plan."

Bagram Airfield, Afghanistan – 11:35 PM AFT

The 60-Whisky Black Hawk covered the five hundred miles from the Wahkan Corridor in near record time by pressing the chopper to 300 km/hour, just under the maximum allowable speed. The landing was picture perfect, but still hard.

"I think he's stable," the medic said through the intercom.

"E-vac team coming to port side. Open the hatch."

He slid the hatch back, flooding the cabin with the wash from the rotors spinning overhead. The medics released the tethers holding the stretcher and passed it with the sergeant to the hands of four medics standing on the tarmac. A thumbs up signaled the transfer was complete, and the stretcher bearing the wounded sergeant was whisked away into the darkness.

The turbines began their slow decrescendo, and the crew began the process of shutting down the systems on the Black Hawk. The sequence of putting the bird to bed was as important as the start-up procedure. There was a method for everything.

A second crew approached the helicopter with a different mission from the first. The destination of their charge was not to the emergency room, but to the morgue.

The chopper medics carefully moved the body bag holding the remains of the lieutenant to the side hatch. Without speaking a word the transfer was made to the men on the ground. The lieutenant was carried by the four soldiers to a waiting gurney with great care. He had completed the mission and paid the final and greatest price. Every one of the men knew the value of that sacrifice. It was not chosen, but it was endured.

Roosevelt Room, White House – 3:50 PM EST

President-elect Ronald Hunter stood in the room alone. He was pleased with the day. In fact, he was very pleased with the last two years. The inception of the idea for a presidential run was the most stellar event of his life.

For years he had prepared himself. For decades he had considered the impact his choices might have on something like this. Of course, he did not imagine himself as president of the United States of America back then. He just knew he was destined for something great.

His wife was one of those choices. He knew, almost instinctively, his wife must be attractive, but not too pretty. Certainly, she must not be a blonde. He was particular about how much red or blond should be in her natural hair color. Some was fine, too much would detract. She must be educated well enough to be a professional, but motherhood needed to be the priority. She also needed to be tall, but not more than five-ten. Up to that height she would look good next to his six-foot-four-inch frame.

He had found his mate in Susan. She was educated at Cornell in political science, had light auburn hair, and bright eyes reflecting keen intelligence. She stood one-half inch short of his maximum height, loved to run to maintain her figure, and wanted children someday.

That day had come at the right time on two occasions. Their son was conceived during Ronald's first campaign for a seat in the Virginia State House of Representatives. The campaign blossomed with her pregnancy. Their daughter was born three years later as his campaign for the senate was just getting underway.

Ronald Hunter's political picture as a father and family man was secured. Of course, he loved Susan and the kids. They were wonderful people: smart and exciting children and a vivacious woman who continued to excite him. His family was the perfect answer to his plan and chosen life. They were exactly what he had wanted.

After serving the State of Virginia for fifteen years, the offer for a run for the presidency was timed perfectly. The kids were twelve and nine, old enough to be cute but not yet teenagers. Susan had aged beautifully and maintained her energy for everything Ronald pursued. She was his best cheerleader.

He paused and caught his reflection in a mirror on the wall. He looked great. His temples hinted slightly of strands of grey. It was just enough to reflect his wisdom without making him look worn. Yes, he was handsome. The time was right. His time had come.

He reached into his suit coat pocket and pulled out his cell phone. *Should I? I mean tomorrow I am the president. Why not?*

He typed in the number he had longed to call. It was a call that marked his level of achievement. After all this time he could do it. He smiled and let out a deep breath. The phone rang on the other end.

"Hello?"

"Hi, it's Ronnie."

"Why are you calling today?"

"I'm here. I'm in the White House, and tomorrow I will be president of the United States, that's why."

"It's too early."

"That's redic—"

"Call me tomorrow."

The call was clicked off on the other end.

Ronald Hunter was surprised. He was even a little angry.

I'm the president of the United States! Didn't you hear me?

He gripped the phone tightly in his hand and gritted his teeth.

We'll see about you. We'll just see!

chapter 9

Qala-e Mufushad South Face – 12:10 AM AFT

Descending the south face of the mountain in daytime was dangerous. At night most would call it foolhardy. Failak Jahnangir feared nothing. He had made the trip many hundreds of times for supplies. He knew delivering this package was important. He wasn't going to wait for the others to return and send someone untrustworthy on this mission. This had to be done properly.

The road down into the south valley was just over two kilometers and could be done on foot as quickly as he drove the treacherous mountain road. As he arrived on the valley floor, the landscape opened into a wide stone-washed plain. The roadway was nearly level most of the time, but spring floods often forced massive stones to the most inconvenient locations.

As Failak drove the valley floor toward the river he could see the silhouettes of the Korakoram Range in the east against the night sky. In a few hours the morning sun would strike the high peaks of the Hindu Kush Mountains to the west. The early morning reflection from the mountain peaks was one of the wonders of this mountain region he loved.

People who did not live in the mountains did not understand the beauty they held. Their rugged, barren majesty was like none other. It was these mountains that gave birth to the great Himalayas to the southeast. Failak knew Allah had given him this special understanding of his mountain home. Infidels would never comprehend this truth.

The mountain people were unique. Although borders of different countries wove through the mountain ridges and snowmelt-washed valleys they meant nothing to the people of the mountains. Their allegiance was to the mountains. If a country or kingdom made any difference, they preferred Tajikistan, one hundred kilometers to the north. It was an ancient kingdom locked into the eternal grip of the massive peaks.

At some point along the descent of the south face, Failak had crossed into the People's Republic of China. It did not matter. The Chinese were far away from him and no longer were interested in the far corners of their country. Before the sun came up Failak would leave Chinese territory and enter Pakistan. No border guardhouses would stop him. No borders would constrain him. These were his mountains, his home, and no nation would ever succeed in claiming them.

He would follow the river road for just under eleven kilometers before arriving at the Running Arabian Mining Company. The huge profile of an Arabian stallion in a full run stood above the ten foot high fence surrounding the company compound.

Failak did not know what the company mined, nor did he care. They could all be Chinese spies for all he knew. He had learned that sizeable stacks of money could purchase enduring friendships in these mountains. Friendships that endured until a larger amount of cash came on the scene. Loyalty required a price, and he had spent years making certain his price was the best price.

The Running Arabian was useful to Failak and his soldiers because of the two helipads the company had built years before. Samples of their mining results were often carried off by large helicopters. Failak simply timed his need of supplies to the company's need to deliver mineral samples to their home office. They brought the supplies for Failak and his men and returned to Sonikot Gilit and their company offices with the mineral samples.

Before leaving his demolished compound on Qala-e Mufushad, Failak had placed one phone call to ensure the helicopter would be waiting for him at the mining company. He was going to do this job himself so it would be done correctly. He no longer cared about the destroyed communications compound. He had already made up his mind. He wasn't going back.

White House, NSA Office – 4:25 PM EST

Mike Trapper and Steve Granger sat patiently with the outgoing president of the United States watching the monitor and the feed from Langley. From outer space everything on the ground moves painfully slowly. And any moment Langley would re-aim the satellite and the trail of the backpack containing the device would be lost.

"If it moved any slower I could convince myself we were on pause," Granger said with a hopeless groan.

"All is not lost until it actually is lost." The president grinned at his own witticism. The other two men hung their heads in mock shame. "Hey, I'm almost a former president. Show some respect."

"Yes, sir. Right you are, sir," Mike said offering a crisp salute.

"Where do you think the device goes from here, mister-almost-former-president?" Granger asked. The light banter did manage to brighten the glum mood.

"No ideas here. Mike?"

"My guess would be their headquarters in either Pakistan or Iran. It really depends on who the guy with the backpack favors the most. Loyalties are pretty diverse at this point."

"Can we anticipate this a little bit? Where is the most likely path, or paths this guy might follow?" President Makin asked.

"I'm not sure I can answer that one, Mr. President. The one thing I do know is that the pickings are few in that region."

"Meaning?" Granger asked.

"Driving anywhere is a long and frustrating process. The roads are bad and sometimes the only connection they make is with a footpath that leads to another road. Not very efficient. My guess is there might be some arrangement to fly the device out of the mountains. Choppers are the most effective, simply because a helipad is easier to build than a runway."

"How can we find a helipad nearest the compound?"

"Mr. President, *that* is why God invented maps." Granger hopped from his seat and left the office.

"I suppose he's off on some mission to make me look my age, right?"

"No, sir, Mr. President. He just got an inspiration. Let's go."

The two men leaped to their feet and followed Steve Granger. Fifteen seconds later the feed from Langley zoomed away from the Hindu Kush mountain range and the screen went black. Whether they knew it or not, they were done.

OCT Little Rock – 3:40 PM CST

Keith Dillon strode toward Colonel Stevens's office. His face was intense and focused on the papers he carried. Colonel Stevens had long been concerned about Keith's deeply focused attention, even to the point of safely passing through an open door. There were frames on either side that would not give if Keith happened to score a direct hit.

"What do you have, Keith?" he said before the technician entered the office.

Keith looked up, adjusted his trajectory a half step to the right to avoid the doorframe, and entered his boss's office.

"Colonel, me and the guys have been looking the hardest at biometrics and how they might help us find this guy."

"Biometrics. You mean things like finger prints and spit, right?"

"Yes, sir, and no, sir. Yes, fingerprints and saliva analyses are part of the realm of biometric science. But we have no way of looking at those two disciplines at this point. The other methodologies available include facial recognition, when we know what his face looks like, gait analysis, hand geometry, even handwriting biometric recognition—"

"What's that?"

"Handwriting analysis always looks at the shapes and commonality between letters, biometrics analysis and recognition takes things a couple of steps further. It tries to determine the speed at which the letters were formed, the intensity of the pressure from the writer, and if the differentials in the handwriting are consistent or deliberate efforts to disguise a signature, for example."

"You can do that?" Stevens asked somewhat amazed.

"Well, no. I can't. But it is possible with the proper equipment."

"What else can we check?"

"If we can find a starting point we can always do a retinal scan or even iris recognition for that matter. Vein matching and voice analysis are other possibilities. Then there is the old standard signature recognition."

"How can anyone possibly put all that together to make a positive ID?"

"It's kinda new, but then again not. People in the field use a program called a *fuzzy extractor*. The program converts biometric data into random strings of data that are applied to cryptographic techniques creating a profile of an individual."

"A profile."

"Yup. Every time a person travels, checks into a hotel, or walks through customs that information can be assembled in the database."

"We do this?"

"You mean here in the States?"

"Yes, in the general sense that *we* means *us*, and us is, well, our side. Do we do this?"

"Sorta. The federal program is called the United States Visitor and Immigration Status Indicator, or US-VISIT."

"Isn't that cute. Do you think they pay folks extra for that crap?"

"I have no idea, sir. It's just an acronym."

"Okay, you've identified something we might begin with, but where do we begin?"

"That's what we are doing right now. Since we have only one word to relate to this person, *kouzen*, we're looking at any regularities and consistencies with that word showing up in our target countries."

"So, the needle in the haystack."

"Oh, no sir. It's the needle in all the haystacks in most of the industrialized countries on the planet."

"So, the computer is on it."

"Right, sir. We don't do this by hand anymore."

"What are you expecting to find in all this?" Colonel Stevens asked leaning back in his chair.

"A consistency, sir."

"A consistency."

"Yes, sir."

Stevens looked at Keith both annoyed and a little amazed. "Have you found one yet? I mean something that is consistent with something else."

"Well, yes. We are consistently finding nothing of any regularity in the target countries."

"Does that mean taking those countries off the table and ignoring them?"

"No, sir. Just to back-burner status."

"But then where do you go for your data search, if I may ask?"

"Glad you did ask, colonel. We have a first level target we are looking into."

"And that is . . . ?"

"India."

"India? Why India?"

"India is a nation that does more surveillance on its millions of people, as well as individuals coming and going in their country, than anyone else. They even have biometric files on people who have never even come to India, but indicated through their travel habits that someday they might come to India."

"You're kidding, right?"

"Nope, it's what they do, colonel."

Stevens stared at Keith. "Whatever . . ."

One of Keith's technicians walked down the hall toward him.

"What is it, Bobby?"

The young, bespectacled tech held up a slip of paper and spoke softly to his supervisor.

"That's good . . ." Keith said. The chubby tech muttered more to him. "Very good. That's very helpful. Tell the guys they did good work."

The young technician smiled and hazarded a glance at the colonel, then retreated down the hall toward his cubicle.

"And . . . ?"

"We have a consistency."

Trapper Home, Washington DC – 4:55 PM EST

"Hi, I hope I'm not too early."

"Not at all, Sam. Come in. Gosh, it seems like forever."

The two women hugged. It had been almost forever. Sam and Elli shared a friendship that had been through very difficult times, but were always hoping for the good times ahead.

Samantha Long had decided to take a break from her high-stress life working for the State Department. The events of three years ago at Oak Mountain, the invasion of the Southwest, and the Chinese incident in Washington had left her a broken person. The stress had been too much. After some serious soul searching, some therapy, and a long-term friendship with Steven Granger, her world had finally found a resting spot.

"How long has it been?" Elli asked.

"Almost forever. But in real time, two years in March."

"Well, that's you and Steve. When did we have you guys over last? Was it that barbeque last fall?"

"I think it was," Sam said taking off her coat.

"Wait a minute!" Elli exclaimed taking a step back. "Now that is a baby bump!"

Sam blushed. "Yes. Arriving in a week or so."

"Wow. How exciting can life get?"

"Hopefully, not exciting at all." Sam smiled softly. "The less excitement I have to deal with, the better."

"I can agree with that. Adventure is best written in history, not in the present." Elli blew out a breath, and looked Sam in the eye. "You're looking great, I mean . . . really great, Sam."

"Thanks, Elli. Do you know when the guys will get here?"

"No, but I've been promised they will arrive sometime."

"Can I help with anything in the kitchen?" Sam asked, fully aware she knew little about cooking.

"Sure. When Mom and Dad lived with us I went through an intensive training course to learn her secrets. Even Mike tells me I'm doing better."

"Good. Then you can teach me."

"I would really like that, Sam. The kids will be very happy to see you, too."

"Robbie's what, ten now?

"In April. Technically, according to him, he's nine and nine-twelfths."

Both women laughed. Elli loved having Sam around. She was a real, adult female friend. She kicked herself for not insisting she and Steve come over more often. But life is busy at its best.

"Robbie and Sara will be home from basketball practice soon. With those two it is run, run, run. High school looks terrifying to me."

"And there are two more right behind them," Sam added. "I can't wait."

"Don't ask me why, but it seems to come at you like a freight train, and, according to my parents, you tumble along with it until it all plays out. In other words, they do grow up."

"That's the hope, anyway."

The phone in the hallway rang.

"Hello? Hi, Sam just got here. . . okay, there's no rush. . . fine. See you then."

She turned to Sam. "The boys won't be here for a while. So it's just you and me for now." *Time for girl talk.*

And that was fine.

chapter 10

Running Arabian Mining Co. – 1:10 AM AFT

Failak Jahnangir arrived at the mining company in the dark of night. A single bulb lit the parking area outside the company office.

He crawled from the old truck and stretched. Two and a half hours banging down the mountain roads had taken a toll on him. He didn't have any idea when he might sleep and told himself it didn't matter. His cargo had to be something important.

Failak walked to the office door and opened it. The manager greeted him with his customary gruff voice and surly attitude.

"You are working nights, now, huh?"

"We work when work needs to be done. And work needs to be done all the time."

"The chopper radioed a few minutes ago. If you had been here you would know when he will arrive."

"But I was not. You were here. Now tell me when he will arrive."

Their comradeship was not built on affection or kindness. The two men did not like each other. Nor did they like or care about the other's business. They only liked the money and that they were working against the white Europeans and Russians. Any mention of America brought a look of contempt and a spit.

"Fifteen minutes. You have time for a smoke."

"Do you have coffee?"

"I would have to make it."

"How long would that take you?"

"Fifteen minutes, so why bother?"

The two men glared at each other.

Failak turned away and looked out the window. He decided the solitude awaiting him outside was more inviting than his present company. "I'll wait at the helipad."

"Suit yourself."

Failak stepped outside and pulled his jacket tight around him. The helipad was fifty yards to the east. He retrieved the pack from his truck and swung it onto his back. As he walked toward the pad he glanced back at the office. Through the window he could see his host was making coffee.

"Bastard." He continued toward the helipad.

OCT Little Rock – 4:20 PM CST

Colonel Stevens had spent the last hour reviewing the Internet traffic reports on known criminals and terrorists. Communication by normal channels had erupted after the attack on the compound in the Wahkan Corridor. His concentration was continually broken with curiosity about what Keith and his subordinates were discovering. He had to do what was in front of him, but the suspense was driving him nuts.

"Enough of this." Stevens stood to leave his office. Keith Dillon beat him to his own door.

"Colonel. We've got him."

"What? You've captured him?"

"No, oh no, sir. No way." Keith stopped in his tracks, surprised at the colonel's conclusion. "Not captured sir, but I think we have enough data to create a biometric file."

"Okay, not caught, but identified."

"Not quite, sir. No identification can be confirmed until the biometrics pick up a subject. Then we might have enough to ID him. Or, maybe, *her*."

"Fine. Then tell me, what part of 'we've got him' do we have?"

"I will, sir. That's why I came to your office."

"And thank you. Whatcha got?"

"We matched a handwriting biometric and a voice analysis."

Stevens was stunned. "What? You were able to find two E's that resembled each other? What do you mean?"

"Well, sir, they were actually S's, and they both were linked to the same voice print of the word 'yes' spoken in very clear American English. Colonel, this is really big and we were very, very lucky."

"Well, that's fine. What's next?"

"The two pieces of data are entered into a complex formula known as the Reed-Solomon Code. The data goes in as the polynomials with a coefficient message, which is secret, and the program searches other data bases for the same, or nearly the same data."

"Poly-whats?"

"Polynomials, sir. But that's not the big thing. The fuzzy extractor takes the data and works through other databases around the world to find matches or near matches to the original data."

"Wait a minute. You're telling me that all this information is stored by countries and governments everywhere?"

"Yes."

"Doesn't that just kinda violate the Constitution somehow? It *has* to. This is the most egregious violation of privacy I have ever heard of."

"Not really, sir. You see the information is collected like, oh, say *hair*. A person has hair—or not. It's just a fact about that person. There is no way to ID someone from the fact that they have hair.

Now when all the bits begin to come together we might be lucky enough to put it all together and match a person to it."

"Hopefully the right person."

"Well, sure. Do you remember the couple in California who shot up a Christmas party and killed fourteen people?"

"Who doesn't?"

"And do you remember the picture of the couple as they entered the country a year or so earlier?"

"Sure."

"That picture alone gave us five biometric indicators that went into the system: facial recognition, height, iris recognition, retinal scan, and vein matching. Every person who enters the United States is asked a handful of questions. The expected answer to those questions is "yes." The answers are recorded and matched. Everyone must walk to the counter, and from that we collect *gait analysis* data. Then they have to sign a card declaring anything they are bringing into the country. That activity gives us eight of the ten biometric indicators we need to match and catch the bad guys."

"So why didn't we catch those two?" Stevens asked.

"DHS didn't take the time to run the data. Now, it's done automatically. But we still don't use all ten indicators like they do in India."

"And if they answer *no* to all the questions instead of *yes*?"

"Well, then it's a foregone conclusion that they're terrorists. We send them back."

Colonel Stevens paused momentarily before he saw the curl in the corner of Keith's mouth. "Right. Got it." Stevens smiled at the joke.

"Colonel, the fuzzy extractor needs more time to gather information. If the person we are looking for moves around a lot, he's left plenty of data out there. We will get a match."

"And if he traveled through India . . . ?"

"His goose is already cooked, sir."

Oval Office, White House - 5:35 PM EST

The maps were scattered across the Resolute Desk in a most un-presidential manner. The president along with Mike and Steve were hunched over the cartography examining the terrain around the destroyed mountaintop communications center.

"We watched the tracker lights as he moved down to the lower valley and probably caught this road by the river." Mike muttered his thoughts as he traced the line with his finger.

"There's only one direction a person can go from there, you know," the president said. "Downhill."

Steve snickered. "From where he started there is no up-hill available, is there?"

Mike traced the road as it wound through the valley. "What do you think this is?"

The three men moved close together, squinting to see the map.

"We need to look at this on Google Earth," Steve said reaching for the laptop on the credenza behind the president's desk. "Is this one on any super high security?"

"Nope. This one's mine," the president said.

Steve quickly opened Google Earth and directed the program to the Wahkan Corridor in eastern Afghanistan. The pictures of Qala-e Mufushad had not been updated since 2003 and held no imagery of the compound. They were not necessary.

He scrolled along the path the tracking system had taken until he found the road. Then again down the mountain road until they found the rectangle.

"I don't know what resolution we can get, but . . . there. It looks like some buildings, and a silo, or tower of some—"

"Wait," Mike interrupted. "What's that?" He pointed to an image and shadow of a running horse. "Who in the world would have a horse ranch out in the middle of nowhere?"

"And to be seen from a satellite that thing has to be what . . . thirty feet long?"

"But what's important is over here," Steve said directing the focus of the image farther east. Less than two hundred yards from the building were two concrete slabs, each about one hundred feet square. "There's the way out. Helipads."

"Simple. Have someone fly up and pick up the backpack and the handler."

"But Mike," the president said, "where to then?"

"I saw an airport down south somewhere." Steve widened the screen and scrolled south. "Google Earth marks buildings and things like airports. Makes them easy to find."

He saw it and zoomed in to a small city nestled in the mountain valley.

"Probably the only airstrip within five hundred miles. And look . . ." Half the way down the airstrip an old helicopter sat on a similar concrete pad.

"Hey, can you zoom in on that?" the president asked.

"Sure, but the clarity of the picture drops off pretty fast." Steve eased the view to a lower level.

"Well, I'll be," the president mused. "See the double wing on the tail? That's probably an old Russian Mil Mi-6. Could be as old as an early 60's model."

"I had no idea you were an expert on Russian aircraft, Mr. President. You continue to surprise me," Mike added sitting on the edge of the credenza.

"Old hobby of mine. I can't be sure, but the five overhead blades and that double tail are the identifiers. The Russians abandoned over a hundred of those old crates when they pulled out of Afghanistan, just like the stuff we dumped in Iraq."

"Then all the bad guys need to do is patch 'em up and make them work."

"Nothing safe about an old chopper like that flying around in the mountains. But I would bet my last dollar that's how he would get out of the high country. Bring the chopper back to Kashrote, or whatever the name is, then catch the next flight to civilization."

"My guess would be either Islamabad or Kabul. Then we're back to the loyalty thing. Who is their friend this month?"

"Mike, again, it's more my gut feeling than anything, but the people up in those mountains never cared much for the Afghans.

Didn't want to have anything to do with being part of a nation other than the tribes that have been there for thousands of years."

"You think they would favor Pakistan over Iran."

"I do, Steve. Their homeland, those mountains, are carved up like a Thanksgiving turkey, a part to China, a part to Pakistan, another chunk to Afghanistan. They don't care for any of them."

"But they fought together against the Russians, didn't they?" Mike asked.

"Sure. It's that old 'my enemy's enemy is my friend' business. Alliances shift with the snow in those parts."

"So the most reasonable assumption at this point is a chopper out of the mountains, and a normal commercial flight to Islamabad. Right?" Steve asked.

"Then all we need is a flight schedule for Pakistani Air."

"And you guys can have that in a matter of minutes." Al Makin stood and stretched his back. "It's almost time for me to pack up my stuff and head for the house."

"No special going away parties tonight, Mr. President?" Mike asked.

"No. We can let the youngsters have their celebrations now. We'll get everyone together in a week or so just to stay out of the limelight."

"Thank you, sir. It's been a hell of a ride."

"It has indeed, Mike. One hell of a ride."

Hindu Kush Mountains, Pakistan – 1:50 AM AFT

Failak sat in the metal seat clutching the backpack against his chest. The pounding of the rotors overhead was deafening. He glared into the darkness, still angry at the man at the mining company for not offering him some hot coffee before the flight.

The old helicopter probably had a heating system when the Russians flew it into Afghanistan, he thought. He was alone in the old chopper, except for the pilot. *He must have been paid a pretty sum to make this midnight run.*

The thunderous roar inside the old helicopter would have prevented conversation with anyone. That was fine. Failak didn't care much for people. They were usually in the way or made too much noise. Silence was better. If only it were silence.

Once in his life he had flown on a large commercial airliner. He was amazed during the entire flight. He remembered that he was also warm. His present condition gave him only misery. *It is much different to run through the mountains and break a sweat even when the temperature is extremely cold, than to sit in a metal bucket that is pounded on from the outside.*

He would rather run.

But this trip was necessary. He held in his arms something of great value. He just knew it. The two Americans had died defending it, and the wizardry inside it was beyond his imagination.

His superiors at headquarters would be impressed. *They were impressed enough to command the arrangements for my trip. It must be very important.*

He knew the distance to Kashrote was less than one hundred fifty kilometers. Of course, driving the distance was much farther. And in the lumbering, old Russian chopper it would still take two hours to fly the distance. He had been told the plane would meet him at the helipad and be ready for take-off.

I will believe that when I see it.

The thundering vibrations continued, lulling him to a drowsy state. Before he could resist it, sleep claimed him.

chapter 11

Washington DC, Private Residence Party – 6:10 PM EST

The party was just beginning, and the early arrivals were treated to the president-elect and his wife, Susan, sneaking into the home through the kitchen.

"Hey, congratulations to us all!" Ronald Hunter announced as he led his wife through the kitchen door into the dining room. About thirty supporters and campaign workers burst into loud cheers and swarmed toward the First Couple.

"I wanted to come here to start things off because I heard the food was the best." President-elect Hunter beamed, and the small crowd laughed boisterously at his joke.

But it wasn't the food that brought him. This group of people had been the core of the election effort from the very beginning. It didn't matter if the campaign needed money or envelope stuffers, this crowd shouldered the burden personally or with staff members or employees. They were most loyal.

It was also the most private. The party was early and off the official schedule. The names of the guests were securely kept from view, especially from the press. The guest list of this mix of partygoers was newsworthy, but their privacy was more valued. And it would remain so.

"Congratulations, Mr. President!"

A strong hand clasped Ronald Hunter's left shoulder. He turned to see the chubby, rough-cut face of Bobby Myers, the president of the AFL-CIO.

"Bobby, so good to see you."

"Likewise Mr. President."

"I think I might get used to that title in time," Hunter replied with a false humility. He loved the title.

"You won't be forgetting us after you say all the 'I do's' and make promises about everything under the sun, now will ya?"

"Never, Bobby. Never. Your support has been a huge factor in this election."

"And wouldn't the press be excited if they knew I was here!"

Both men laughed. Myers pounded his hand on Hunter's punctuating his annoying jocularity. Hunter knew how to play the humble part of politics. The big contributors would always be his best friends, whether he liked them or not.

Hunter turned to greet the undersecretary from the Chinese embassy, another financial contributor about whom no one should know. The assistant to the Crown Prince of Saudi Arabia shook his hand with a knowing smile of approval.

The president-elect moved around the room greeting more little-known dignitaries and representatives of corporate America and beyond. He ended his time of pressing the flesh where he began, beside the kitchen door.

August White stepped into the room from the kitchen.

"Did he call back?"

"Not yet. But I don't think he'll call tonight, and I'm positive he won't call your cell, especially here. You need to be in the White House for the best security."

"Not me, Augie. You!" he said pounding a finger into White's chest. The glare flashed in Hunter's eyes for a brief second. Long enough to make his point, brief enough that no one in the room noticed.

White got the message. He moved quickly through the swinging door to the kitchen. Hunter was glad to see him leave. This crowd wouldn't understand the presence of the CIA. Nor would they appreciate it.

OCT Little Rock – 5:25 PM CST

"Colonel Stevens," he said reaching for his jacket.

"Aaron, this is Daniel Sim."

"Hi, Daniel. You just caught me. I was headed home."

"Sounds nice. I just came in from a rare but pleasant breakfast with my wife. But *you,* you might need to hang around for a little while."

"What's up?" Stevens asked moving to his chair behind his desk.

"Well, it's this *kouzen* character. Your boys worked anything up yet?"

"They've been on it all afternoon. Keith came in here an hour ago all excited over a couple of matching voice prints that were linked to a bit of handwriting. Not much more."

"Worked through India?"

"I think so. What's on your mind?"

"We might be a step or two ahead of you, and with what you have we might be able to establish a more complete file."

"Okay, I'm listening."

"About forty-five minutes ago we had a man check in for a flight to Kuala Lumpur at Changi International. We got a full facial image and a short voice print. What set off the alarms was the fact that he used a different name than he did when he arrived in Singapore six weeks ago."

"Same face but a different name?"

"Exactly, Aaron. If we can match his voice to the voiceprint you found we could build an excellent bio-file. If this is the guy we're looking for, he may have tipped his hand."

"When does his flight leave?"

"Already gone. He got to the gate just before they closed the hatch, checked in, and boarded the plane too quickly for any actions to be taken."

"Daniel, since he's in the air right now, I'm sure you have the time the plane is due to land at Kuala Lumpur International Airport."

"That's another interesting point. He's not landing at the larger airport where the security is more sophisticated. He's on a flight that lands up north of the city at a field called Subang. He's on a little double-engine turboprop service used by most of the locals. They get larger planes landing there, but those are private jets. Smaller airport, and less red tape getting in and out of the country."

"Fits the *motis operendi*, doesn't it?"

"And thus, my call. The flight left here at five-ten this morning. So he's been in the air less than twenty minutes."

"Can you have someone on the ground when he arrives?"

"I have two agents on their way now. The flight is expected to land at six fifty-five our time. They have instructions to monitor and follow him. The airport security has been notified to watch for him and send me everything they collect."

"Can they be expected to get much information? I mean at a small airport?"

"Aaron, this is Malaysia. Talk about a police state. We are just a much nicer police state. It's not India, nor is it a flight from Dallas to Wichita."

"I understand. I'll ask Keith to forward what we have to you if you promise to keep me updated."

"Never a problem, my friend. Your concerns are my concerns."

"Thanks, Daniel."

Colonel Stevens sprang from his desk and headed to find Keith Dillon. *Probably should call home so they aren't expecting me.*

Wahkan Corridor – 2:35 AM AFT

The young soldier stood at the edge of a deep ravine. The darkness fell into a bottomless void that could have ended in hell itself. He was at the edge of the world.

"This is as good a place as any."

He drew back his arm to throw the tiny metal piece, but stopped. He opened his gloved hand and looked at the sensor he had removed from the device hours before. He had walked miles climbing mountainsides and sliding down the far side. He had no idea where he was. The darkness had tricked him time and again until he was lost.

"Perhaps I will find my way back when the sun comes up." He gazed intently at the chip. "But someone on the other side of the world knows exactly where you are. I am here and find myself completely lost. What a strange paradox."

His thoughts shifted from the snow and ice surrounding him. He thought of his home, his family. Memories flooded his conscious mind. They were so real he could almost see the shapes of his mother and father projected on the darkness. A smile crossed his lips.

His younger sister had pestered him constantly. Her teasing and pranks left him filled with rage, even hatred for her. She had always been playful. He laughed out loud remembering how she had tormented the family cat. As a ten-year-old she had scanned the Internet looking for new ways to bring terror to their pet. Mother was constantly after them, threatening the most severe punishments for scaring the animal. His sister was the instigator, he was the technical assistant. He smiled at the memory.

A sudden gust of icy wind brought him back to the mountain and the washer-like chip in his open hand.

"What does it all matter? This little toy of a thing that helped destroy years of work. Me. One man stands at the top of the world doing . . . what? It's all so meaningless from here."

He closed his hand around the chip, drew his arm back and flung it into the darkness in front of him. It left his sight in an instant. He knew he would not be able to hear it bounce off the rocks at the bottom, if there was a bottom.

Several hundred feet below him the small metal indicator bounced from stone to stone finally landing on the rocky canyon floor less than two yards from a dead body. More than forty bodies were scattered around the area. The Mujahideen soldiers lay silent in the freezing night. The only sign of life was the *ping* that was jarred from the small tracking device. The signal was noted on the other side of the globe.

The young soldier gazed into the night sky over his head. In his wandering through the darkness he had not walked north. His path had covered a wide arc that slowly turned to the west. Without realizing it he had returned to overlook the canyon where Failak Jahnangir had led a small band in pursuit of two American Marines. He did not know his companions lay dead on the rocks below.

Only a star or two twinkled, but only momentarily. The clouds blew past to obscure them again. The swirl of darkness only reminded him that he had no idea where he was.

He had been awake for nearly twenty-four hours and the exhaustion pressed on him. An unwanted hopelessness sat like a stone, low in his chest. *Tomorrow will be different. I will find my way when the sun is up.*

He looked around for a crevice in the rock he could use for shelter. He knew if he was out of the wind he would stay warm. He climbed back down from the jagged edge of the mountain ridge and found the place he sought. He forced himself against the hard stone and wrapped his heavy coat tight around him.

Sleep was instantaneous. It had been a strenuous day, and his body yearned for the sleep it grasped so quickly. The young soldier remained in a deep sleep even when the wind changed direction to blow hard against the face of stone where he had sought shelter.

Some warriors of jihad find glorious death in the midst of the terrible fight, others more quickly with the flip of a switch hidden in a jacket pocket. This soldier found death in a frozen slumber. His body chilled. His heart stopped.

In a few hours the sun would pass above the eastern horizon, but the warmth that normally accompanies sunrise would be too late.

Roosevelt Room, White House – 6:50 PM EST

August White seated himself at the conference table facing the door that opened to the Oval Office. He wanted his back to the wall. He felt safer that way. Years of undercover work in foreign lands had honed a strong sense of caution in him, even in the White House. He wanted all the action happening in front of him. No surprises.

He pulled his phone from his pocket and called Langley. The phone rang once.

"Proctor."

"Yeah, this is August White. I need an update on the action in Afghanistan."

"Okay, what's your need to know?"

"I've been with the president-elect all day and will have a late night meeting with him. He wants to be on top of all this."

"Gottcha. Hold on a sec."

White was put on hold. *Dear God! They're still playing Christmas music.*

"All right, I've got the report here in front of me. Entries began earlier today, let's see, yup, started at 10:15 this morning at the order of President Makin. And the last entry was made . . . Here it is. The last entry was made twenty minutes ago."

"What was the last entry?"

"Well, you are aware that we needed to re-task the satellite for some of the time, but we went back a couple of times to check things."

"Fine. The last entry, please."

"It reads, 'Status unchanged. Device *ping* was recorded at six thirty-one Eastern Standard Time in the same location previously noted."

"That's it?"

"Yup."

"What about our soldiers who were out there?"

"One KIA, the other guy revived during the return flight to Bagram Airfield. They have him in the OR right now."

"And what about the equipment they were carrying?"

"Well, like I said we had higher priorities for the satellite to focus on, so we were back and forth a couple of times. We got a ping, like I said, at six forty-one from that location. If the tracker on the device you're concerned about pinged us, then I guess one can assume that a piece of the equipment is still there, like I said."

"Assume! But we watched it move away from the scene."

"You must have seen something else. I wasn't here watching that event, but the record shows the pings came during the engagement with enemy troops. Our guys were hit and presumed dead before the extraction team could get there."

"But we saw it . . ." White stopped. *It they think it's still there, maybe it is. Maybe we were distracted by something else. Maybe I should let this go.*

"Sir? Are you still there?"

"Yes . . . yes, I am. The official report indicates the extraction team left the equipment behind, is that right?"

"There is no mention of any specific equipment. All we know is the ping we received at six thirty-one was consistent with earlier pings from any equipment that was on the scene before the extraction. It's still there."

"Hmm, interesting." White was puzzled. He had seen the tracking indicators light up. *Trapper, Granger, the guy from Secret Service, and the president had seen the tracker move. Langley hadn't watched. They missed it. Langley didn't follow the tracker.*

"Is that all, sir?"

White snapped back to the present.

"No, . . . I mean yes. That's all. Except, have a copy of that report sent to President Hunter tomorrow afternoon. I mean everything you have. He'll want to stay on top of all this."

"Fair enough, sir. Consider it done."

White turned his phone off and slowly slid it into his pocket. *This is an opportunity. I need to handle this right. Exactly right.*

chapter 12

Trapper Home – 7:05 PM EST

Mike had immediately assumed the role of grill master when he arrived home. Steve Granger hugged his wife, Sam, and procured two chilled beers from the fridge. So it was official, time to relax.

"I'm amazed the weather has held so we can still grill," Mike said as he filled the steaming, hot surface with burgers, hotdogs and bratwursts. The plan was to always have leftovers that could last a week, if needed.

"A jacket doesn't hurt, but still it's warm for January." Steve pulled two chairs toward the grill.

"Are you going to be upset if the girls join in the festivities?" Sam was bright-eyed and as perky as she had been years before. More recent years had been difficult for her and Steve as well. But together they had found the quiet settled life for which they had longed.

"There's nothing containing alcohol in that glass, is there?" Steve asked gently.

"No," Sam replied, dragging the word out and then growling at him. "I know better than that." The glow of pregnancy poured from her with every look, smile, move, and gesture. Sam was thrilled she was going to be a mom.

"Another exciting day at the office?" Elli asked as she took her seat.

"We could tell ya, but then you know, we'd have to, well you know."

"Worst John Wayne *ever!* You've got to find a new hero voice, sweetie."

"That wasn't John Wayne," Mike protested.

"Well, then who in the Sam Hill was it?"

Mike paused. He could not think of the actor's name. Sam picked up on it.

"Probably best left unsaid, Elli." Sam smiled and laughed as she sipped her iced tea. Everyone laughed, except Mike.

"Gonna let that slide, buddy?"

"Do I have a choice?" Mike asked smiling. He turned back to the grill and rotated the bratwurst and hotdogs.

Kashrote Helipad, Pakistan – 3:15 AM PKT

The landing woke him. The pilot had to stay awake to make the flight, and Failak was certain the harder-than-necessary landing was for his personal benefit. He didn't blame him. No one enjoys working in the middle of the night no matter how much they are paid.

Failak collected the backpack and the few other things he had brought and glanced at the pilot. They shared a mutual sneer. No love lost between them, were any ever to be found.

He climbed from the ancient helicopter and looked toward the terminal building. The entrance was less than two hundred meters away. He would walk and stretch his legs. His thoughts briefly returned to the communications compound high in the mountains.

They should all be back at the base by now. I wonder how long until they figure out that I am not returning. Failak had no idea that no one would return. No one would wonder about him. The handful that had remained would be asleep. It would be hours before anyone knew everything had changed.

He pulled hard on the terminal door and walked toward a lighted room down the short corridor. He didn't expect crowds of travelers in the middle of the night. He did expect someone would be there to meet him.

The phone call he had placed before he left the communications compound would have put everything into action. The prompt arrival of the helicopter at the mining camp confirmed to him that things were underway, but he needed instructions as to where he was to take the backpack. The instructions should be waiting at the terminal.

Failak rounded the corner from the hall into the waiting room. It was empty. A man stepped from the office behind the ticket counter as he entered. Failak walked toward him.

The man behind the counter was a patriot, one Failak knew was devoted to jihad. He was not angry about being awake in the middle of the night. It was a matter of duty, not anything like the attitudes of the first two men who had been paid for their services. This man was not paid to serve. He served out of faith in the cause and in Allah.

"You are Failak Jahnangir, no?"

"I am. What do you have for me?" Failak did not intend to speak as harshly as he did. He cleared his throat. "Please forgive my voice. I have been awake for most of the night."

"I understand, my brother. Allah does not call upon the faint of heart. Your service is well known."

The compliment left Failak slightly flustered. He was not often spoken to with kindness. Admiration, even slight admiration, was not customary. He normally projected terror and the most common response was fear.

"Thank you. Your words are kind and undeserved for this soldier of jihad." His humility was artificial, but an expected response to a flattering remark.

"This message arrived for you about an hour ago." The attendant handed him an envelope that was sealed. "Your plane will arrive here in a few hours. It is being readied in Islamabad as we speak. I have no bed to offer you, but you might be able to rest on one of the benches here. No one will disturb you until people begin to arrive for work at seven in the morning."

"But you do not know the *hour* the plane will arrive?"

"I do not. I am sorry."

Failak took the envelope, thanked the man, and turned to check out the benches. They were all the same, hard. But their location and the direction they faced were important to him. *Back to the wall, eyes on the door,* he repeated to himself as he surveyed the room.

He chose a bench and sat. He opened the envelope to find a significant sum of money and his ticket for the flight to Islamabad. He was pleased.

The only other contact for him was in Kabul. He did not care for the Afghani people. The majority were Pashtun, ancient nomads. Untrustworthy and divided in loyalty and language. They were dirty. He respected the people of Pakistan, the ancient Indus Valley Civilization dating back nine thousand years. To him they were noble and wise, and to be trusted. This was a good thing in his mind. He was pleased to be going to Pakistan.

Koto Kinabalu, Malaysia
Shangri-Las Tanjung Aru – 7:25 AM BNT

Robert awoke abruptly without an alarm. He hadn't used an alarm for weeks and was puzzled that he awakened as he had.

He rolled to his side and saw Yolanda still asleep. He could not help but stare. From the first moment he laid eyes on her, she had captivated him. At that time, she had been terrified by her drive from Dallas. She had been horrified from the morning she had experienced in Dallas. Through all of that, she was stunningly beautiful.

He touched her dark, thick hair and lifted it from her face. She stirred. Her eyes opened, and she smiled.

"You are still here?" she teased.

"Where would you expect me to be?"

"I don't know. Maybe someplace where you can be a big, strong man. Maybe you can save some poor people from terrible danger. Are you too busy for that?"

"Yes." He kissed her.

"You are a selfish man, aren't you?"

"Yes." He kissed her again.

"But we need to get up and pack for our flight home, don't you think?"

"Eventually," he said. "That won't take very long, will it?"

"Not so long," she said.

She threw herself across his chest and rose slowly, straddling him.

"First, you must show me that you really are a strong man." She leaned forward, lowering herself against him. They kissed.

"Don't forget, we still need to pack."

"I forget nothing," she chided. "But it is time for you to forget everything . . . but me." She smiled and sat up straight.

"And I promise, I won't remember a thing. Just you, babe."

The plane will be there, he said to himself. *The bags will be packed. We will make it to the airport . . . all in good time.*

Then, he really did forget everything else.

Trapper Home, Washington DC – 7:40 PM EST

The doorbell rang. The nerve-jangling clatter of what used to be a bell was more an annoyance than the interruption of a quiet evening. *I'm moving that bell to first place on the fix-it list,* Mike thought as he opened the door.

"Wang Zhu. I am surprised to see you here," Mike said extending his hand in welcome. Wang Zhu was the Chinese Ambassador to the States and a personal friend since the incident at the White House. He and his family had visited many times over the years, but an unannounced arrival was unusual and raised Mike's concern. "Please, come in."

"Thank you, Mike. Can we speak privately?"

"Sure." Mike led him into the living room. The laughter from the patio caused Zhu to pause.

"Is this a bad time?" His face reflected unease as he glanced toward the back.

"It's never a bad time to see you. Some times are simply more convenient. What's going on?"

"I'll be brief. An hour ago I received word from Beijing that an entire team of our best espionage agents was found dead."

"That's terrible. Where did this happen?"

"That, I cannot tell you, for obvious reasons. My supervisor would not be happy to know I am talking directly to you. I am bypassing normal channels of communication to come here."

"Don't do or say anything that will cause you trouble, please."

"I have to. This cannot wait."

"Then, let's have it."

"Six of our agents have been killed by a team of Americans."

Mike froze. As NSA liaison to the White House, as of tomorrow, he was the right person with whom to have a discussion. He trusted Zhu, but the meeting like this just felt out of sequence.

"Zhu, I promise you I have heard nothing about this. There is no plan that I am aware of to assassinate Chinese agents, anywhere, for any reason."

"President Makin gave you no indication of any such activity?"

"None. It doesn't sound like something he would do. It's just not him."

"That was my impression, but I had to ask."

"Ask what?" It was Steve Granger's voice that interrupted them. "Sorry, I just came for a beer. I didn't mean to break into an international conference."

"No, nothing official," Mike said in an effort to cover the grave look on his face.

"Steve, please join us. I could use your input," Wang Zhu requested. "Mike, are you all right with his hearing this?"

"If you're comfortable with him, I have no opposition."

Zhu told the story again.

"Do you know when the assault happened?" Steve asked.

"Less than six hours ago."

"But you can't tell us where it happened?"

"No, Mike. The location might come through another channel, but I cannot be that source. I am afraid I have said too much already. I just don't know."

"Okay, so within the last six hours you lost a team of agents . . . somewhere on planet Earth. And every indication suggests they were killed by an American team of assassins. I can only confirm to you that I haven't heard of anything like this coming through the White House. Steve, have you?"

"Zilch. But that doesn't preclude any black ops team from taking action. It could be CIA. Not likely, but it could. Zhu, is there any military objective that may have drawn the conflict?"

Now Zhu became more uncomfortable. He looked back and forth between Mike and Steve. "There is a rumor, and as far as I know that is all it is. It seems that someone made a very damaging attack on a MISC communications compound. Do you know of this?"

Mike paused. The entire CIA mission was Top Secret. Providing information regarding the campaign to an agent of a foreign nation would be treasonous.

"I'm going to say 'yes,' but very carefully. Do you understand?"

"Believe me, Mike, I understand. This is all very carefully considered."

"Do you think this is somehow connected to the murder of your agents?" Steve asked.

Again, Zhu paused.

"I do."

"Can you tell us why you believe that?"

"Our team had just been activated to retrieve some equipment used in the attack on the MISC compound. The notification was sent to them less than an hour before they were killed."

Steve looked at Mike. They both knew the 'equipment' in question was the USURP device. They were both amazed that someone outside the top-secret echelons of the United States government knew about it as well.

"Do you know of some device that is missing?" Zhu asked.

"My friend, this is where I must neither confirm nor deny that I know anything." Mike looked directly at Zhu.

Zhu held his gaze then slowly nodded his head. "Okay, so we have a real problem here, it would seem."

"I think that sizes it up very nicely," Mike replied.

"Thank you, Mike. I must return to the embassy. I will contact you through the normal channels very shortly. Will you be at the White House?"

"Now I will, in an hour or so. And Zhu, I'm sorry for the loss of your countrymen."

"Thank you, again. Talk to you soon."

Wang Zhu made his way quickly to the door and left.

Mike closed the door and turned to Steve. "Holy crap, Granger. What the hell is going on?"

"Not sure. But it looks like we need to find out."

The dinner party was over.

chapter 13

Colonel Stevens leaned over the mapping table in the grid room. Keith was across from him piecing the data fragments together on *kouzen*. The facial analysis and the voiceprint from Singapore had made the match. The two different names used when he had entered and departed from Singapore were sure to help expand the search. They still did not know who this man was.

The biometric file was growing, but not as quickly as Stevens wanted. Waiting for further information from the agents at Subang Airport north of Kuala Lumpur was straining his patience. As he began to give voice to his impatience, his phone rang.

"Colonel Stevens."

"Aaron, it's Daniel. We got him."

Aaron Stevens paused. He had been down this path before.

"But not in custody, right?"

"Oh, heavens no. Even here a person must break a law before they are arrested."

"Okay, then what do you have?"

"My agents videoed him as he approached the exit gate at Subang."

"So, he wasn't boarding another flight immediately?"

"No. He took a cab to the Hyatt Regency in Saujana a couple miles from the airport. He registered under the name Charles Mark Dalton."

"Dalton? What kind of name it that? I mean nationality, of course."

"Probably fake . . . or English, maybe Irish in origin. But certainly an American because that's where just about all of them live. No current records outside the U.S."

"But is that his real name?"

"Probably not, Aaron. But now we can enter all three names into the fuzzy extractor along with a face, his gait analysis, handwriting and a couple of voice prints. I recommend we begin in India."

"You read my thoughts well, Daniel."

"It's only reasonable, Aaron."

"Fine. At least you have confirmed I am a reasonable person. Let us know what you find."

"I may not be back to you very soon."

"Something else giving you trouble?"

"Might say that. We have six dead Chinese citizens and, I must assume, agents in the Marina Bay Sands hotel."

"That's not good. Be careful."

"As always. Talk to you later."

The line went dead.

Keith Dillon looked up from his work. "What's new?"

"We got him," Stevens said without looking up.

Keith stifled a snicker. "Good. He's a rotten S.O.B. anyway."

Kashrote, Pakistan Airport – 5:10 AM PKT

Failak awoke to the whine of a jet engine as a small plane turned sharply on the tarmac outside the tiny terminal. He shook the fog of sleep from his mind and looked toward the ticket counter. The agent was looking out the window also.

"Your plane is here sooner than I thought."

"Is this the plane that comes here every day?"

"No, this one is much newer."

Failak grew concerned. *If this wasn't the plane that was expected should I board it? Who is on that plane?*

The terminal door opened, and a large man with a shaved head stepped through.

"Are you Failak Jahnangir?"

"Yes."

"You are to come with me."

"What about my ticket?"

"You don't need it, just get in the plane."

Failak shouldered the backpack and walked boldly to the open door. His skin prickled under his clothing. Any sudden move from this man and he would react with deadly force. He was not sure this man was a friend. There was only one thing to do with an enemy. Kill them.

He stepped outside into the bitter cold. The wind had picked up and blew icy particles against his face. It was colder than when he arrived. It was always colder just before dawn. The morning sunlight reflected off the high peaks to the west casting an amber hue. The two men walked quickly through the morning twilight Failak had known and loved from childhood.

The plane was less than twenty-five feet from the terminal. He walked with keen awareness of the man just behind him. He came to the steps of the small twin-engine jet and climbed them quickly. The inside of the plane was spotless and glowed with indirect lighting. *Surely, this is from Paradise.*

"You sit here," the bald man ordered.

Failak took the seat, buckled himself in, and set the backpack at his feet. The steward pulled the door shut, and the jet began to move toward the runway.

"It is not safe for the pack to be free to slide about the cabin. Please, let me put it in the luggage area," the large bald man said standing over Failak.

"I don't know you. How can I trust you?"

"I am not here to harm you, Failak. You are a great warrior for jihad, known to many for your bravery and service. Please, the backpack is not safe sitting on the floor."

"All right." He lifted the backpack and handed it to him. Failak watched carefully as the bald man carried the pack to the rear of the plane, opened a small bin and carefully placed it inside.

The large bald man spoke softly to the cabin steward and took his seat across from Failak. As he sat, the plane lurched forward, speeding down the runway. In seconds the nose lifted and the rumbling of the wheels on the runway fell silent. They were airborne.

The small plane sliced through the amber glow of morning twilight and quickly leaped into full sunlight. Failak winced at the brightness and pulled back from the window. His ears popped as he swallowed.

"There is a shade on the window," the bald man said as he lowered the blind in his window.

Failak fumbled with the sliding shade and lowered it. "How long until we get to Islamabad?"

"You do not know?" the bald man asked. "We are not going to Islamabad. Where we are going you will not need your heavy coat."

Before he could ask a question, the steward placed a plate of steaming hot food in front of him. Failak was speechless.

"Eat," his companion said with a broad smile.

Failak ate. *Perhaps I am not going to die today after all.*

Hyatt Regency Hotel, Saujana, Malaysia – 8:20 AM MYT

The two agents who had been dispatched by Deputy Commissioner Daniel Sim to follow the suspect *kouzen* at the airport, sat calmly in the lobby of the busy hotel. The desk clerk had allowed them to take a picture of the man's signature, the customs card he had filled out, and the registration papers. The agents knew his room number and would be told if any phone calls were routed to the suspect's room.

Such a call had been received shortly after the suspect's arrival at the hotel. The agents were confident the suspect's arrival had been monitored by someone in the lobby. They were also certain that person was no longer on the premises.

The desk clerk had delayed the call long enough for one of the agents to monitor and record it. From the call the agent learned of a meeting in a tea salon about a block from the hotel. He was also able to determine the men he was to meet were American. No question. The recording was immediately forwarded to Commissioner Sim at the Singapore Department of Investigations and Intelligence.

The agents' attire was informal. They did not dress like government men. No black suits and white shirts. One was dressed very casually with a light sweater over his shoulders. The other wore a sport coat and an open collared shirt. They communicated with very simple gestures, and kept fifty feet between them as they executed their mission.

The elevator door opened, and their suspect exited into the lobby. The younger agent wearing the sweater stood and moved slowly toward the hotel entrance. He looked down the street as if he were expecting someone.

The suspect walked swiftly across the lobby, past the agent and through the doors onto the street. The agent in the sweater slowly followed him out the door. The older agent in the sport coat left his newspaper beside his seat as he stood. He pressed a small pager in his right hand. Immediately, a car pulled to the front of the hotel. He entered the car and instructed the driver to take him to the TWG Tea Salon two blocks down.

As the car passed the suspect, the young agent in the sweater followed on the sidewalk across the street. The threesome continued to their destination, two of them scrutinizing every move of the one they followed. The suspect walked more confidently that he should have and was unaware he was being followed.

He entered the tea salon. The older agent in the sport coat was already seated at a table that provided a clear view of the entire salon. The maitre'd was instructed by the older agent to direct the suspect to a specific table.

The suspect was smiling when he entered and politely asked for a table for six. He was directed to a table that seemed private but one that could be monitored.

The younger agent entered, without his sweater, and greeted the older man. They appeared to be a father and son, or uncle and nephew meeting for morning tea and pastries.

Five minutes later, six American men in business attire entered the salon and greeted the suspect at his table. They were not boisterous like Americans generally were. They appeared happy to see each other but spoke softly.

The older agent held a new cell phone in his hand with a tiny earphone in his ear. He spoke loudly enough to be convincing, commenting on the final plays of the football game just past halftime in Kansas City, Missouri. It was a ruse.

The 'phone' was a sensitive listening device that was recording every word at the suspects' table. They were Americans. They were on schedule for their mission. The Chinese were out of the way. They would wait patiently until further instructions arrived.

The two agents, as well as the Deputy Commissioner of Investigations and Intelligence in Singapore, knew they were killers. They knew the men were dangerous. They also sensed something else was in the works.

The Trapper Home, Washington DC – 8:50 PM EST

Sam and Steve had been gone for twenty minutes. The fun had come to an end far too soon. Elli's mood reflected the disappointment.

"I'm sorry, honey," Mike said swinging her into his embrace. He pulled her close against his chest. She let out a plaintive sigh.

"I know. Something big has just gone down and the world needs Mike Trapper to fix it. I get it." She looked up at him with a pained look. "Sometimes I think the world could just go to hell and leave us alone."

"Elli, it does go to hell, every day, all on its own. People like me all over the planet work very hard to keep it from falling completely apart. You knew—"

"Yes, I know. This was just such a great evening with Steve and Sam. I hate to see it end too soon."

The phone in the hallway rang. She looked down the hall toward the phone, and then back at Mike. Her mouth was skewered to one side with her lower lip out a bit.

"No. I am not surprised." Elli gave a futile shrug and stomped into the kitchen. Mike smiled as she imitated four-year-old Riley's huff when he didn't get his way. Her disappointment was real, though. The huff was her humorous way of dealing with it.

"Trapper."

"Hi, Mike. Aaron Stevens in Little Rock. I am very sorry to interrupt your evening and call you at home."

"You're lucky you caught me here, I was just headed back to the White House. What's up?"

"I think it's time I bring you up to speed on the day's events."

"The White House is falling behind, again?"

"It's something of a tradition."

Mike chuckled. "What's going on?"

"Ever since the initial explosion of data this morning, we have continued to be buried in new information. The stuff of most interest has come to me from Daniel Sim in Singapore. Is this line safe for this kind of discussion?"

"It took a while, but with my moving from the Secret Service to the NSA it finally was approved. You may speak freely. No more taps."

"Good. Daniel alerted us to a double-agent working between the US and Russia. I should say, working the two sides against each other. No one knows who he is, but his existence has never been in question."

"This is what you called me about this morning, isn't it?"

"Exactly. Singapore Intelligence picked up a call from near the site of the attack on the compound this morning. It seems someone in MISC has contact with this guy. I mean, he's a ghost. But through the day we've collected more intelligence on him. Right now we are running his biometric file with information from India."

"Good. Where does all this lead us?"

"It seems there has been chatter about some technical equipment that has gone missing. This secret agent we only know as *Kouzen* is on the move. He just met with a small group of Americans in Kuala Lumpur. Plus, I just learned that a team of Chinese operatives was found dead in Singapore."

"They were in Singapore?"

"You knew about them?"

"Well, yes. But I didn't know *where* they were."

"But, how did you—"

"Can't go there. Okay?"

Colonel Stevens paused. "All right. As we reviewed the information it was peculiar to us that this suspect just happened to leave Singapore shortly after the murders of the Chinese occurred. Add in the phone call from a very secret spot in the Hindu Kush Mountains that just happened to be destroyed only hours earlier. Finally, we discover we have some highly sensitive equipment missing, and we have a mystery."

"How connected are they?"

"Right now, only by circumstances. It all happened in, what, the last twelve hours?"

"Thirteen."

"Thirteen hours?"

"Anything else?" Mike looked at Elli in the kitchen.

"We're following up with Devanagari, the Indian Bureau, on some of the biometrics on *Kouzen* as well of some of their own skullduggery. They went to their highest-level alert this morning when all hell broke loose."

"Do you have a file you can send me on all this?"

"It will take half an hour to reduce it to a file, but yes."

"Good. I'll be in my office shortly after that. And thanks, Aaron."

Mike placed a quick call to Steve about meeting at the White House in about forty-five minutes. Then he walked into the kitchen. A certain little woman was still in a pout over the events of the evening.

He stepped behind her and slid his arms around her waist. He could feel her smile. He pulled her close.

"Not now. I'm busy," she said in a falsely gruff voice.

He turned her gently to face him. He kissed her. She melted against him.

"Too busy to comfort a lonely soldier headed to the front?"

She snickered and buried her face in his chest.

"Oh, I suppose. If I *have* to." The snicker became one of those shoulder-shaking silent chuckles. She was warm in his embrace.

Slowly, she took his hand, turned, and led him toward the stairs.

chapter 14

Streets of Washington DC – 9:05 PM EST

President-elect Hunter sat in the back seat of the limo with his wife Susan as they sped down Rhode Island Ave. Their eyes met, and they both smiled. He grabbed her hand.

"We did it," he said jubilantly.

"We did. But we had a lot of help. Don't forget that little fact, darling."

"Oh, yes. The little people."

"Ronnie! Don't even *joke* like that." Then she smiled and chuckled a little. "I know you're jesting, but many in the press corps would kill you over such a comment."

"And that would make them even littler people. Small minds mind small matters."

He settled back and gazed out the window. "Remember how much we hated to come to this town?"

"When I think about it, I do. It's funny how circumstances change one's view."

He looked at her. "Tell me just how you mean that comment, Madame Almost-President?"

"Just that. We're in an entirely different position. You know I have always had a bad taste in my mouth for politicians and their hordes of minions. I like creative people who dare to challenge the odds and win."

"Like me."

"Like you." Her reply was solicitous with a hint of seduction.

"And yet, I'm surrounded by minions."

"That's fine, dear. Just as long as you leave them at work."

"They will be scurrying around one floor below our new home. How in the world are you going to deal with that?"

"Same way I deal with you, my dear."

He paused turning his head to the side and looking at her. *How does she deal with me?* "And how is that, darling?"

"I'll smother them with kindness."

"Genuine kindness?"

"Most of the time. You can never tell, can you?"

"I guess not." The phone in his pocket rang. "Hunter."

"Mr. President, this is August White."

"Augie, my main man." He turned to Susan and mouthed, *Little people.* She giggled. "What can I do for you?"

"Nothing for me, sir. I wanted to bring you up to date on the issue in Afghanistan from this morning."

"Great. My first security briefing. Whatcha got?" He winked at Susan.

"The device that was of so much concern is still up in the mountains at the site of the conflict. It seems that MISC did not carry it off."

"But you said you tracked it with Makin and the guys that worked for him. You said it appeared to have been taken to the compound. What is it? Did they get it or not?"

"Mr. President, we did watch what we believed to be the signals from the device, both in and out of the backpack. But the official record at Langley is that the last ping they received on the device was in the mountains near where the attack occurred. I cannot explain it, but I think it's a stroke of good luck for us."

"How so?'

"If they don't have it, we don't need to explain it, and how it came up missing."

"But the others did see it, didn't they?"

"They saw what they wanted to see. You and I both know the official CIA record of the event carries more weight than what someone believes they have seen."

Hunter paused. *Maybe, just maybe.* "So technically, the device doesn't exist so it couldn't be lost."

"Pretty much, boss. At least for now."

"Good. Tomorrow is a big day, Augie. We can talk more in the evening. Good night." The president-elect turned off his phone.

"Big business, already? Shouldn't all this secret stuff wait until tomorrow?" Susan asked pulling herself close to his side.

"Naw. Small potatoes." He patted her arm with his hand and looked out the window again. *I hope it's small potatoes.*

1004 19th Street NW, 3rd Floor, Washington DC – 9:15 PM EST

"We got that, right?"

"Every word."

"We are on the up and up, aren't we? I don't want to be involved with anything un-American, if you catch my drift."

"We are as American as apple pie, my friend." His eye never left the monitor, his hands never stopped typing.

"But what if we find out we are being used to do something we shouldn't."

"Are you complaining about getting paid, or what?"

"No. I don't know, it feels kinda funny."

"Your perspective is wrong."

"How's that?"

He turned to face his assistant. "You're looking at all this as some sort of violation of privacy. Buddy, we're recording history as it happens. We are historians *for* America. This is a public service we're doing."

The assistant cocked his head at the revelation. "Oh. So we're just making a record of the new president *for* the country. That makes sense."

"Good. Now get the field team out to the next location. I'd like them be there before the president-elect arrives."

"I'm on it boss. I'm on it."

NSA Office, White House – 9:30 PM EST

Mike was at his desk when Steve Granger entered. "You're not going to like this."

"Like what?" Steve tossed his jacket on the back of a chair.

"The CIA report on the attack at the compound."

"Why? Did they skip over something? Like maybe the other shooter on the grassy knoll?"

"Ha. Their report concludes the USURP device never left the site of the battle the Marines fought. They say there was a ping at . . . wait, I saw it here . . . *'a ping, consistent with the device in question was registered at six forty-one p.m., Eastern Standard Time.'"*

"That's nuts!" Steve said dropping himself into a chair. "We *saw* it. We watched it go back to the compound. We saw the trackers come on when they removed it from the backpack."

"We did. Apparently, they didn't."

"So, according to the 'official record,' what we saw, along with the president, didn't happen."

"Pretty much sums it up. Remember, they had higher priorities they wanted to focus the satellite on. They were busy elsewhere."

"But it was a CIA operation!" Steve was livid. "Why wouldn't they watch their own mission? This makes no sense at all."

"I agree. Their operation was complete, and the Marines extracted. They're done with it. But we need to work with what we have. For the next twenty-four to thirty-six hours, no one is going to be doing much besides watching the Inauguration of a new president. We have time to do a little digging on our own."

"Did we keep a copy of the feed we got from Langley?"

"Of course. But that isn't going to change the official report until we can collect more information."

"But it *shows* the device being moved."

Mike turned to his friend. "Steve, you know how this town works. Nothing is fixed, everything is fluid. For the moment, the stream of political thought has moved on. Sometime soon it will need to be re-directed to what actually happened. That will be our opportunity to make our point, and hopefully embarrass the crap out of the CIA."

Steve let out a breath and looked at Mike. "I just don't get it."

"That's fine for now. Let's go back over the facts we know. Maybe we'll see what could happen."

The two men spread area maps on Mike's desk and brought the video up on his computer. The twenty-four-inch screen helped them match the topography and pin point the locations of the pings they had tracked through the afternoon.

The route marked on the map followed a rugged mountain road back to the MISC compound.

"Okay, we are certain they went back. The rest of this is speculation."

"But reasonable speculation, Mike."

"Yes, it's reasonable." Mike traced the road on the map into the valley and then to the mining company with the helipad. "Again, our best guess is the chopper flight to Kashrote."

"Then where?" Steve asked, leaning back in his chair.

"Initially, I'd guess Kabul or Islamabad. After that, it's anybody's guess."

Mike's phone rang. He reached for it and looked at the screen. "It's OCT." He answered, "Aaron, thanks for calling back. What else do you have for us?"

"We're still waiting for a call from the Indian Bureau in Mumbai. The guys should be sending you the complete file any minute."

"Can you check on one more thing for us?"

"Sure. What is it?"

"We have lost the trail on a suspect."

"From the attack this morning?"

Mike paused. "Yes. We believe someone left the compound with a piece of equipment we need to get back."

"The USURP device."

Mike was surprised. "I didn't realize you knew about that."

"Mike, it's what we do."

"Okay, yeah, that's what we're concerned about. We believe he left a mining company up in the mountains by helicopter and flew to Kashrote. That's the closest airport, anyway. We need to know of any flights that are leaving or have already departed, and where they're headed."

"We can tap into radar and check with friendly countries about anything unusual."

"Like India?" Mike interjected.

"Precisely. They watch everything, you know."

"Yeah. So, I've heard."

"One question before I go."

"Shoot."

"Do you think this ties into the dead Chinese agents in any way?"

Again, Mike paused. "I have it from a very reliable source that the agents were activated by Beijing to acquire a piece of equipment linked to the attack this morning."

"The USURP device," Aaron said softly.

"Yes. And we believe the person bringing it to them is the guy we followed through the mountains. The same person who took a flight out of Kashrote to someplace. We need to know about that flight."

"Got it. Mike, this could get pretty ugly before it's over."

"A lot depends on who killed the Chinese."

"Or if we don't get that device back."

"Yeah." Mike's thoughts trailed off into a frightening future. Just then his fax machine chirped to life. "Looks like that file is coming in, Aaron."

"Good. Throw it all in the mix of data, and I'll get back to you when we hear anything about a flight from Kashrote."

"Thanks, Aaron."

Mike hung up his phone and turned to begin sorting the papers from his fax machine.

OCT Little Rock – 9:40 PM CST

Aaron Stevens walked quickly toward the grid room where he knew he would find Keith Dillon hard at work. He wasn't disappointed.

"Keith, what are you working on right now?"

"I'm trying to piece together the information we have on *kouzen* in different ways to see if we would come to a different result. Also, I'm introducing scenarios to anticipate what we might get from IB."

"India Bureau?"

"Yeah. That's what they call it. A lot easier to say 'IB' and eliminate all the extra syllables." Keith looked at Aaron with his normal dead pan stare.

"Okay, fine. But we need to track some radar data going back a few hours."

"Local or overseas?"

"Since everything is happening over there right now, let's begin on the other side of the planet."

Keith's stare turned to his bank of screens. Two taps on the keyboard opened a display of flights over Iran, Pakistan, and western India. "This is present time. You want to see earlier, right?"

"Yes," Aaron replied. "Let's go back four hours and see what we can pick up."

"This is a composite of land radar and satellite imagery that should show us everything that is in the air, even up in the mountains. Can't hide behind a mountain from space, you know."

"I suspected as much. How did you get this set up so quickly?"
"I sorta figured you might want to look at this. I mean if some guy is trying to get away with our secret stuff, we need to know what he's up to, right?"
"You figured correctly, Keith."
"Usually do, Colonel."
The screen fast reversed in time. Tiny dots representing commercial and military aircraft spun wildly back to their points of origin.
"You do understand that air traffic is very limited at night. Four hours ago puts them at roughly one thirty in the morning." Keith looked over his shoulder at Aaron Stevens.
"That's what I suspected."
"Here we are at one-thirty a.m. Pakistani time."
"Can you zoom in on northern Pakistan?"
"Sure can."
The picture dove into the sparsely populated region of Pakistan-controlled Kashmir. The rugged mountains did not show on the screen. Military and commercial traffic flew at altitudes higher than the mountain peaks. Smaller aircraft and helicopters were required to follow the canyons between the high ridges maintaining lower altitudes and longer flights between two points.
"We're looking for anything moving in the air." Aaron winced at his own obvious remark. Keith politely acted as if he didn't notice.
A single dot of light moved southward and a little to the east.
"This right here is the mountain where the attack occurred this morning," Keith pointed out. "Do you want me to see if I can bring in the topography?"
"Yeah, do it."
The small point of light continued to move in a straight line to the south, southeast, away from the mountain compound. After half a dozen keystrokes the craggy mountains pixeled into view.
"That's cool."
"Just superimposed Google Earth. Pretty slick, actually."

The two men watched the point of light follow a weaving path through the mountain valleys.

"Moving that slow that has to be a helicopter," Keith observed. "Not too many aircraft could maintain enough lift to keep them airborne in that high altitude going that slow. Gotta be a chopper. Where did you say we think it's headed?"

"I don't remember saying, but the only airport in the area is at Kashrote."

Keith typed in the query, and a dot identified the small town.

"It's amazing," he mused. "These folks are flying through Chinese airspace, probably undetected, and will move into Pakistan with little notice. And they probably do it all the time because nobody cares."

"Let's hope that's the case. I'd hate to have that chopper blown out of the sky and the Chinese get their hands on that equipment." Aaron knew they were looking back in time. His hope to regain the device forced him to disallow a threat from another nation.

The dot changed course, turning to the west. The next stop would clearly be the helipad at the airport in Kashrote. Keith sped the video up and the dot charged ahead to the suspected landing spot.

"Let's keep going ahead at a faster speed," Aaron advised. "We don't know how long he waited to be picked up, or if he's still waiting."

They watched in silence as an hour of time passed on the screen.

Another small dot appeared at the bottom edge of the screen. It moved faster and in a straight line toward Kashrote.

"This is our guy, Colonel."

"How do you know?"

"He's at a high enough altitude to fly over the peaks, thus the straight line, probably a jet, and his transponder is turned off. If this was a legit private or commercial flight, the screen would show the transponder number so the plane could be properly identified."

"So, he's intentionally avoiding an ID."

"That means whoever this is, he's up to no good."

chapter 15

Shangri-La Tanjung Aru, Koto Kinabalu, Malaysia
10:05 AM BNT

Yolanda, Mrs. Robert P. Hitchens III, was beginning to pack. Robert had been ready for at least an hour.

"Honey, we need to be ready to go."

"I am almost ready," she replied nonchalantly.

"But you're not packed."

"Robert, should I wear the shawl you bought me on the beach yesterday?"

"Sweetheart, you are beautiful without it. Be comfortable. It's just a short flight, and we will have time to rest and dress up for dinner. Just wear comfortable traveling clothes."

"What about this one?" Yolanda swept into the main room of their cottage wearing a lace baju kurung in purple. She spun gently, allowing the skirt and overblouse to billow around her before wrapping gently around her feminine form. Her little parade had the esired effect. She looked at Robert and saw the breath leave his lungs.

"Uh—you're—just —"

She sashayed toward him seductively.

"I thought this was a good color on me. What do you think?" She spun again.

"I—it's very—uh, I mean, nice."

"Nice!" she retorted. "Oh, Robert, you are such a—*a man.* What is wrong with you? I come to you as a *woman*, in this *beautiful* dress, and you say *nice?*" She turned and stomped into the bedroom. *"Por todos los cielos. Los hombres son imposibles. Yo deberia haber excuchado a mi madre!"*

Robert followed her with a very confused expression on his face. He held his hands out in a plea for understanding. "Honey, wait. Hold on."

Yolanda angrily slithered out of her kurung and overblouse throwing them on the bed. Her anger melted when she felt Robert's hand on her bare shoulder. He gently turned her to face him.

"Yolanda, you are stunning. You surprised me. I couldn't even think—I couldn't begin to put how—oh, my gosh, I still can't. You're an angel. You are everything a man could ever hope for. I'm sorry, but I just couldn't find the words."

"Really?" She stepped toward him and took one of the buttons on his shirt between her fingers.

"From the first moment I first saw you I knew you were nothing less than magnificent."

"And after last night? —"

"After every night." Robert gently lifted her chin and drew her lips to his. They kissed. "Sweetie, I don't want to share you in any way. Look stunning for me. Please wear jeans and a sweatshirt on the plane."

She drew back from him.

"You don't want me to be beautiful in public? Is that it? You want me to hide in ugly clothes all the time?"

"It is impossible for you to *not* be beautiful. People notice you everywhere we go. The only way I could hide you from the world is put a basket over your head, and I would *never* do that."

"Is that what you think?"

"Of course. When we're out just doing normal stuff you don't need to try at all to be gorgeous. You *are.*"

Yolanda smiled and coyly turned from him. She was enjoying this.

"Babe, I want you to wear that outfit tonight when we go out for dinner," he said. "Every woman in the place will be jealous, and every man will be speechless. I guarantee it."

She spun around and threw her arms around his neck. She paused and looked into his eyes. "And this will never end?"

"Never."

She kissed him as he lifted her from the floor.

"Okay. I've got to pack. Go on, put me down and get out of here. Shoo!"

Robert lowered her to her feet and stepped back into the living room. Much to her delight, the bewildered look returned to his face.

OCT Little Rock – 9:15 PM CST

Keith Dillon and Colonel Aaron Stevens had monitored the flight of the unmarked plane as it crossed most of Pakistan. They were still almost an hour behind real time. The single dot moved much too fast to be a small, single engine plane.

"Does Pakistan not care about an unidentified aircraft passing through their airspace?" Keith asked.

"If they did they would have shot it down by now. They are either watching and waiting, like we are, or they already know who is on board and where they're going. My guess would be the latter."

"India doesn't have the same gracious attitude I would imagine."

"Especially with a plane coming from Pakistan. Those two countries do have a history, you know."

"It will be interesting to watch if it crosses into India."

Just as he finished speaking the transponder data flashed onto the screen.

"And there's your answer. Looks like any other private flight to me."

"Yup," Keith replied as he scratched the numbers on a slip of paper. "I'll check the registry and see what I can find on the flight plan."

Aaron Stevens remained hunched over the screen. He spoke to the dot they had been following. "Once we know where you are going, we'll be sure to have someone there to meet you."

It was only a guess based on circumstances. But it was a good guess in Aaron's mind. The evidence raised too many questions, especially in light of the attack earlier that morning. *This has to be our guy. It just has to be.*

38,000 Feet Over Uttar Pradesh, India – 7:35 AM IST

The Learjet 75 cruised at five hundred thirty-five miles per hour over the plains of central India. Failak had never ridden in a private jet. He had never known such luxury.

Earlier he had watched in awe as the Himalayan Mountains slipped silently past his view. He had read about them, but to see them with his own eyes was little short of miraculous. The majestic peaks make those of his homeland look small.

Failak had no interest in the people of India. He had heard from some who had traveled there that the land was dusty and always hot. He had also heard that both the food and the people of that strange land smelled odd. He wondered if the people made the food smell, or if the food the people ate made them smell. He didn't know. Much more so, he didn't care. He would never go there to find out.

But the mountains were incredible. He knew mountains, but none as large as these. He was spellbound by them.

The plane banked slightly to the left, holding the position for several seconds. *We are turning.* He was beginning to feel the motion of the plane like one feels the movement of a strong horse at a full gallop. The coursing strides of the powerful animal became smooth when it ran fast. So it was in this amazing machine, ever thrusting itself forward through hazy blue skies, never challenged or hindered.

The bald man walked toward him. He was smiling. Failak relaxed.

"The pilot has just made our first course change turning us toward our destination." He sat in the seat just across the aisle from Failak. "I am sorry we were not able to tell you where we are going. In truth, neither I nor the pilot knew until a few minutes ago. Sometimes security requires us to be overly cautious."

"I understand," Failak replied. "Can you tell me where it is we are going?"

"Yes. In a few more hours we will land in Kuala Lumpur, Malaysia."

Failak's eyes widened with shock. His heart pounded in his chest. His breath became shallow.

"You are surprised."

"More than surprised. How am I to return home? Who is requiring this of me?" Questions spun in his mind. He felt dizzy. "I was not expecting this."

"Nor was I. You will see that the people we are working for are very kind. They are gentle, as long as we do our part."

"And what is my *part* in all this?" Failak didn't know if he should be angry or afraid.

"Your part is to deliver the backpack you brought on board this plane." The large bald man smiled assuringly at him.

Failak looked down. He felt by instinct that he should do something to take control of his situation. He could kill the large bald man, but that would accomplish nothing. The man had been nice to him. And he certainly could not kill the pilot. Killing the cabin steward would be senseless, and Allah would not be happy with that, not that Failak cared what Allah thought.

He looked up at the bald man and nodded his head.

"I will do my part, and expect them to do theirs. It is a matter of respect and duty. If they do not return me to my home, then I will kill them."

The large bald man smiled and nodded his head. "That would be exactly what I would do in your situation. You will be well cared for, I can assure you. But there is more that you must know."

"I was hoping there might be."

"When we arrive, you will be given a ticket for a flight to your final destination. I am told there will be six other men on the flight who will make themselves known to you. They are there to protect you and make sure no one disturbs you in your travel. I do not know who these men are, but you will meet them after your flight has left Kuala Lumpur."

"Where will I go from there?"

"That, I cannot tell you. I do not know myself."

"Your part is to deliver me to them. My part is to deliver the backpack to someone else."

"Yes." The large bald man smiled. Failak thought that under different circumstances he would be a friend to this man. But the circumstance was not different. After they landed in a few hours, he would never see him again.

Failak nodded and turned back to the view through his window. The scenery had changed slightly. The mountains were behind them and plains had given way to dusty hills covered with scrubby trees and small villages. He was pleased he was not required to travel through the dirty land filled with people who smelled odd.

International Airport Koto Kinabalu, Malaysia
10:45 AM MYT

"Robert, you are making me run to keep up with you," Yolanda complained.

"And if we don't run and catch our flight we will have to swim home."

Robert was not happy with how long it had taken to leave the hotel. He didn't voice his complaint, but he knew his bride was well aware of his frustration. To make matters a little worse, she seemed to be irritated at him for being frustrated.

"Robert, please walk a little slower. I cannot keep up with you."

He stopped.

"Sweetheart, we are about to miss our flight. If we miss our flight here we may not be able to catch our plane in Kuala Lumpur. That's the one that takes us back to the United States. We want, rather, we *need* to be on that plane. We must hurry."

"Do you know what gate we need for our flight?"

Robert fumbled with the tickets, managing to keep the six bags he was carrying from falling off his shoulders. "Gate Eleven. We need to go. *Now.*"

"But, Robert—"

"No, honey. We don't have time to stand around."

"Robert!" Her stern demand stopped him dead in his tracks. He turned to her.

"What?" Both he and his tone were exasperated.

Yolanda smiled and turned slightly to her left saying, "Do you mean like that Gate Eleven?"

He looked up with a blank gaze and realized they were twenty feet away from Gate Eleven. The very same Gate Eleven he was rushing to find and nearly walked past.

"Yes. That's probably the Gate Eleven we need." He swallowed hard. "It seems we're here."

"And we are here exactly on time. See, I knew we would not be late. Things work out for me like that. I am never late. Robert, you must learn to trust me." She turned and walked away with a smart little wiggle that made Robert smile.

OCT Little Rock – 10:00 PM CST

His desk phone rang. "Colonel Stevens."

"Aaron, I'm glad you're still working. Do you ever go home?" asked Daniel Sim.

"Just like you, my friend. We work until the job is done. What can I do for you?"

"We just got the ballistic reports from the murder of the Chinese agents. It isn't very good news."

"American?"

"Yes. All the bullets came from Springfield 1911s, standard CIA handguns."

"A pricy little weapon."

"A very efficient and very American weapon."

"Right. Sorry about that, Daniel. We have bad guys, too."

"But we never expect them to come from the CIA."

"Has that panned out to be true?"

"No, we only suspect that the men who met with our elusive stranger are CIA. And we don't know if they are actually carrying 1911s."

"Have you questioned them or taken any of them into custody?"

"Eating lunch, even with suspicious people, is not against the law in Malaysia."

Aaron smiled. He knew his friend had cause for suspicion but not proof to detain the suspects. "So, we're sort of in the same place."

"With the exception that the Chinese agents were all killed by weapons commonly carried by the CIA."

"No prints on the scene. No disposed weapons you've stumbled upon, right?"

"Exactly, Aaron. Nothing unusual. The only other thing is that the six men arrived together for lunch with *Kouzen,* but they left separately. I had only two men at the location, so we lost them when they left."

"But they kept up with *Kouzen*, right?"

"As I learned in your country many years ago, 'like a duck on a June bug.' *Kouzen* returned to his hotel and has remained there."

The door to Aaron's office swung open. Keith Dillon stood in the opening, both hands braced against the frame. His eyes held a wild look that startled the colonel.

"Just a minute, Daniel." Stevens covered the mouthpiece and said to Keith, "What is it?"

"We just heard back from India Bureau. They ID'ed him. We know who he is."

chapter 16

NSA Office, White House – 11:10 PM EST

Mike and Steve were still huddled over the desktop. Kabul and Islamabad had long been discarded as points of interest or concern regarding the USURP device. Although the device had emitted no transmissions identifying its location, they were very confident it was on the small jet flying across India.

"What's the range of a Learjet 75?" Mike asked.

"Probably a couple thousand miles," Steve said looking up from the map. "That doesn't help much, does it? I'll Google it."

He stepped to the credenza and the laptop resting on it. After a few keystrokes he said, "Just over two thousand miles."

"A heavy payload would reduce that," Mike said.

"But we're probably talking about a handful of people and a backpack."

"Right. How far could a person go with a light cargo?"

"From the start point in Pakistan, and headed southeast, about a thousand miles out in the Indian Ocean, or the Bay of Bengal."

"As long as they maintain that heading."

"Right."

"I suppose they could refuel in India."

"Or Myanmar." A dispirited tone hovered over their conversation.

"It's late. Maybe we should—" Mike's phone rang. "Trapper."

"Mike, this is Aaron Stevens. I know it's the middle of the night, but we have news."

"I'm in my office. You're not interrupting anything. We were about ready to head home."

"You'll probably want to reconsider that. We have identified this guy *Kouzen*."

"What? You know who he is?"

"Just confirmed it. First, I need to let you know the ballistics from the bullets taken from the Chinese agents are from weapons like those carried by the CIA. The folks in Singapore are convinced that some of our guys did the killing."

"That's a bit of a smudge on our reputation in the South Seas."

"Yeah. All from 1911s."

"Springfields?"

"Standard CIA issue."

"Okay, what about *Kouzen*?"

"Well, as you might have expected, *Kouzen* isn't his real name. The Indian Bureau identified him as Mikael Edwin Kohen, goes by Mick, sometimes Ed. He is an American citizen, Special Forces trained, retired Army. He went home to Illinois after he left the service, blended into the countryside for a few years, and then vanished."

"Until today," Mike added.

"Right."

"Any linkage with the Chinese agent killings?"

"Circumstantial. Commissioner Sim pointed out that he was in Singapore at the time of the attack, *Kouzen* left immediately after, then met with six men in business suits in Kuala Lumpur a few hours later. We have video and muddled audio of that meeting, but it wasn't much help."

"Where is he now?"

"In his hotel room."

"I will assume that Singapore has agents on the scene."

"They have two, and more on the way. I don't think Mr. Kohen is going anywhere any time soon."

"What about the six guys he met with?"

"Mike, Daniel had attached two agents to *Kouzen*. The six men arrived together at the restaurant, but left at different times and in different directions. The two of them were unable to keep up with everyone."

"Nothing in the travel records in Malaysia to link them in any way?"

"They're working on it right now. If there is something to find, they'll do it."

"So, what were the Chinese up to that got them all killed?"

"You already know they were activated this morning, just after the hit in Afghanistan. Do you think the Chinese could have been some kind of rapid deployment team to go after the device?"

"We have them, why shouldn't they? As big at the attack was, I think we need to assume everyone else found out about it the same way we did."

"The up-tick in traffic?"

"Or, they are still able to listen to every word spoken in the White House."

The conversation paused.

"That's a little unnerving," Aaron said.

"Tell me about it. Up until a couple of years ago they could. We never figured out how, but they could. After the Chinese incident in the White House we cleaned out everything we found, but nothing is ever perfect."

"So, it remains an unknown."

"Yes, it does." Mike tapped the eraser end of a pencil on the notepad in front of him. "Have you run any more recent background searches on Kohen? Are there American contacts, family, wives or ex-wives? Anybody?"

"I have a team doing a background search right now. We're looking for anything we can find on his pre-military life."

"Okay. Oh, I need to ask you what our suspicious jet from Pakistan is doing."

"It just passed out of Indian airspace."

"No refueling stops?"

"None. We don't know if they are going to follow the coast, or just where they plan to land."

"The flight plan didn't have a destination?"

"Oh, sure. It's a requirement. But that doesn't mean that's where they'll go. They haven't made the course correction to arrive at what was filed for crossing India."

"That's odd."

"It's also criminal to file a false flight plan."

"Let's see where they end up. Call me if it looks like they're stopping for fuel."

"Will do, Mike."

He closed his phone and turned to Steve Granger. "It's not like a game of chess, for sure."

"What do you mean by that?"

"Too many pawns, one king whose identity we know, but is about to be taken out of service, and we still don't know who we're playing with."

Washington DC, Private Residence Party – 11:35 PM EST

Ronald Hunter worked the crowd of friends and supporters as he had for years. But this was a different crowd made up of international business people, low-level diplomats, and foreign lobbyists. While fundraising was little spoken of in this group, the volume of finances dwarfed in-country contributions.

"Mr. President! *Kak vui pozivyet, moi druk?*"

"Dmitri! *Ochen xorosho, spaciba. Ie vui?*" Ronald Hunter gripped the large hand of Dmitriyev Vetrov Fyodorovych, a leader among Russian lobbyists in Washington.

"We are all very excited with your election victory. It is a new era for our countries, do you not agree?" Dmitri smiled broadly as he pumped the president's hand.

"Well said. And I do agree. We have some great days ahead for us."

"Great days, indeed."

Hunter grinned as widely as he could. In all honesty, his face was beginning to hurt from all the grinning and glad-handing. He was ready to be alone. Maybe even with Susan for a while.

"Mr. President," Dmitri said as he leaned close to Hunter. The president-elect wasn't sure if it was the smell of vodka on his breath, Russian cigarettes, or beets and borsch, but the overpowering odor made him nauseous. "Mr. President, we will need to have a meeting as soon as possible. We have many common interests to discuss."

"Absolutely, my friend. Perhaps the day after tomorrow. Breakfast and coffee. Would that work?"

"Of course, of course, that would be very fine. I know you are a busy man with this Inauguration and all the people, and the parties. You must be exhausted. We have time, but . . . not too much of it," he added leaning even closer.

Dmitri's eyes bore into Hunter's. The sparkle that was there moments before glazed to a cold, hard stare. A shiver ran down the new president's spine.

Something's up that I don't know about, Hunter thought.

"Fine. Very soon. As soon as I can get past all of this." Hunter waved his hand at the activity around him and squinted a dismissive face. Then he smiled.

Dmitri erupted in laughter. "Something the both of us can look forward to." He slapped Hunter's shoulder, nearly spilling his drink, and laughed harder.

"Xoroshi nochni, gospodyn prezidyent." Dmitri stepped back from Hunter laughing boisterously.

"And good night to you. Please give my best to the ambassador."

"Konyeshno, and good night."

Hunter made a half turn and found his left arm firmly gripped by his wife Susan.

"Who the *hell* was that?" she asked under her breath.

"Only one of the three most powerful men in the Russian Federation."

"What a dreadful man. Can we go?"

"Most certainly. I feel like I need a bath."

OCT Little Rock – 10:45 PM CST

"Mikael Edwin Kohen."

"Or, just good ole Mick," Keith Dillon responded across the colonel's desk.

"I like 'good ole Mick.' But now that we know who he is, how much value will he be to us?"

"Hard to say, sir. I guess it depends on who he gets his orders from."

"Yeah." Aaron Stevens nodded his head. The mystery was not solved by knowing the man's name. "I'm getting a little foggy. Let's do a recap."

Just then, the phone rang on Colonel Stevens's desk.

"Colonel Stevens."

"Aaron, this is Daniel Sim."

"Sure, Daniel, what's new?"

"Not a lot, just a couple more pieces. If we're all looking at the same pieces we might discover more."

"Right. What did you find?"

"We were very curious regarding the methods used in uncovering *Kouzen's* real name. We had put out feelers to several of our operatives around the world, but we had only one solid reply. It came from our man in Russia. And it came with what felt like some bad blood."

"You think *Kouzen* screwed the Russians somehow?"

"That's about what we've concluded. You remember I mentioned we have suspected him to be a double agent working the United States and Russia against each other."

"Yes, I remember."

"Well, if he was working the two against each other, and suddenly receives a call from someone up in the Hindu Kush Mountains, why were the Chinese agents in Singapore activated?"

"I'd think he would summon the Russians to demonstrate his loyalty."

"So would I, Aaron. Unless someone brought a better offer to the table."

"The Chinese?"

"They were the ones who got all excited. Activating a high-level team so quickly has to mean there was something big happening."

"And just as soon as the Chinese team is activated they all get shot by people we believe to be CIA, or Americans, at the very least."

"That's the other bit of information."

"What's that?"

"Four of the six who met with *Kouzen* this morning in Kuala Lumpur are ex-CIA, not current."

Aaron Stevens let it sink in a bit.

"I guess that's better than active CIA agents doing the killing."

"Either that or it reflects poorly on the benefits and retirement paid to former agents."

Aaron half-laughed.

"The stew just gets thicker and thicker, Daniel."

"It does. But every little piece has a place to fit together. Please, keep us up to date with any news from your end, okay?"

"Sure. Are you going to pick up *Kouzen*, or Kohen any time soon?"

"Not unless he makes a sudden move. We're watching him very closely. He won't be leaving town, I can assure you."

"Good. Thanks for your call, Daniel." He hung up.

"So, let me see if I got all this right?" Keith asked quietly. "*Kouzen*, Mickey Kohen, gets a call from up in the mountains shortly after we destroy a secret communications hub for the world's most dangerous terrorist network. The Internet explodes with terrorist chatter. Then some top secret equipment goes missing, and we believe we've watched that equipment make its way across India in a very suspicious aircraft. Shortly after that, the Chinese activate a team of super spies in Singapore, and within an hour, they're all dead, killed by Americans. Finally, out of nowhere, the Russians out a secret double-agent working between Washington and Moscow."

"So far, so good, Keith."

"But why?"

"Because, we still have a bucket of that good old midnight oil to burn."

Keith sighed and let his head hang. He stood slowly and left Colonel Stevens's office. There was more to do. Always more.

chapter 17

Hyatt Regency Hotel, Saujana, Malaysia – 12:00 PM MYT

The two agents of the Singapore Secret Police waited for additional officers. Their suspect had remained in his room for several hours and showed no indication of when he might show himself. The agents were well trained. They would not lose contact with the man they watched.

The hotel had graciously provided a room adjacent to the suspect's room. The plan was almost complete. After that time, the wall between the two rooms might as well have been made of glass.

Shortly after taking the room the agents began setting up infrared imaging devices a few feet from the wall itself. These cameras were very different from the night-vision goggles or thermal-vision instruments seen in the movies. Advances in infrared spectroscopy allow clear detection of objects regardless of bright sunlight or moonlight. The new infrared devices metered the absorption or transmissions of photons in a given specific range. The measurements might come from a single cell growing, dividing or mutating, or from the variation of light from a distant star indicating the existence of an orbiting planet.

It wasn't simply the advances in hyperspectral imaging using near-visual infrared waves that made the difference, but the combination of terahertz infrared, or T-rays that brought dramatic clarity to the images collected. If needed, the technician could zoom in on an individual's watchband and count the links.

While considered a violation of privacy by many nations around the world, nothing would stop the agents of the Malaysian Secret Police from gathering every possible detail from a suspect.

The image was displayed on a forty-inch ultra-high-definition monitor with a 4096x2160 resolution. Nothing that happened in the room was unseen. However, as in any surveillance operation there was downtime.

At the moment, their subject, whether his name was Dalton, Kohen or *kouzen*, was napping.

Andaman and Nicobar Islands, Bay of Bengal – 10:15 AM IST

The Learjet 75 floated to a perfect landing on the ten-thousand-foot runway of the Veer Savarkar International Airport in Port Blair on the southern end of Smith Island. The entire system of islands had grown to attract an upscale clientele for vacationers and honeymooners from Dubai to Hong Kong. It was a true island paradise.

Failak stretched and stood as the plane came to a stop. His host, the large bald man exited the pilot's cabin and smiled at him.

"You will certainly need a change of clothes before you go very far." He smiled and retrieved a comfortable looking shirt, new slacks and sandals for Failak to put on.

"Thank you. *Jazakallahu khayran.*"

The bald man laughed. "He may reward me for the good I do, as long as he forgets my evil deeds." He laughed even harder.

Failak decided that man was about as much a believer as he was and laughed as well. The clothes were fresh and lightweight. He shed the heavy pants and coat he had worn in the mountains for weeks. *A bath would be good when there is time.*

After he was dressed he climbed down the short stairs to the tarmac. The plane was being refueled by the local grounds crew. The sun beat down; its heat was amplified by the concrete surrounding them.

Failak looked into the bright blue sky and shielded his eyes from the glare. *The sun is bright like this off the mountain snow, but it is never this hot.* He was not sure he could live in such a climate year round. The warmth was fine, but he loved the cold.

"They will be through filling the fuel tanks in a few minutes. Would you like to join me inside for a drink?" the large bald man asked.

"Thank you, but no. I would prefer to stay with the plane." Failak did not want anyone to enter the aircraft without his seeing who it was. The backpack was still in the luggage cabinet, and he didn't want to be blamed for losing it.

"As you wish," the large man said as he turned and walked toward the modern terminal.

Trust was a commodity in short supply in Failak's character. With his men he would spend months watching them, listening to them express themselves, and observing how well they could run through the jagged mountain rocks. Before he began to trust he felt he needed to see a man's confidence in his own ability. If they lived, worked, and fought with the same convictions they spoke about, he would someday trust them.

Several minutes passed while he contemplated the bald man with whom he had flown from northern Pakistan. He was confident he stood a fair chance against him in a fight. Failak might even win and kill him. It wasn't necessary. Their destination was only a few hours away. *There might be someone I will need to fight there. I will save my strength for what is unknown.*

"The plane is ready. Will you please come aboard?" His host was standing at the base of the short stairs, and was smiling warmly at him.

Failak quickly climbed the steps to the Learjet. He was excited to fly again in the marvelous aircraft. As he passed his host he smelled the distinct odor of whiskey on his breath. It lowered Failak's esteem of the man, but not enough to prevent him from flying again.

Once again, he determined his ways and the cause he served to be higher and more noble than those of this large bald man. *He has weaknesses. Weaknesses that I would never allow in myself, or my warriors.*

He buckled himself in as the cabin steward raised the steps and closed the hatch. Moments later the small jet raced down the runway and leaped into the crystal blue sky.

Kuala Lumpur, Malaysia – 12:30 PM MYT

Robert and Yolanda rode in the rear seat of the old Mercedes taxi cab. The windows were down, and the warm subtropical air washed over them, cooling them. The ride to their hotel would be brief. Their stay at the hotel would also be brief. Hourly rates were common for a number of reasons. In their case, they needed someplace comfortable to relax before their long flight back to the States. A quiet afternoon, a last exotic dinner, and then the interminable ordeal of an all-night sojourn through the night sky.

"I think I want to go swimming. Will you come with me, Robert?" Yolanda's eyes sparkled with excitement.

"Sounds great," he replied.

"And then later we will have a fabulous dinner, and I will wear my new baju kurung." She smiled. Robert loved to see her smile.

"I think we have a wonderful evening ahead of us."

"And then a thousand hours in an airplane." Yolanda sighed and turned to look out the window of the taxi.

"Yeah, well, we can carb-up at dinner and sleep the first ten hours of the flight. How's that?"

She faced him with a fresh smile. "You can do that every time."

"Do what?"

"Say some silly thing that forces me to smile. It's almost irritating." She giggled.

"It's what I do, little lady, it's what I do. You'd better get used to it."

The taxi swept into the driveway in front of the Shangri-La Hotel. The streets around the hotel were narrow and cluttered, exposing the cramped reality of Southeast Asia. Small shops of every imaginable kind were scattered along the streets, packed together and teeming with shoppers and tourists.

It was strange to Robert to find a hotel in the middle of a market, but that was the best description. Directly across the narrow street stood a coin-operated laundry, a computer store, and a mini-mart. *Nope, this ain't Wichita.* Robert smiled.

The couple exited the taxi with the small amount of luggage they would need for the afternoon and evening. The rest of their belongings were five miles away at the airport, checked and ready for the flight.

Yolanda grabbed his hand and pulled him into the lobby. It was going to be their last few hours in paradise, and she was determined to make them count.

Hunter Residence, Washington DC – 12:41 AM EST

"Thanks for dropping me off, honey. I'm dead on my feet," Susan Hunter said as she kissed her husband's cheek. "I'm going to have to get myself in better shape for the parties tomorrow night."

"You get some sleep. I have a feeling it will be at least a month before we find our *normal* life again."

"If ever . . . I don't know if I remember what *normal* is." She smiled and left the vehicle, followed by her ever-present swarm of bodyguards.

Hunter smiled. *She's perfect.* "Take me to the café, if you would, Thomas."

"Yes, sir." Thomas Young had driven presidents through the streets of Washington for over thirty years. Experienced drivers were a rare commodity, especially when it came to chauffeuring presidents. President Hunter would be the sixth president Thomas had served, and Hunter had requested him specifically. Thomas had a reputation for knowing when to speak and when to keep quiet. Hunter appreciated that.

The drive through the early morning streets of the Capitol was eerie. Hunter knew he was going to govern the nation, and, in so doing, influence most of the world one way or another. In the morning he would become one of the most important men on the planet. He would command the most powerful military on Earth, and oversee the greatest economy ever seen by mankind. He was eager to leave his mark as others had in the past.

The presidential entourage was not easy to miss. Hunter's limo was flanked by two SUVs in front, and two in the rear, all with lights flashing. Motorcycles seemed to swarm around them. But the train of vehicles would not follow him to the café, according to a specific plan. The president-elect's arrival at the café was to always be low-key. No flash. No pizzazz. No press. Just Thomas and the president.

Hunter climbed from the limo and stepped quickly into the café. He was expected. His favorite tea was served immediately upon his being seated, and the waiter left the room.

He breathed in the soft aroma, allowing the steam from the hot liquid to fill his lungs. He began to relax. He needed this time. Hunter thrived in the crowds and the adulation that came with them, but deep inside he loved quiet.

He sipped the tea and allowed it to slowly burn down his throat and into his stomach. He relished the warmth.

One phone call needed to be made. Hunter removed his private phone from his pocket and dialed. It rang softly in his ear twice.

"Yeah."

"Holy crap, you sound sleepy."

"No. I'm fine. What's up?"

"I just wanted to check on tomorrow. Everything set?"

"Yeah. We had a glitch earlier, but we took care of it."

"Good. I'll be looking forward to your report tomorrow afternoon."

"Yup."

The line went dead.

NSA Office, White House – 1:05 AM EST

Mike and Steve sat on either side of his desk. They shared an impending deja vu to which neither would admit. The haunting dread that they would miss something, be too late, or once again find themselves helpless to remedy a situation hung over them in the palpable silence of a deserted White House.

The old building popped and cracked in the quiet as heating ducts cooled or warmed. Distant chirps and buzzes broke the night silence, sounds that were usually covered by the noise of everyday activity. Every one of them drew Mike's attention from the pages of notes in front of him for a moment.

Muffled voices down the hall alerted his senses. He shivered. Then the rhythmic shuffling of a man walking—no, two men—came to his ears. The distraction forced Mike to put his papers down and look to the doorway. Someone was coming.

"You both still here?" President Makin said entering the office. He was wearing a robe and slippers and had probably been trying to go to sleep. Immediately behind him was Matt Kreiter, Secret Service Agent to the president. "Yeah, I brought my puppy," he said nodding toward Kreiter. "One would think that a full-grown man could walk around his residence without being shadowed by security. I mean, is that too much to ask?"

"Obviously, in this circumstance, it is too much to ask, Mr. President." Mike and Steve smiled.

Matt Kreiter shrugged his shoulders and said, "Mr. President, I think you are completely capable of walking around all by yourself. It's those other guys I have to work with. They're impossible."

"You're off the hook, Matt," the president replied. "What do you have for me?"

"A lot of stuff. No obvious plan. No conclusive actions. You know, pieces."

"Thanks, Steve. Mike, you look like you have the list in hand. Bring me up to speed."

"The plane we believe to be transporting the USURP device just refueled, but we still don't know where it's going. We do know about six dead Chinese agents in Singapore, but we aren't sure if there is a connection. The only possible link to the killings involves weapons that are like those the CIA issues. Our mystery man *Kouzen* is actually an American by the name of Mick or Ed Kohen, and—"

"Kohen? Did you say Mick Kohen?"

"Yes. Why?"

"Sounds familiar . . . but, I can't place it."

"Someone here in the White House?" Steve asked.

"No, I don't think so. But . . . well, it'll come back to me. What else?"

"Not sure why the Chinese came to high alert when we took out the compound in the Wahkan Corridor. Don't know why *Kouzen*, rather Kohen, was contacted, nor do we know by whom."

"And you think sitting here in the middle of the night is going to bring you two a revelation of some kind?"

Mike and Steve looked at each other.

"Yeah, maybe." Mike knew the president was chiding him. "I don't know, maybe a phone call."

"And that's why we invented answering machines and e-mail. You two need to go home and get some rest. You aren't worth squat when you're overworked."

"Yeah, he's right," Kreiter interjected leaning against the door post. "Then I can return to my post in a straight-back chair and suffer through the rest of my shift."

"See, boys," the president said through a grin, "I appreciate your devotion, but this young man needs his rest." Kreiter groaned.

"Okay. You made your point. Let's get out of here, Steve."

"You're the boss, Mike." Both men stood and began gathering their things. The notes would remain on Mike's desk, undisturbed. The rest was out of their control until something else came to light.

"You said Mick Kohen, didn't you?"

"Yes, Mr. President."

"It will probably keep me up the rest of the night now."

"Sir, you came down here all on your own, I didn't call—"

"No, you didn't, Mike. Now, you two get out of here. Tomorrow is going to be a mess, and you will have all the time in the world to do your work. Now, scoot. Go home."

chapter 18

OCT Little Rock – 12:20 AM CST

Colonel Aaron Stevens was asleep at his desk. His feet were propped on his desk and his chair leaned as far back as possible without toppling over. The ringing of his desk phone wrenched him from a warm sleep.

"Colonel Stevens."

"Aaron, this is Daniel. Our man over here, Mr. Dalton, or Kohen, whatever, just got a phone call."

Aaron scrambled, righting himself, and scoured his desk for a pen.

"*Kouzen*, I mean Kohen, was called in the middle of the night?"

"Well, we were just getting ready to break for lunch over here. But yes, in the middle of your night."

"Who was it? I mean—"

"Did I wake you? You just don't seem up to your normally concise self."

"Yes, I was sleeping. Sorry." Aaron took a deep breath to clear his head. "Okay, Daniel. I'm ready. How much do you have on the call?"

"I just sent it to you. The whole thing."

"But it was definitely Kohen, right?"

"We have been watching him the entire morning. And I mean literally watching him. The call was from the States, and I think you should run a voiceprint analysis on this one."

"Who do you think it is? Did Kohen call him or the other way around?"

"Aaron, Mr. Kohen received a call from someone in the States. I have sent you the recording of the call, and I recommend you run a voiceprint analysis."

"Right. Thank you, Daniel. I'll download the file and get right on it."

"One question for you, Aaron."

"Shoot."

"Do I sound like you just did when you call me in the middle of the night?"

Aaron paused. *He had never sounded like he had been sleeping.* "No, Daniel, you don't. I apologize."

"No need to apologize, my friend. You just work yourself too hard. You need to pay attention to that. Go home and sleep in your own bed. Let someone else take your calls for a couple of hours."

"Good point, Daniel. Right after I review your new file and get this mess cleaned up. I promise."

"I'm sure you will. Talk to you later, Aaron." The line went dead.

Aaron rubbed his eyes forcing blood into them and wiping away the sleep.

"Keith!" he shouted into the intercom.

"Yes, sir?"

"I have a new audio file from Daniel Sim. We need to do a voiceprint and see if we can match it with anyone."

"Can you forward it to me?"

"Consider it done."

"Oh, before I forget. Two things. We have absolutely confirmed *kouzen* to be Mick Kohen."

"I thought we already did that?"

"It was mostly hard science with a bit of conjecture."

"Mostly science?"

"Yeah, the highly likely kind of hard science."

"But now you have proof."

"Yes, sir, the definitely positive kind of hard science."

"And that consists of . . . ?"

"A complete biometric file with ten out of ten possibilities as positives."

"And you got all this data from . . .?"

"Both Russia and India . . . independently. They completed our file for us, but neither is aware of the other's information."

"That's pretty slick. How did you do that?"

"Just by being nice, chief. Besides, the Ruskies are pissed at him for some reason, and the India Bureau is very eager to impress us with their advanced capabilities."

"Fine. What's the other thing?"

"Our little jet that flew across India and refueled in the Andaman and Nicobar Islands?"

"Yes?"

"Well, they just turned their transponder off again."

White House, NSA Office – 1:40 AM EST

August White walked calmly into Mike Trapper's office. He had waited until Mike and Steve Granger had left the building. Then he waited a little longer to confirm they weren't coming back. They hadn't returned.

White stood behind Mike's desk scanning the papers and documents strewn across it. To him it was all bits and pieces. Mostly pieces. He couldn't make a connection. *Why are they tracking a plane across India? What does any of this have to do with Singapore?*

He leaned over the desktop and looked closer at the various pages. The killing of the Chinese agents in Singapore was news to him. *But where does it all fit? Why was it done? And by whom?* He pulled his phone from his pocket and started taking snapshots of the documents.

"Don't you think you should ask Mr. Trapper before you survey his personal property?"

August White spun toward the open office door. Matt Kreiter leaned casually against the doorframe, silhouetted by the light from the hallway.

"Oh, no . . . I was just following up on some details—"

"In the middle of the night? Really, Mr. White, it seems to me there are procedures for things like this." Kreiter didn't budge an inch.

"Yes, there are . . . but none of this takes effect until after the Inaugur—"

"White House security is an ongoing service, Mr. White. I will not be doing anything different tomorrow before or after the Inauguration. We will be on duty to keep this building safe for the current president and the new one we will have in a few hours."

"Glad to know that. I'll check with Mike in the morning about the latest information they've received. So, if you'll excuse me—"

"Mr. White, since you are highly placed in the CIA and assigned to the White House, I will let this slide. But I will include this event in my daily report. I will inform Mr. Trapper of this event. And you must keep in mind that I will be paying attention to you from now on. Am I clear?"

"Of course. And again, I apologize. I'll straighten this out with Mike in the morning."

Matt Kreiter took a half step back allowing August White just enough room to squeeze past him and to the hallway. "Have a good evening, Mr. White."

"And the same to you," White said over his shoulder. *You can bite me you, little bastard.* August White was mad. Embarrassed and mad. He had been caught red-handed snooping through Mike's papers. *I will get past this. I don't know how, but I will.*

He left the White House and walked toward the parking lot. Had he turned around or looked over his shoulder he would have seen Matt Kreiter watching him through the window. But he didn't need to turn around. He knew he was being watched, and that he would be watched . . . all the time.

Trapper Home, Washington DC – 1:45 AM EST

Mike slipped into bed as quietly as he could. Elli stirred and rolled over to face him.

"Sorry, I didn't mean to wake you," he said.

"Honey, I heard you when you came into the garage." Elli smiled.

"It's like radar, isn't it?"

"All moms have radar. One for kids . . ." she leaned over and kissed him, "and another one for husbands."

Mike smiled and pulled her close against his chest. She melted into his embrace and pressed her face against him.

"Did you save the world, today?"

"Most of it. Some parts of it go to hell all on their own. Can't be saved."

"I know people like that."

"Yeah." Mike sighed and buried his face in her hair.

"So, are you free until sun-up?"

"As long as my phone doesn't ring. Then, no one knows."

"But until your phone rings, I can claim ya, right?"

"Yes, ma'am. I am at your disposal."

She raised herself over him. She smiled, and suddenly she was naked.

The breath left Mike's lungs. He ran his hands up her sides caressing her soft skin. She kissed him with a long, deep kiss.

Mike's phone rang.

His hands dropped to his face. "Who the heck could that be?" He reached for his phone he'd put on the night stand. Elli rolled to her side of the bed and pulled the blankets over her.

"Trapper."

"Sorry, Mike. This is Matt Kreiter."

"Are you still at the White House?"

"Yeah, I've got the overnight shift. You know, tuck the president in and make sure no bad guys stop by."

"I know the routine. Did you catch a bad guy?"

"Not one that would surprise you," Matt said. "I caught August White digging around on your desk a little while ago."

"That's rude. Did he say he was sorry for violating my privacy?"

"Sorta. I waited until he left, but I couldn't tell if anything was missing or not."

"He was probably overcome by curiosity." Mike rubbed his forehead, then he reached toward Elli and touched her hip. "I will look at it in the morning. I don't think there was anything classified sitting out."

"Kind of what I figured. I thought you would want to know. It seems the new administration might be a little more nosey than the last one."

"Thanks for keeping me informed, Matt. Now go make sure the president is getting a good night's sleep on his last night in the White House."

"Yes, sir. See you in the morning."

"What was that all about?" Elli asked.

"Just some internal stuff going on at the White House. Nothing important." He replaced his phone on the nightstand and rolled to face her. "Now we were discussing something important here, weren't we?"

"Yeah, but I lost the mood."

"What?"

"Just kidding." Elli attacked him.

OCT Little Rock – 1:05 AM CST

"I'm not getting a good feeling about this," Keith Dillon said. He and Colonel Stevens had monitored the flight of the Learjet across the Bay of Bengal.

"It would seem the next point of contact is one of the airports in Kuala Lumpur."

"Or Singapore."

"Only if they fly over land."

"My best guess is it will be one of the smaller ones. Either place."

"Less traffic, lower security."

"Right."

As they watched, the plane's transponder signal once again identified the small craft as it approached Malaysian airspace.

"That was a good move. They won't have the Malaysian air force escorting them to the ground."

"Strange that they would shut down the transponder like that, though," Keith said.

"Who knows. Inexperience, poor judgment. You can never know what's going on in someone's head."

"Maybe he thinks it saves fuel," Keith added with a sardonic smile.

"I doubt we're dealing with people that incompetent."

"But we still believe the reason for the flight is the USURP device?"

"That's what brought this whole thing to our attention, Keith. The CIA won't loan us one of their satellites to confirm the device is on the plane. Maybe things will change later, but I rather doubt it."

"They could have dropped the device off when they refueled."

"Then why continue to Kuala Lumpur or Singapore?"

Keith shrugged. "Should we alert Daniel Sim about this?"

"Something tells me he already knows, but, yes, we should when we know where the plane is headed."

The two men sat in silence watching the tiny radar dot that identified the Learjet. If the destination was the Changi International Airport in Singapore the plane would need to cross over the Malaysian peninsula, and the Gulf of Thailand. The approach to Changi International was from the northeast into the southwest prevailing winds. That change of course could happen anytime, and the move would indicate the pilot's intention. If the destination was Kuala Lumpur the approach would be direct.

"The Malacca Strait separates Malaysia and Sumatra. If they stay over the water my best guess is Kuala Lumpur."

"If he's going to catch an international flight, I would agree. If he plans to pass the device to some contact they could land in Taiping or any other of a dozen modern airports along the west coast."

Aaron felt dismay begin to take hold. The reality of their situation was that after the plane landed, the device could be taken just about anywhere, and they would be unable to follow it.

"We really need a satellite to scan the area, don't we?" Keith said.

"Yeah."

"I'll call Daniel and let him know about the plane."

chapter 19

Subang Field, Kuala Lumpur, Malaysia – 2:15 PM MYT

The Learjet had come to a stop in the area reserved for private planes. Failak unlatched his seat belt and stretched. He had slept, but not enough.

The large bald man came out of the pilot's cabin and walked toward him. He was smiling.

"Welcome to Malaysia," he said. "Have you ever been here before?"

"No. I have never been anywhere before."

The large bald man threw his head back and laughed.

"I have something for you." He withdrew a large packet from his vest pocket and held it toward Failak. "This contains everything you will need."

"Thank you. But what do I need? I don't know what is going to happen next."

"There is enough money to take care of you for a long time. Once you leave the plane you will be met by a man wearing a black hat. He will drive you to the international airport on the south side of

Kuala Lumpur. Take the backpack with you. Your ticket is also in the envelope. You can find the flight and wait for it to board."

"Where will that take me?" Failak asked. He was far from his home and concerned about getting back.

"I do not know where you go next. Your ticket will have your next destination printed on it. Once you are on that plane and airborne you will be contacted. Six men will escort you on the remainder of your trip. They will treat you well."

"And after I deliver the backpack?"

"You are a free man and can now afford to go anywhere you please."

Failak examined the contents of the large envelope. In contained his ticket and some money, a lot of money. He had never had much use for cash and was astonished at the amount he had been given.

"I . . . I don't . . ."

"You will figure it out, my friend. It is time for you to go."

Failak rose from his seat and climbed down the short steps of the plane to the tarmac. He felt like he was in a stupor, sleep deprived, confused, and rich. He pulled the backpack onto his shoulders. In the distance he saw a man wearing a black suit standing beside a black Mercedes Benz. The man waved to him.

There he is. Failak took a deep breath. He was in a new land. He had no idea where he would be when this day was over. He didn't know if he would live to see the day come to an end. *I will be ready. If I have to fight, I will win.*

Failak turned toward the plane and nodded farewell to the man standing in the hatch grinning at him. He smiled back. Then he turned and walked toward the car.

White House Parking Lot – 2:30 AM EST

August White sat in his car, alone. He was embarrassed to have been caught snooping around on Mike Trapper's desk. The after-hours foray had been a bad idea. The whole incident was simply unprofessional.

He dialed President-elect Hunter's number on his phone.

"President Hunter, here."

"That sounds good when you say it, Mr. President."

"I'm sure it does, Augie. What keeps you up so late?"

"Just getting ready to head home."

"Me too. Actually, almost there."

"I wanted to let you know I checked up on what Trapper and his minions are up to. He left his desk in a mess, and I thought I would see what they were working on."

"Augie, all you had to do was wait until morning, and we'll be in control of everything. Did anyone see you?"

"Yeah, that short Secret Service guy. You know, the one who speaks Chinese."

"Kreiter?"

"That's him. All of a sudden he's watching me from the door all spooky like."

"You were out of line. Trapper is going to be the National Security Advisor's liaison by noon tomorrow, and now you've set him on edge. That's going to create a wedge that we don't need right now."

"It'll straighten out."

"No, *you* will straighten it out. First thing tomorrow you will apologize to him and help him in any way you can."

White paused. "Do you think that is wise?"

"Yes, August, I do. If I didn't, I would not have said it." Hunter's tone was brittle and cold. "We're in the middle of all this, and you want to start pissing people off? We cannot do that at this point, Augie. We have to play the game a little. Am I clear?"

The last thing he wanted to do was agree, but he knew Hunter was right. They were almost there. "All right. I'll do a little bending and try to get on his good side."

"No, you won't try. You'll *do it.*

White was quiet. Sucking up to someone like Mike Trapper was not what he called strength. He wanted to roll right over him. Just get him out of the way.

"You're probably right. I'll be as helpful as I can be."

"Good. Tomorrow is a big day Augie. I need you at your best. Get home and get some sleep."

"Yeah. Okay, chief. You do the same."

August White gritted his teeth. *I can do this. Don't want to, but, yes, I can.*

OCT Little Rock – 1:45 AM CST

Aaron Stevens sat in the Grid Room staring at a yellow pad fully covered in scribbles. Keith Dillon lay flat on his back on the floor in the middle of the large room snoring softly. The overnight crew was still monitoring Internet communications of known terrorists and activists in the States and Europe. The boards were ablaze with traffic.

What is the common link? What am I missing? On the pad he had written 'The device' in the upper left corner; 'Kouzen/Kohen' in the upper right. In the center of the page he had listed 'Chinese agents killed in Singapore,' 'Private jet to Kuala Lumpur,' and 'Six Americans.'

His call to Daniel Sim was a non-starter. Daniel knew about the private jet, but had no reason to stop it, seize it, or search it. Aaron was unable to provide proof of any wrongdoing. Suspicion would not work in international relations. Reason and proof carried more weight. He really needed a satellite.

Then there were the Russians. *Why did they turn Kohen in? Why did they give us information that would compromise one of their resources?* That part did not make sense to him. *Did Kohen double-cross them?*

The phone on Keith's work station beeped and flashed to life. He awoke instantly and answered the phone before the third ring.

"Keith Dillon, OCT." He looked at Aaron and motioned for him to pick up as well.

"Yes, this is Terry Mengis at Langley. Did you recently send in a request for a voiceprint?"

"Yes, I did. Do you have it for me?"

"We made the print, but we have some questions we'd like answered."

"Certainly. Go ahead."

"Where did you obtain this recording?"

Keith looked at Aaron with alarm. *Why would they want to know that?* his eyes asked. Aaron shrugged and nodded his approval.

"We received it from Malaysian intelligence through a contact we have with the Singapore Secret Police."

There was silence on the other end. Keith waited.

"Are you still there?"

"Yes, we're here." Both Aaron and Keith could hear soft whisperings they could not understand. Then the voice on the other end was clear.

"What was the reason for submitting the recording in the first place?"

"Well, we had an ID on one of the two in the conversation and wanted to know if you could help us ID the other guy."

Again, there was a long pause.

"We also have one of the parties clearly identified. The other voice we can't match with the database."

Keith looked at Aaron and wrinkled his brow.

"Well . . . which person can you ID?" His expression turned to one of a person playing a guessing game.

"The one placing the call, of course. The man he called is unidentifiable."

"So, who was the one placing the call based on your investigation?"

"The president-elect. Ronald Hunter. Didn't you know?"

Keith nearly choked. Aaron was speechless.

"Well, yeah . . . of course. That's what we had—just was curious about the other guy." Keith's eyes were wide with astonishment.

"Can you tell me why the people in Singapore are recording the president-elect?"

Keith stammered. No word escaped his lips. He swallowed hard.

"We were wondering the same thing, Mr. Mengis." He mouthed, *What do I do?*

Aaron mouthed back, *Dump him!*

"We'll let you know if anything comes up." He hung up the phone.

"Holy crap! The most mysterious double agent in the last twenty years is linked to the murder of six Chinese agents and gets a call from the president-elect? What the *hell* is going on?"

"Two things," Aaron began. "The thing Kohen said about a *glitch*, and when he asked if everything was set for tomorrow. What was the *glitch*?"

Keith shook his head, his eyes wide. "The Chinese agents?"

Aaron was stunned. He grabbed his phone and dialed Daniel Sim in Singapore.

"Commissioner Sim."

"Daniel, did you know the other guy on that call was President-elect Hunter?" His voice betrayed that he was nearing panic.

"Yes, Aaron. We knew. But you had to confirm it. It's outside my jurisdiction."

"Have you linked Kohen to the murder of the Chinese?"

"Only circumstantially. No one saw them enter the building. None of the security video shows their entry or exit. They just happen to be in town the same day six Chinese agents just happen to die when shot by American bullets."

"But this—this call *from*, not to but *from*, the president-elect of the United States. Can you bring him in for questioning?"

"Aaron, we have had this very discussion for the last hour or so. We have decided to bring *kouzen* in today. If he makes any attempt to leave we will arrest him immediately, but if he stays put, we'll pick him up in a few hours."

"But why wait? Things are on the move right now, aren't they?"

"Yes, Aaron. We aren't convinced how many of these elements are connected."

"You did check out the plane, right?"

"Yes. It is locally owned by someone we know well. Very up and up, nothing funny it seems."

"But the guy that flew in that plane from Afghanistan, are you following him?"

"Yes, he was picked up by a charter driving service and is on his way to the international airport in Kuala Lumpur. We've got him if we need him."

"What we don't have is exactly how they are all connected. Especially now that our new president is somehow involved."

"And thus, we wait."

It hit Aaron hard. "We have to do this exactly right. If we're off by a millisecond we could miss everything."

"Yes. If we were napping, we could miss something. Aaron, I have more than fifty highly-trained field agents working on this. We're on it."

Aaron let out a breath. "I know you are, Daniel. We'll stay in touch." He hung up.

Keith stepped toward him. "So, what do we do next? Do we, or can we, delay the inauguration of an elected president tied to an international murder?"

"I don't know," Aaron replied. "And is that all there is to it?"

"Who do we even talk to? Is this connected to the device?" It may have been exhaustion or shock, but both men were pale.

"I don't know, Keith. I simply don't know."

The Hunter Residence, Washington DC – 3:00 AM EST

Ronald Hunter slowly slipped between the sheets of his bed. His wife stirred beside him.

"You're coming home late. Everything all right?" she asked.

"Yes. Everything couldn't be better. I was just taking my last night of freedom to stretch my legs a bit." He breathed in a deep breath and let it out slowly. He folded his hands behind his head and stared at the ceiling. "It's a funny thing."

"What's that?" Susan asked as she turned on her side and put her head on his shoulder. "What's a funny thing?"

"It's odd that a person can rise to the top of the free world and find oneself in a prison of political duty, not free at all."

"Pretty philosophical for this late hour. Are you having regrets or just over-thinking things again?"

"No regrets, I can assure you. I am just convinced that I can do more if I'm not some political puppet. I don't want to have some senator or, God forbid, a member of the House, crawling over my shoulder all the time for political treats. Somehow we have to be above that."

"Sounding a little imperial, dear." She smiled and ran her fingers across his chest.

"Does *emperor* really sound all that bad?" They both laughed.

"As long as it's you, my dear. As long as it's you."

chapter 20

Robert watched Yolanda as she fought off sleep lying in the warm sunshine at poolside. Two weeks of luxury had softened her. She preferred to nap. Swimming was fine as long as it didn't require too much effort. She wasn't a lazy person, but on her honeymoon, she had fully enjoyed her sumptuous surroundings.

"Should I borrow a large spatula and flip you every ten minutes or so?" he teased.

She swatted at him and made a face. "Keep your hands to yourself, buster. I can flip all on my own." She smiled.

"Madame, it's just that I sorta like getting my hands on you."

"Not out here in front of everyone. I am a beautiful woman who is not enamored with public displays of affection . . . that includes touching."

"Yeah, but I'm just a poor boy from Oklahoma who likes pretty girls like you."

"Listen, cowboy, I am not a side of beef you can just toss around."

He saw the corners of her mouth curl slightly. He knew that behind her sunglasses Yolanda's eyes were dancing with delight from her little game.

"Well, ma'am I think I'm fallin' in lov—"

"What happened to *madame*? Just a minute ago you called me *madame* and now you talk to me like I'm some middle-aged spinster?"

"No, uh . . . Madame. I was just remembering my humble beginnings, that's all."

"And don't you forget it either."

On the other side of the pool, Robert noticed six men who had exited the hotel and were taking seats around a small table. They didn't fit in here. All of the men wore suits, and he could tell from experience the bulges at their sides were made by handguns.

The men kept to themselves and through sunglasses they watched the women decorating the poolside. They smiled and talked among themselves. One could imagine their jestings were based on promiscuous insults about the women.

Through his sunglasses he watched them, his head turned at an angle. Unable to see his eyes they would not know that he was watching them. Robert's eyes never left the group of six men.

At his side, he felt Yolanda roll from her front to her back. One man leaned forward and spoke to the rest. All six pairs of sunglasses across the pool simultaneously turned and looked at her. Their stares lingered.

Robert's heart skipped in alarm. He slowly turned his gaze directly at the table of six men. As abruptly as their leering at Yolanda had begun, it stopped.

He held his eyes on them. He began to memorize their shapes, how their hair was cut, how they moved.

He watched them for several minutes. Occasionally, one would glance his way, but only for a moment. With every glance, his suspicion grew. After each man had looked at them, Robert had had enough.

"Okay, babe. I think it's time for us to leave."

"No, Robert, just a little longer. This is so nice."

He lowered his voice. "Honey, it's not the sunshine I'm concerned about."

"But I think I could sleep just a little bit."

"Yolanda, sweetheart, there are six men wearing suits on the other side of the pool that have taken special notice of you. I think they have seen enough."

"Six men—" She started to sit up. He stopped her.

"Here's what we need to do, honey. I'm going to stand and hold your robe for you. Then I want you to get up and put it on."

"Oh, Robert. You are being silly. You don't think—"

"No, I don't. I want to get us out of here. Now."

He stood and lifted her robe. She got to her feet and allowed him to help her put the garment on.

"I just don't see why you are such a big afraidie-cat all of a sudden." She shrugged her robe on her shoulders and tied it at her waist.

"It's not *afraidie-cat*, it's just fraidy-cat. Now, let's go."

He slipped his arm around her and led her to the door to the lobby. He turned to the table of six men. All six men were staring at them.

Hyatt Regency Hotel, Saujana, Malaysia – 3:35 PM MYT

Commissioner Daniel Sim patiently watched his suspect on the UHD monitor. Not very much was happening in the room on the other side of the wall. He had about decided the man should be taken into custody for being boring. *What a waste of valuable time— time watching a suspect do nothing.*

"Sir, don't we have enough to detain him for questioning?" his assistant, Inspector Danish Wan asked.

"Of course. It's simply all circumstantial evidence. We know he had a discussion with some suspicious men this morning. We know he had a short conversation with the president-elect of the

United States a few hours ago. Coincidently we have six murdered Chinese killed by what appears to be American CIA weaponry. It's just too loose."

"The information is unclear as to any guilt, but the associations have got to mean something."

"Danish, if we move on this too quickly we could lose everything. I don't want to do that."

Daniel Sim's phone vibrated in his pocket. "Commissioner Sim."

"Commissioner, this is Zara. We received the filtered recording from the tea salon this morning."

"Anything conclusive?"

"Yes, sir. It is very clear the six Americans he met with killed the Chinese agents. Not a shadow of doubt, sir."

"You have the recording in our office, and you have listened to it yet?"

"Yes, commissioner. We have also run voice prints on Mr. Dalton, or Kohen, and it matches the voice speaking with the president-elect."

"Thank you, Zara." He turned off his phone. "Danish, we have him on tape. When we go in we must address him as he is registered at this hotel. As Mr. Dalton. Let's take him in."

Inspector Wan spoke quietly into his radio, and the twelve-man SWAT team left the stairwell and entered the hallway. Four more officers waited on the two adjoining balconies. If Kohen bolted for his only way of escape off the balcony, they would stop him. The suspect's plans for the evening were about to change.

Daniel Sim and Inspector Wan turned from the recording equipment and walked to the door. Wan spoke again into his radio. "Take him."

The arrest of Mr. Dalton, a.k.a. Mick Kohen was nothing spectacular. The SWAT team crashed through the door, and the balcony was swarmed by four officers. Kohen didn't flinch.

Commissioner Sim entered the room. "Mr. Dalton, you are to be detained for questioning about the murder of six Chinese citizens."

"Will anything I say be used against me?"

"Probably, Mr. Dalton."

"May I call a lawyer?"

"Later, perhaps. For now we would like to have a nice talk," Commissioner Sim said as Inspector Wan applied handcuffs.

Kohen smiled. "You might have me for an hour or—"

"Sir, may I remind you that you are in Malaysia. You are no longer in the United States of America. Follow me, please."

Kuala Lumpur International Airport – 4:10 PM MYT

The airport was the largest Failak had ever seen. The vaulted ceilings were higher and brighter than those of the mosque he had grown up attending with his family. He recalled the awe he had for the grand swooping arches and the ornate mosaics that decorated them. These arches were even more splendid.

He forced himself to turn his attention from the architecture and look at the people around him. *Should I look for someone in Muslim dress? The man on the plane was not dressed in traditional clothing. Perhaps they look like westerners.*

He swung the backpack onto his shoulders and walked slowly through the crowd of travelers, families on vacation, businessmen, and students. They all seemed busy. They also appeared to know where they were going.

Failak checked his ticket and found the flight number and the gate where he would board his plane. *That's the place where I will find the people I need.* He quickened his pace looking at the signs hanging above the gates as he passed.

The backpack was not heavy, and he moved easily through the groups of passengers. He did become aware that most of the people carried only small pieces of luggage as they waited for their flights. He hoped the backpack was not too large.

Perhaps those he was to meet would recognize the backpack. The thought encouraged him. *The man on the plane said I would be met by someone. They should recognize me.*

Failak slowed his pace. He moved into the center of the vast terminal concourse making himself as visible as he could. There was plenty of time. He was confident he would be found.

After several minutes at his more casual pace he arrived at his gate. He carefully checked the numbers on the marquee identifying the next flight. The numbers on his ticket matched. He found a seat against the wall beside the window and sat. He placed the backpack on the floor at his feet. *They will easily find me now.* His wait began.

Central Intelligence Agency, Langley, VA – 4:15 AM EST

"Captain, we need to reposition the satellite over the South China Sea. The guys upstairs are concerned about exactly what the Chicoms are placing on those islands they're building."

"You'll need to give me those coordinates again. The last time we checked was days ago."

"Where have you been since? Don't we keep track of that stuff?"

"Lieutenant, we've been all over the map. We have that thing in Afghanistan the president got his shorts in a wad about, then east Africa, you know Somalia, Yemen. All of it a mess. Even Oman is getting into some scary stuff."

"Fine. You have to be caretaker of the Middle East. We are all proud of you. Now, can I get some work done here?"

"All right. Exactly where in the South China Sea?"

"South Thomas Shoal. 9°43'51.5"N, and 115°51'43.2"E.

"At least you're specific."

"Nothin' more than sand that sticks out of the ocean by a little more than a foot."

"What's all the fuss about?"

"They tell us that China is manufacturing islands to control one of the world's most important shipping lanes."

"This will take a minute or two."

"I got time. It's beyond me why they are dumping tons of rock and dirt. I mean, what's the point? Another tiny island nobody can live on? Give me a break."

"Or an airbase. Or submarine base. Who knows what the Chinese want."

"Do they really drink beer in China? Just think, sitting out in the middle—"

"What was that?"

"I don't know. Why are you askin' me?"

"Just a sec."

The path the satellite scanned covered the southern tip of India and the Bay of Bengal. As the sensors crossed into Malaysia toward Indonesia something registered on the captain's screen.

"Hold on a bit."

"This is priority, Captain. Do I need to remind—"

"No, Lieutenant. Do I need to remind you that I out-rank you? Hold on a second."

"Yes, sir." He paused. "What did you see?"

"Not sure." He focused the scan on southern Malaysia. The screen lit again. "I have to call this in, Lieutenant. Tell your boss to hold his water, and I'll get back to you."

"Wait just a minute—"

"No. You will wait. This is marked Special Access Protocol. That means it's over your security clearance. Now, please get off my line. I have to call Washington."

Damn. How did that thing get all the way down there?

Shangri-La Hotel, Kuala Lumpur, Malaysia – 5:00 PM MYT

Robert led his wife into the four-star restaurant for an elegant meal. It was early, but the wait staff obliged and brought their best style to serve them. Yolanda appeared to float across the floor wearing her light purple lace baju kurung. As Robert had promised, every eye in the room was drawn to her.

"You are such a wise man," she said as he seated her.

"Did you ever doubt me?"

"Of course. Isn't that my job?" Yolanda's napkin floated into her lap at the hand of one of the attending waiters. A second served them water. The wine steward presented Robert with the wine list as the head waiter patiently stood to the side waiting for his turn to present the selections on the evening menu. Yolanda smiled at her handsome man. She felt like royalty.

"Oh, Robert, this is like a fairytale."

"Nothing but the best, even for just one evening, one meal, one memory."

The steward poured a Japanese wine called *koshu*, known for its fruity and delicate bouquet, and the meal commenced. Trays of sushi and fruit swarmed the table. As soon as they emptied one, another selection of delicacies replaced it.

"The bites, they are so small," she said as she examined a rice-stuffed shrimp.

"That's so they can serve a whole bunch of these things at a dollar a piece."

Yolanda stopped. "They're charging a *dollar* for a bite?"

Robert had to laugh. "Sweetheart, I'm glad you haven't lost your penny-pinching ways in the midst of all this elegance."

"I'm not a penny-pincher," she said with a feigned pout of injustice.

"Kidding, honey. I'm kidding."

Yolanda knew she was not a lavish spender, except on some things. "For tonight they can charge us *two* dollars a bite. I won't mind."

The main course arrived at the right time, just before they were full but after their palates had experienced the culinary treasures of Malaysia.

The presentation was breath-taking. Three large crab legs rested on a bed of fine pasta bathed in a light, lemony sauce. Thinly-sliced grilled chicken, or what she believed was chicken, edged the right side of the plate, while sautéed sliced mushrooms bordered the left. Fresh limes, cut in the shape of a star provided color and that extra, tangy splash for the roasted bronze croaker, the entire fish, head, fins and tail, that was placed at the top of the plate surrounded by steamed bok choy. Tomato slices curled into the shape of a rose rested in front of the fish. Everything was decorated with mints, parsley and other herbs, and just behind the fish, an orchid.

"Robert, this is too *beautiful* to eat!" The waiter leaned over her shoulder and with a small knife slit the scales of the roasted fish, exposing the steaming hot white meat inside.

The steward held a bottle of Australian wine from the Beelgara Estate Range winery for his approval. "The sauvignon blanc you requested, sir."

He poured a sip into Robert's glass, and upon his approval filled Yolanda's glass, and then Robert's.

"To our last evening in paradise," he said lifting his glass toward her. She touched his glass, making a soft clink. As Yolanda drew the glass to her lips she froze. The sparkle melted from her eyes. Her heart stopped.

"R—Robert . . ."

"Yolanda, what is it? You're absolutely white. What is it?"

"The man . . ." Her words staggered. She licked her lips. "The man from the pool."

He spun and looked behind him. The man immediately stepped back out of their view.

"Robert, why is he here? Why was he watching us?"

"I don't know, honey. I don't know."

OCT Little Rock – 4:35 AM CST

"So, why didn't that information come to us as well?" Keith Dillon was more than angry even though he never let it show. "I mean, sir, we're pretty much running point on this whole exercise. Why would Langley not tell us about the ping?"

"I'm as frustrated about it as you are, Keith. How much time do you suspect we have lost by their delay in notifying us?"

"Just over an hour, colonel. But it means we knew exactly where the device was an hour ago. Where is it now?"

"Did you get the location?"

"Kuala Lumpur. I told you."

"Let's try *where* in Kuala Lumpur?"

"The international airport."

"I will take a risk and assume it was in the airport and not the airport parking lot or an adjacent hotel. How am I doing?"

"Very well, sir." Keith knew exactly where the ping had originated. He knew the exact point. He was confident the location would have changed in the hour that had passed since the ping was detected. He also enjoyed frustrating his supervisor.

"Thank you. Now perhaps we could request some additional help from Langley. Does that fall within the realm of possibility?"

"It does. And I have tried. Twice."

"You have asked the CIA to sweep the Kuala Lumpur airport twice, and they said no? You didn't think that was something I would like to hear about?"

"I just told you, sir."

"Okay. Well, I'm afraid I'll just have to go over their heads, or at least to the other side of their heads and have someone else yell in their ear."

"That would be my recommendation, colonel." Keith grinned as he typed. He knew he was tormenting his boss, and he enjoyed it.

"Thank you for your approval. I need to make a phone call. Don't you have something at your workstation that needs attention? Anything?"

"Now that you mention it, I do." Keith stood and turned to leave Colonel Stevens's office. A smile crossed his face. Doling out information in small bits and pieces was his favorite game. He rationalized that the bits-and-pieces procedure forced attention to every specific part of the picture. Everything was discussed. Every bit was acknowledged. *The devil is always in the details.* His smile broadened. It had been a long day, but it had been a good day.

chapter 21

Police Department, Kuala Lumpur – 5:50 PM MYT

The interrogation room was stark and colorless. Mick Kohen sat on the single chair in the room. His hands and feet were shackled. The chair was anchored to the floor. Kohen had been in the room for an hour, and no one had spoken a word to him.

Daniel Sim stood in the observation room with three secret police agents. The older man, who had followed and recorded Kohen in the tea salon, and his young partner silently watched Kohen. The third man was the chief of the local police department.

"How long before you begin the interrogation, Commissioner Sim?" the chief asked.

"In a little while. He's far too comfortable at the moment." Daniel Sim knew he was up against a master of deception. Mick Kohen had eluded authorities on five continents for years.

"We could advance the time with some extra measures, Commissioner Sim."

"We could, my friend. I'm very confident he is fully expecting us to do so."

"Just a thought. In the old days we could have this canary singing loud and clear."

"Yes," Sim replied as he turned to face the older agent. "And if you'll remember, in those days the interrogations usually ended with a corpse."

The older man smiled a knowing smile. "Indeed, commissioner. Effective but often deadly."

"And, in spite of the fact that he would protest reality, he is an American citizen. We don't want to muddy those waters."

"So, we wait?"

"We wait and watch."

The purpose of the wait was to observe the man and his natural motions and actions. The camera would record if he showed restless behavior, if he was placid in waiting, or if he was suspicious about why he was being interrogated.

Daniel could hold the man for forty-eight hours for just about any reason. He hoped that would be enough time. He was also aware that Kohen knew how long he was allowed to be held. It was a game, a waiting game.

Hunter Residence, Washington DC – 6:00 AM EST

The alarm jangled in its customarily annoying clatter. Ronald Hunter lurched from his deep sleep in response. His wife, Susan was jolted awake by his sudden movement.

"Ron, are you all right?"

"Are you kidding? Today I become the president of the United States. Am I all right? Wow! I feel great."

"I just have never seen you bolt like that to the alarm. Goodness."

He rolled toward her and drew her near. "My dear, this is what it has all been about. These last twenty years have brought us to this day. We are on top. It's like waking up and being king of the world."

She returned his smile with approval. "You have done well, and I am proud of you."

"I will collect my reward from you, you voluptuous little tart, later tonight."

"I love it when you talk dirty." She laughed at her own exaggeration.

"No, sweetie. The last time I talked dirty you took away my dessert."

Susan swatted at him as he rolled out of bed.

"Gotta hit the shower. This is the biggest day of our lives." He half-jogged into the bathroom and relieved himself. The shower quickly steamed the room as he shaved, then hopped into the scalding hot spray.

"Oh, yes! Burn me up if you can." He loved hot water in the shower, not the tepid warm spray Susan preferred. It took only one adventure as newlyweds to make the separation. Once that preference was understood and agreed upon life went on swimmingly. Showering was a separate event.

"Did you decide which suit you are going to wear today?" he yelled from under the steaming blast.

Susan stuck her head into the foggy room. "Yes, I'm wearing the violet one."

"Good. I think I have a tie that will complement that color even with my dark grey suit."

"You're not wearing the navy blue?"

"Nope. Didn't Al Makin wear dark blue? I don't want any possible comparison made between me and that man." He turned the shower off and grabbed his towel. "We are going to be the best thing in Washington DC since Bill Clinton. The parties are going to be grand and lavish. Nothing dark blue with me."

"Whatever you say, dear. I mean, you are the president."

He poked his head from behind the shower curtain displaying a playful smile. "I'd rather be king."

Susan laughed. "And so you've said many times, my dear. Don't forget, here in the States we don't have *kings and queens*."

He walked up behind her and threw his arms around her waist. "Until now, my dear. Until now."

She spun around and kissed him. "You are certainly my hero among men. If ever we needed a king, and if ever a man was worthy of the title, you are the one."

He kissed her long and hard. *I am the one. I am the one.*

International Airport, Kuala Lumpur, Malaysia
6:10 PM MYT

Failak sat quietly near the gate entrance with the backpack at his feet. No one had approached him. No one had spoken to him. Being alone did not bother him. Most of the time people were an annoyance with which to be dealt. He did not enjoy companionship.

He had decided he would ignore his hunger. As soon as he sought something to eat, he was certain the person he was to meet would pass by and miss him. So he waited, not yielding to the growling in his abdomen.

He did not desire to know about the people who passed by him. His only interest was the person who would recognize him. That person would help him onto the plane and let him know to where he would next travel.

His ticket showed a destination of Hong Kong, but he assumed that would only be a stop. He would have nothing to do with that capitalist sewer of a city. The glamour and lights were only advertising of a morally bankrupt culture. If that was his destination he certainly wouldn't stay there long.

A man wearing traditional Iranian clothes walked toward him. Failak felt his pulse increase. Was it him? Was that the man he was to meet? He did not acknowledge Failak. His passing was as casual as his approach. The alarm the man's approach had caused alerted Failak to how tired he was. He could not let down his guard.

It had been nearly thirty-six hours since the explosion in the compound had awakened him. He had not eaten since he had been given food on the Learjet. Between the lack of sleep and little food, he felt uncertain, even slightly suspicious of everything around him. Perhaps he would sleep on the plane.

For now he would need to keep watch. He had to find his contact person before boarding the flight to Hong Kong. He still had more than an hour. He could stay awake. He would not need to eat.

Shangri-La Hotel, Kuala Lumpur, Malaysia – 6:15 PM MYT

The ride in the elevator up to their room was smooth and quiet. The dinner had been remarkable, but Yolanda had remained strangely quiet after seeing the suspicious man watching them.

"Robert, do you think those men want to hurt us?" Her voice was soft, hinting at the lingering fear of the unknown.

"I don't have any idea of why they would be watching us. Well, except for the obvious fact that you were a knock-out in that bikini, and the fact that every man and woman in the restaurant couldn't take their eyes off you. Just like I said."

Yolanda smiled, blushed a little, and dropped her gaze to the floor. "I know you said I was beautiful. But I also know you do not have an objective opinion."

"It didn't take objectivity to see everyone look at you. It was wonderfully obvious." He pulled her chin up and kissed her.

"Robert, we don't have time for that. We have to get to the airport."

He sighed. "I know."

The elevator stopped at their floor and the doors opened silently. Their room was the third door on the right side of the hall. They walked to the door, and Robert inserted his card. The light blinked green, and the latch popped.

"There you go. Our last moments in paradise are given to collecting odds and ends and putting on comfortable clothes for the trip home."

She quickly slipped out of her light purple lace baju kurung. She held it up and said, "I can't imagine where I will wear this beautiful outfit in Wichita."

"I know. You can wear it for me around the house anytime you like."

"You would like that?"

"I would. Of course I prefer what you're wearing now."

"Dirty minded old man!" she teased as she pulled on her jeans.

"Just stating the obvious."

They dressed quickly and gathered the rest of their belongings to place in their carry-on luggage. It was time to go.

She stepped up to her husband, and put her arms around his neck. "Robert, this has been a wonderful time, and we may never be able to do this again. I want to tell you how much I love you and how excited I am for the next fifty years."

"Only fifty? I was hoping for more like one hundred and fifty."

"That's okay with me," she said.

They kissed. The honeymoon was over. Now it was time for real life to begin.

He picked up their small carrying case and opened the door into the hall. The elevator doors slid back, and Yolanda stepped in. Robert cast a short glance down the hallway.

The shadowed shape of a man stepped back and out of his view.

NSA Office, White House – 6:25 AM EST

Mike had slept for no more than four hours. The call from Colonel Aaron Stevens had woken him and prevented further sleep. After a long shower and a quick breakfast with Elli he had headed back to the White House.

The fact that Langley had recorded a ping on the USURP device both excited and aggravated him. The fact that August White had been caught looking through the papers on his desk while he was away infuriated him. To top it off, he had a headache.

"You look a little worse for the wear."

Mike looked up to see President Al Makin peeking around the doorframe into his office. He shook his head and rubbed his eyes. "Mr. President, you're up pretty early, aren't you?"

"No earlier than usual, Mike. Just going to check my abbreviated schedule for today."

"Did you hear about the ping of the device in Kuala Lumpur?"

"I saw it on the PDB I got this morning."

"Did your briefing tell you if Langley was going to move this to a higher priority?"

"No, it did not. But that's something we can take care of in short order."

"There's something else from last night."

"You mean White thumbing through the papers on your desk?"

"Yeah, how'd you know?"

"Kreiter. He's sort of my right-hand man these days. You know, nose to the ground, eye on everything."

"Sorta cagey?"

"The best. I might even try to take him with me. You know, on my lifetime security force."

"Yes, sir, I do." Dozens of memories flashed through Mike's mind. He was going to miss Al Makin. Their start had been at a difficult time, but their friendship had become genuine.

"Mike, I'm going to be in my office for the next hour or so. Then I'll be tied up with the Inauguration until they whisk me away to some unknown location so they can de-president me." He smiled and jested, "I don't think they'll do a memory wipe or anything on me."

"I'm sure I'll speak with you a couple of times before you are decommissioned and set out to pasture, Mr. President."

Al Makin left, and for the last time walked toward the Oval Office.

Mike picked up his phone. As of 6 a.m. he was officially the National Security Administration liaison to the president. He decided he would take advantage of the position while he still served a president he knew. He called Langley.

"This is Mike Trapper, NSA liaison to the president in the White House."

"Yes, sir, Mr. Trapper. We received your clearance notification about half an hour ago. What can I do for you this morning?"

"Yesterday we monitored the results of a CIA attack on the communications compound in the Hindu Kush mountains south of the Wahkan Corridor. We lost two good men and a highly-classified piece of equipment. I also am aware that a locator ping was registered from that device a couple of hours ago. I want a live sweep of Kuala Lumpur and an active search for that piece of equipment."

"Yes, sir. I have updated information for you. The ping we received was from the International Airport in Kuala Lumpur. We are working through channels to ask for assistance from the secret police in Malaysia. They seem to be involved with a murder of—"

"Excuse me. That's all fine. But right now I need an immediate sweep of the last area where the device was seen. That's all. We need to find the device. You can use the link we had from you yesterday. But I need it right now."

"Yes, sir. I'll see to it immediately."

Mike hung up his phone. *I wonder exactly what 'immediately' means to the folks at Langley?* He flipped on the monitor he had watched the day before. He saw nothing but a blue screen. *Well, that figures.*

The screen flickered and a satellite image of Malaysia appeared. *Huh. Today at Langley immediately actually means immediately.*

As the view zoomed in on the International Airport no pings registered. The backpack was either not being worn on someone's shoulders, or it was gone.

chapter 22

Kuala Lumpur Police Station – 6:30 PM MYT

The door to the interrogation room opened slowly, and Daniel Sim entered carrying a small table with two bags from a nearby Burger King. The younger agent assisted him in placing the table in front of Mr. Dalton, or Mick Kohen, and then brought a chair into the room for Commissioner Sim.

"I thought you might find an American cheeseburger to your liking, Mr. Dalton," Sim said as he sat across from him.

"That's very kind of you, inspector, but the chains prevent me from reaching the table." Dalton pulled the shackles around his wrists to their maximum length raising his hands a mere inch over his knees.

"Commissioner, not inspector," Daniel Sim said as he stood to loosen the restraints. "I am Commissioner Daniel Sim."

"Oh, well, pardon me, please. Commissioner."

"You should be able to reach your dinner now."

"Thank you." Dalton brought his still-shackled hands to the table top and carefully unwrapped his burger.

"Sorry we have not been able to give you the attention you may have required, but we have had a busy day. Lots of . . . you know, crime." He took his first bite and smiled at Dalton.

"I certainly understand, Commissioner. Crime takes no holidays, as I am sure you know." Dalton watched his would-be interrogator carefully.

Behind the one-way glass the three other agents watched Mr. Dalton even more carefully. They knew what they were looking for, and the three cameras would provide the recorded proof when the reactions occurred.

"Have you enjoyed your time in Kuala Lumpur?" Sim asked reaching for a French fry.

"I have. I needed some time away from business. You know, time to rest and relax. Recharge."

Daniel nodded as he chewed another bite of his burger. He intentionally avoided eye contact with him, presenting a more casual attitude at the beginning of their discussion. "I know exactly how you feel. My wife threatens to move all my things here to the station and come here for conjugal visits once a month." Both men chuckled softly.

"That is one burden I have not chosen to bear: marriage. Too many fish in the sea, if you catch my drift. I prefer more of a free, less encumbered lifestyle."

"I see your point. I waited a long time before I married. I had her picked out long before, but I just didn't see how to make it all fit together."

"So, how's it working for you?" Dalton asked.

"I'll just say she is a very understanding woman." He took a sip from his drink. "So you needed a little rest from your business and came here to find it. I hope you did."

"Oh, yes," he replied dipping a fry into a small packet of catsup. "I love to come here. You know . . . the languid pace of the south seas."

"If you can get out of the city," Sim said.

"True. The countryside is absolutely beautiful."

"How long have you been in Malaysia?"

"Four or five weeks? I think. Maybe longer. I sort of lose track of time when I come here."

"You've been here before?"

"Oh, yes. Several times."

"On business . . ."

"Usually." Dalton took a huge bite of his burger.

"That's odd. We keep very good records of who comes and goes in our country. When you arrived six weeks ago it was the first time we registered a Charles Dalton coming across our borders."

"Huh," Dalton nodded and muttered through a mouthful of food.

"Perhaps the last time you came through you were known as Mikael Kohen."

Dalton choked on his meal.

On cue, the door opened.

"Commissioner, you have a phone call."

He stood and immediately left the room.

Outside the room and far from the earshot of Mick Kohen, Daniel Sim was surrounded by his agents. The phone call was a ruse.

"Sir, we have just learned the six men who met with this *kouzen* guy, Mick Kohen, are preparing to board a flight at the International Airport."

"You're positive? You've confirmed the information?"

"Yes, sir. That's why this is so rushed."

"What flight is it? Can we have it stopped?"

"It's MH 425. But it's an international flight that we cannot stop unless we're there. We must hurry."

A small army of agents charged out the door of the station to their waiting cars. Mick Kohen finally cleared his throat and found himself alone and ignored in a stark and colorless room.

Gate 11, Kuala Lumpur International Airport – 6:45 PM MYT

"Robert, shouldn't we get in line to board the plane?" Yolanda's casual approach in getting to the airport had changed. She was more insistent. "Shouldn't we get on?"

"They will board us next to last. Maybe even last. We're kinda far back."

"We're not flying first class?"

"Not on this flight. When we change planes in Hong Kong we will be in first class. This is just a short flight."

"But the crowd is very large. Won't it take longer if we wait?"

"No honey. We'll just be standing up a lot longer." He ran his fingers through her hair and down her cheek. He wanted to go back to their beachside bungalow in Tanjung Aru. He wanted it to begin all over again.

Yolanda stopped her protest and smiled at him. He knew she was preparing to change her direction of attack and state her position differently.

"Robert, darling, we are going to be sitting on a plane for the next twenty-eight hours. I think we would be fine if we stood for a little while."

He laughed under his breath. She won.

"You're right. And we could stand right over there with all those other people who are getting on the same airplane we are. What a coincidence. Maybe we'll make some friends."

She giggled in her victory and stood to her feet. Robert stood as well and picked up their carry-on bag. He loved her smile. Her eyes sparkled with excitement. She wasn't excited about the flight home. She was just full of life. She was exciting.

The people waiting were from every culture imaginable. Many were Chinese and probably headed home. Others were dressed in business attire, while most, like Robert and Yolanda wore casual clothes. Robert wondered what sort of lives they had. Did they have families waiting for them in Hong Kong or any of a hundred other airports scattered across the globe? Where would all these people end their common journey?

Yolanda tugged on his shirt sleeve.

"Did you get my magazine off the night stand at the hotel?"

"Yes, dear. It's here in the bag."

"Okay."

"Are you nervous? You seem jittery all of a sudden."

"No. I mean, yes, sort of. Just a little bit."

Her smile seemed forced.

"Do I need to do something, honey?" he asked.

"No. We just need to get on the plane. I'll be fine then."

Robert looked toward the door to the ramp that led to the plane. People were beginning to board. That was when he saw him. He was one of the men from the hotel; one of the guys that stared at him and Yolanda; one of the men who was armed at the pool.

Are his friends on our plane, too?

White House – 6:50 AM EST

Mike entered his office to find August White standing in the middle of the room. He pulled up short in mid-stride, stopping just inside the door.

"Look, we got off on the wrong—"

"No, you look," Mike said stepping directly in front of White and planting his index finger in the center of White's chest. "I don't know what your game is, but you are going to find yourself with few friends if you continue to act like you did last night. This is a private office that from time to time will hold sensitive information to which you are not privy. Taking advantage of any such information will get you banned from working in the White House, remove you from gainful employment altogether, or land your sorry butt in jail."

"I know." White held his hands up as if to ward off the impact of Mike's words. "I am sorry. It was a lapse in judgment."

"Mr. White, your antics in the past are well known by the people who work here and those of us who have been in the White House for a few years. We know you were the source of the misinformation regarding the Oak Mountain event and the incident with the Chinese. The week that those events occurred you were in South Africa. You do not have firsthand experience with what went on here, in the Southwest, or with any of that. Your effort to discredit President Makin as well as the White House staff has caused serious credibility issues for every White House employee. You are not considered a secure part of our team, and, in all honesty, I don't know why you still have a job."

"I have a job because I'm *good* at my job," White snarled in his own defense.

"Not good enough to get it right." Mike inched closer to White.

"Hold on here!" White took a step back. "You can't treat me like some kind of criminal, I have—"

"You have nothing. Mr. White, the security of this nation and of this building is not a game of spy versus spy. Lives are at stake. Billions of dollars are at risk with every decision, and every discussion that goes on in this place. You work for a department of this government whose primary function pertains to things *outside* this country, not on my desk."

August White was blanched with rage. "Not everyone thinks that way anymore," he said through clenched teeth.

"Then they have a problem with a little item we call the Constitution." Mike was inches from White's face.

"I'm not going to let you—"

"No, you're not going to do anything except get out of my office. And I mean *right now*."

August White stammered and sidestepped Mike. Then he left without another word.

Mike's fiery gaze followed him out. Molly had come in just after Mike and heard the whole thing.

"Are you all right, Mr. Trapper?" she asked timidly.

Mike took a deep breath and let it out. "Yes, Molly." He grinned at her. "I think I'm just fine. And, good morning to you."

International Airport, Kuala Lumpur – 7:00 PM MYT

Yolanda was eager to get to their seats. Their delicious meal was weighing on her, and as after a Thanksgiving feast, she was getting sleepy.

"Robert, everyone is so slow," she said softly leaning against his chest.

"Honey, you know these things take time. Relax."

"That's the problem. If I relax I will fall asleep." Her eyes were closed. She kept her head against his chest.

"Then I'll just hoist you over my shoulder and carry you on."

Yolanda snickered. "I think I'm too big for carry on luggage."

"The line is moving. Come on. Wake up."

Robert ushered her forward with additional complaint from her.

"Feels like I'm dragging a kid to the dentist. Come *on*, sweetheart." He put his arm around her waist and shoved her toward the attendant at the gate.

Once past the check-in and inside the gangway, Yolanda stumbled down the ramp.

"Am I almost there?"

"Yes, and your lightly cushioned airline seat eagerly waits to cradle your backside."

"That doesn't sound very nice, Robert."

"I could have said it like guys talk in the Navy. Is that what you want?"

Yolanda looked into his eyes. Her eyes were blurry, but she could manage a glare.

"You talk to me like those Navy men do and you will find yourself in the doggie house." She nearly tumbled to the floor.

"And thus the re-phrasing of my comment. Sweetie, people are going to think you're drunk."

"I don't know them. I don't care what they think."

Robert carefully helped her through the main hatch and onto the airliner. Their seats were about two-thirds down the plane. As the crowd thinned and took their seats he led her and finally deposited her in the proper location.

"There. Now buckle up, lady."

Yolanda rolled her eyes at him without smiling. "I need a pillow."

"Soon enough, my dear. Soon enough."

Robert took his seat on the aisle next to her. Yolanda struggled to latch her seat belt looking every bit like a drunk. He leaned over and latched her belt.

"Thank you, Robert. You are such a gentleman."

As Robert clicked his own belt, Yolanda's head fell heavily against his shoulder. He smiled and settled back into his seat.

The last of the passengers were entering the plane. One man carried a rectangular backpack. He slipped it into the overhead storage and sat down.

Then Robert looked down the aisle toward the front of the plane. His blood ran cold. A shiver shook him. The six men he had seen at the hotel pool boarded and took their seats in first class.

This time he recognized one of them.

chapter 23

Steve Granger and Mike sat at his desk reviewing the satellite feed from Langley. The ping that had registered through the satellite was identical to the ones recorded the previous day near the Wahkan Corridor. The device had covered a lot of ground overnight. The question was, with whom?

"That proves it was on the plane the guys at OCT tracked," Steve said as he stood and stretched his back.

Mike noticed. "Your back bothering you?"

"Oh, no. Not very much anyway. I don't know, maybe I pulled it moving a box or something."

"Or something?"

"Don't go there, buddy. Pregnancy has a way of slowing down an adventuresome love life. You should know that."

"Not me. Every time Elli was pregnant I was in Iraq." He smiled. Teasing Steve about his beautiful wife was an ongoing taunt.

"I'm just happy she's happy. I've never seen Sam so settled."

"It is a good thing."

President Al Makin entered Mike's office unannounced, followed by Matt Kreiter. The president's mood was light as he was finally coming to his last day in office. "Good morning, gentlemen. What's the latest?"

"Morning, Mr. President," Mike said as he stood. "Glad you brought your puppy."

"Will you guys give me a break?" Matt complained, and everyone laughed.

"I feel for him," the president said. "They've got him glued to my hip until I get on that chopper this afternoon. I kinda feel sorry for him."

Mike turned the attention back to the more serious matter.

"Sir, we had a ping on the device late last night from Kuala Lumpur. At the International Airport. It confirms the device got there on the plane we tracked yesterday."

"Good. Any news on the man they're holding down there?"

"You mean the *kouzen* guy?" Steve asked. The president nodded. "Nothing yet this morning, sir."

"Well, keep me up to date, at least until they put me on the chopper and haul me out of here." President Makin turned to leave but stopped when he heard a sound.

The fax machine on Mike's credenza beeped and quickly printed four pages.

"It's from OCT about the people *kouzen* met with. Colonel Stevens says he spoke with Commissioner Sim moments ago, while he was on the way to the International Airport. Those six guys are booked on a flight leaving Kuala Lumpur in the next few minutes."

"The same guys who are suspects in the Chinese shooting?" Steve asked.

"Same ones. It's flight MH425 heading to Hong Kong."

"I don't like the sound of that," the president said.

"Me either. Do we have anyone there who can get involved?"

"Mike, the only people we have on the ground are CIA." Steve's eyes locked on Mike's.

Mike looked at the president who was unaware of August White's midnight intrusion into Mike's personal papers. "Yeah, that might be difficult."

"Excuse me, Mr. Trapper," Molly said walking to the open door. "Mr. Wang Zhu from the Chinese embassy is here to see you."

President Makin exchanged a surprised look with Mike.

"Ambassador Wang, good to see you again. Please, come in," Mike said as he greeted his friend.

"Morning, Mike. Mr. President, I'm surprised to see you. But I am also pleased you are here." The ambassador and the president shook hands.

"What can we do for you this morning?" the president asked.

"I actually came to speak with Mike, but I think you are high enough in the government to hear what I have to say." Ambassador Wang's expression was serious.

"Thank you, Mr. Ambassador."

"You *are* the president. But I'm afraid this is not very good news."

"What is it Zhu?" Mike asked stepping toward him.

"You remember the murder of our agents in Singapore yesterday?"

"Of course."

"The team of agents was activated only yesterday. A deal had been struck to purchase a certain piece of equipment from some rather nefarious characters. Our team was to meet a courier, or in this case, the man actually carrying the equipment, at the International Airport in Kuala Lumpur. Then, our people were to escort him to Hong Kong."

"But someone got to them first, before they could contact the courier," Steve said.

"Yes. And now they're dead."

"Your people were in contact with the individual bringing the equipment to Kuala Lumpur?"

"Not exactly, Mike. At least, they were not *yet* in contact. We made arrangements through a person we thought was a third party.

We later discovered he was the same individual with whom we made the original deal."

"Who did you make the deal with? Do you know his name?"

"Only by a code name. We had dealt with him before, and he was known to us as *Táng Di*."

"First . . . cousin?" Matt Kreiter said haltingly while his eyes darted from face to face.

"Or, *father's younger cousin*, an important relation in our country. But, please forgive me, I don't understand the reactions on your faces. Do you know of something of which I am not aware?" The tension in the room increased.

"It's . . . a difficult subject Zhu," Mike said glancing at the president.

"I think we need to clear the decks here, Mike. Sometimes more information helps with the proper assessment of the problem."

"Yes, Mr. President." Mike immediately laid out for Zhu the concerns he had with a man known only to the US government as *Kouzen*. He also revealed the man known as *Kouzen* had met with six Americans, four of whom were former CIA agents. The pieces started falling into place.

"Our largest concern, Mr. Ambassador, is that the six men we have not been able to identify, are preparing to board a plane in Kuala Lumpur at this very moment. We also are concerned that the piece of equipment is at that airport and could be on the same plane."

"And you know this how?" the ambassador asked.

"Commissioner Daniel Sim, Singapore secret police."

"Yes, I know of him."

"Mr. Ambassador, may I ask if you know what happened to your deal with this *Táng Di*?" Matt Kreiter asked.

"We can only assume someone made him a better offer. Probably the Russians."

An uncomfortable silence fell on the men in the room. The realization of what could be underway was terrifying; the international impact unimaginable.

After a prolonged pause, Mike spoke. "Just moments ago we heard from our Office of Counter Terrorism that Commissioner Sim and a number of officers were in route to the airport to stop the plane's departure."

"Let us hope he makes it in time," the ambassador said.

Gate 11, Kuala Lumpur International Airport – 7:40 PM MYT

Failak had waited calmly for his contact to contact him. No one had. The large crowd he had observed was boarding the plane. Still, no one approached him. As the last of the passengers cleared their boarding passes, he stood and swung the backpack onto his shoulders. He would be the last person to enter the plane.

The ramp to the main hatch was nearly empty. Only a few passengers had brought carry-on luggage aboard. His pack seemed large and out of place. Hopefully he would be allowed to keep it with him.

"May I see your ticket, please?" the stewardess asked. "We are very full and may have some doubled bookings. We hope you are not inconvenienced in any way. Is this your only luggage?"

"Yes, this is my luggage. If I may, I would like to keep it near me."

"I'm sure you will find space in the overhead bin." She smiled at Failak, something to which he was not accustomed. "Your ticket is fine. Your seat is next to the aisle on row twenty-three. Thank you for flying Malaysian Air."

Failak retrieved his ticket and made an attempt to return her smile. He just wasn't very good at smiling. He struggled down the aisle toward his seat. The plane was full, overly full in his estimation.

He continued to look for his contact, for a visual response from someone with a knowing look, anyone who would make eye contact, perhaps a nod of recognition. But no one paid the slightest attention to him.

Finally, he found his seat. He lifted the backpack into the overhead bin. It fit, but just barely. Failak sat and buckled his safety belt. He was thankful the seat next to him was empty. He ignored the person in the window seat.

Outside the window, the ground crew prepared the plane for departure. It seemed unnecessary to him; too much fussing and busyness. Life in the mountains was simple. It had taught Failak how to survive. Whether it was the extreme cold or a gunfight with a foreign soldier, he knew how to win. He also knew how to kill.

All the activity and foolishness he had seen at this airport was beyond his grasp. He wanted nothing to do with any of it. He wanted to do his job, deliver the backpack, and go home.

The flight would only be a few hours. He hoped someone would contact him when they landed. He laid his head back against the cushioned headrest. *Perhaps I will sleep for the entire flight.*

White House - 7:55 AM EST

President Al Makin peeked into Mike's office to see if he was still there. He saw Mike and Steve hunched over a Google Earth map of Southeast Asia. Their voices were hushed but urgent.

"Mike. Steve. May I interrupt for a moment?"

"Of course, Mr. President," Mike said as both men stood erect and turned to him.

"I'm ready to leave for the Inauguration, and I wanted to talk to you guys before I left."

"We're happy you stopped by, sir."

"Thanks. Listen, I just wanted to say one more time how much I have valued your service over the last few years. I don't know how all this would have turned out without you. Both of you."

"We appreciate that, Mr. President," Steve said.

"And I don't know how it's going to go beginning tomorrow when President Hunter takes the office. He has a much different style of personnel management than I, and, most likely, more effective."

"Sir, we know it is going to be a big change, but I imagine we'll adapt," Mike said as he looked at Steve. "We've done a lot of adapting over the years."

Steve smiled. "Mr. President, you have no idea how much this guy changes things up all the time. I've learned to make big changes very quickly. We'll have each other's back."

"Good." Al Makin extended his hand to Mike, then to Steve. "I can't imagine what all you'll be facing. Hunter is something of a renegade. You know, new face, new attitude."

"We've seen lots of attitude, that's for sure," Steve said taking a seat on the corner of the desk.

"How's it coming on recovering the device? Have you heard anything new? This is probably the last tidbit of secrecy I'll ever hear."

"Who knows? We did hear from OCT that the device was in Kuala Lumpur, and just minutes ago White confirmed the CIA believes the guy carrying it will soon board a flight in Kuala Lumpur." Mike gestured with both hands then dropped them at his side.

"So this guy carrying the device, has he actually sold it to the Chinese?"

"Well, Mr. President, we think that was the initial plan." Steve shot a glance at Mike.

"The dead Chinese agents in Singapore."

"Yes, sir," Mike affirmed. "I'd say the second guess is the Russians, but the only other people we know anything about are those six men Singapore suspects did the killing. Still no proof."

"What about this *kouzen* fellow?" the president asked looking back and forth from Steve to Mike. "Anything more there?"

"Still in custody and being questioned. That's all we know."

The phone on Mike's desk rang. "Trapper."

"Mike, this is August White. I'm at Langley."

"What can I do for you, Mr. White?" Mike cast a knowing glance at Steve Granger.

"I wanted you to know the device pinged again at the airport in Kuala Lumpur."

"What does that tell us, Mr. White?"

"It indicates that someone probably placed the pack on their shoulders. And based on the fact that it has moved less than fifty feet from the last location, we've concluded the device is probably on a passenger airliner."

"And do you have a particular flight that you suspect the device to be on?"

"Yes. Malaysian Air 425. Its destination is Hong Kong."

International Airport, Kuala Lumpur – 8:05 PM MYT

Commissioner Daniel Sim and eight agents of the Malaysian Secret Police raced down the concourse toward Gate 11. The airport was crowded. People from around the globe jostled each other making their way to a gate for boarding or to the baggage carousel.

"Please! Move out of the way!" Sim yelled pushing his way past one traveler after another. "Move! Quickly! Out of the way."

The crowd pressed against him. Planes at Gates 7 and 9 released more passengers onto the concourse. The number of human beings moving to different locations came to a near standstill.

"Police! Get out of the way!" Sim demanded.

The people immediately around him tried to step back but there was nowhere to go. The bottleneck at the main concourse and the concourse to the gates was impassible.

"Police business!" Sim yelled again. "Please move aside."

Somewhere something changed and people began to move. The large crowd pressed against the walls and Commissioner Sim and his agents were able to force their way through.

They ran to Gate 11. The seats in the waiting area were empty. One ticket agent was busy behind the check-in counter.

"Flight 425. Has it left yet?"

Through the large glass window a Malaysia Air Boeing 777 roared down the runway, rotated, and was airborne. The agent pointed over his shoulder.

"You just missed it."

chapter 24

The Boeing 777 raced from the runway into the brilliant blue sky. The steep angle of ascent pinned the passengers firmly into their seats.

Failak was confused that no one had come to meet him. He feared something had gone wrong. He was worried he might find himself in a difficult situation that he didn't know how to get out of. The plan the bald man on the Learjet had told him about seemed to be unraveling.

He looked around the plane at the passengers. No one stood out. No one made eye contact with him. *Surely someone on this plane is looking for this backpack.* Failak waited in his seat. The seatbelt light was still on, and the plane continued to climb to its cruising altitude. *Sit tight.*

He was glad to have a seat on the aisle. Should something go wrong he could quickly get to his feet. His senses prickled at the thought of close combat. How would he fight? And with what?

Perhaps I could get a knife from the galley? A weapon has to be somewhere in this huge plane. He felt anxiety rising inside. His pulse hammered in his temples. The changes in the cabin air pressure made his head ache. He swallowed to make his ears pop and release the tightness behind his eyes.

He let out a big breath. He was being paranoid. True, no one had approached him. But also true was the fact that no one had shown any aggression toward him. The people on the plane were quiet, even sleepy.

You are running ahead of yourself. Stop this. You have barely had any rest in two days. You are too tired to think clearly.

Failak took a deep breath. The seat next to him was empty, and the person sitting by the window was already asleep. *What are you worried about? Get some rest. There is nothing to worry about.*

He closed his eyes.

Hunter Residence, Washington DC – 8:20 AM EST

President-elect Ronald Hunter stood in front of the full length mirror in his bedroom. He liked what he saw. He stood tall and smiled at his reflection.

"Pretty magnificent, Mr. President." His wife, Susan stepped behind him and slipped her arm under his arm and around his chest. "I think you will make a splendid leader of the free world."

"Should we stop there? Just the free world? There is so much more to roll over, don't you agree?" He adjusted his tie.

Susan laughed at his brag. "You are such an arrogant ass."

"I know. And I love how observant you are." Hunter turned to face her beaming smile. "I think we are going to have a great run here. I don't know if we will change the world, but we sure can have an effect on this country."

"As long as everyone sticks with you and the plan." She kissed him.

204 Stephen T. Gerdel

"Well, that's nothing we need to worry about today." He turned again to the mirror and pressed the lapels of his suit coat against his chest while eyeing himself closely. "Today . . . is all about *me*."

"You do have a vice president, you know. He's going to be part of the team. He has to be, right?"

"Well, yeah. I can get David to handle him though. As long as everything appears to function along normal lines we'll be fine."

"I hope so." Susan took over the mirror as Ronald Hunter walked to his dresser to collect his wallet and cell phone. "What time does the limo arrive?"

"Eight-thirty. We need to get downstairs." He opened the bedroom door for her.

She stopped in front of him. "Ron, I want you to know I'm with you all the way. One hundred percent."

"That's all I can ask, babe. I want nothing more than that." He kissed her and took her arm, leading her down to the arriving limo.

International Airport Kuala Lumpur – 8:25 PM MYT

Commissioner Daniel Sim stood at the larger window overlooking the tarmac for what seemed a very long time. The agents who accompanied him formed a loose perimeter around their superior. The commissioner clearly needed some time to think.

His phone in his pocket chimed that he had received a text from his office. His train of thought was broken, and he turned on his phone to see what had been sent to him.

The text contained information about the man who had brought the device in the backpack to Malaysia. It was nothing surprising to Daniel Sim. The man was known as a Mujahideen warrior. Nothing about him was distinctive. Nothing threatening other than that he was a ferocious fighter for his homeland.

Daniel actually respected that in a man regardless of the land in which he fought. Warring to keep one's home free from occupation by a foreign power was a noble endeavor. He would do the same.

"Excuse me, commissioner."

"Yes, what is it?" Daniel asked turning from the window to face the agent.

"Another plane will be coming to this gate shortly. I thought perhaps you would want to leave before it arrives."

"You're right. I'll make a phone call first." He dismissed the agent and dialed Colonel Aaron Stevens at OCT in Little Rock. The phone rang twice.

"Colonel Stevens."

"Aaron, this is Daniel."

"What's up?"

"Well, we missed the plane. It left only moments before we arrived."

"That stinks."

"Yeah, but not a total loss. We know the plane is headed to Hong Kong and no one is getting off that aircraft until it lands. We can have people at the gate to meet this guy."

"You ID'ed him?"

"Nobody official. He's a Mujahideen fighter in his mid to late fifties. Tough as they come, but alone, probably confused, and with no idea of what is next. He might be open to a friendly face."

"You're not volunteering to jet to Hong Kong, are you?"

"No, but we have a good team that can meet him. They might be able to convince him they are his contact or something."

"What can you send me?"

"We know his name is Failak Jahnangir and the only picture we have of him is twenty years old and pretty grainy."

"Besides that, he's probably got a full beard and a tribal pakol hat like a hundred thousand other Afghani men."

"No, the airport security video shows him dressed in tropical clothing. At least we think it's him. We have footage of one man with a full beard carrying a large backpack. Didn't see his face, however."

"Only one?"

"People don't use backpacks very often when traveling here. We're more like small cases with thongs and bikinis in them. You know . . . vacation stuff."

"Someday I may have that opportunity. Thanks for the update, Daniel. I have a sneaking suspicion the folks in Washington will want to set up a greeting committee in Hong Kong as well. Let's try not to get in each other's way, okay?"

"I'll let everyone know."

Daniel Sim turned off his phone. An Air India passenger liner was pulling up to the gate. He signaled his men, and they hurriedly made their way down the concourse.

Malaysia Air Flight 425, Over North Malaysia – 8:45 PM MYT

"Did you see that guy we saw at the hotel pool?"

"Yeah, but are you sure it's the same one?"

"Definitely. I know him."

"You *what*?"

"I *know* him. I've been wracking my brain trying to remember his name."

"How the hell do you know the guy?"

"We were both SEALs. I knew him in my last tour in Afghanistan. We saw some real nasty shit."

"Are you sure?"

"I would be if I could remember his name. I just can't quite tag him."

"Is he going to be a problem?"

"Doubt it, but you never know. Besides, how could anyone know what's coming?"

"Yeah. Well, keep an eye out for him."

"Okay you two, enough of the chit-chat. I don't care who you think you know. We have to move before they start serving drinks. Like we planned, we take the front of the plane. The others will move to the back when we get up. Any questions?"

The other two men echoed affirmative replies and sat back in their seats. It would not be long.

NSA Office, White House – 8:50 AM EST

"We need only a handful of men to meet this guy in Hong Kong. Can't we just use embassy staffers?" Steve said as he placed his steaming mug of coffee on a coaster on Mike's desk. "Maybe some embassy Marines?

"For one, we don't know exactly who the courier is. Or what he might do if he was met by a band of Americans. We know he's from Afghanistan and that he enabled communication with terrorists groups around the world. I would assume he doesn't like us very much." Mike sipped his coffee.

"But we should at least have someone on the ground to see who he meets, right?"

"Yes. But I don't want this to run through Langley. I'd prefer to use someone else."

"Didn't Ketcham take a position in Hong Kong when he retired?"

"I think you're right, Steve. How do we find out where?"

"I'll call Matt. He worked pretty close with him after he transferred from St. Louis."

Steve opened his call list on his phone and selected his number. After two rings he heard Matt Kreiter's voice.

"Kreiter."

"Hey, Matt, Steve Granger."

"Are you going to be nice, or should I hang up right now?"

"No, no teasing on this call. Hear me out."

"Good. What's up?"

"You remember Bill Ketcham don't you?"

"Of course. Why?"

"When he left the Secret Service didn't he take a job in Hong Kong?"

"Yeah. He's the executive director for the American Chamber of Commerce."

"Good. We need someone we can trust to do a little leg work for us. Do you think he'd be open to a little surveillance?"

"The Chinese over there think we're all spies regardless of our job titles. He'd probably consider it a treat."

"Do you have his number?"

Matt provided Bill Ketcham's cell number, and a plan to watch for the courier was hatched.

OCT Little Rock – 7:55 AM CST

Colonel Aaron Stevens walked into the Grid Room where more than twenty analysts had spent the night tagging terrorists' communications and locations through Facebook and Twitter. SWAT teams were being dispatched in every major city to the identified positions.

"Do we have them on the run?" Stevens asked Keith Dillon.

"Most of them were still eating their breakfast." Keith smiled a shallow grin.

"Don't celebrate with too much vigor. You might scare off the hired help."

"I'm too tired to celebrate."

Stevens's phone rang.

"Colonel Stevens."

"Aaron, it's Mike. I need your help."

"Sure. Fire away."

"Thanks." Mike took in a deep breath. "You probably know we're expecting the USURP device to be sold in Hong Kong to an unknown buyer soon after the plane lands. I was wondering what assets you might have available?"

"Might get sticky with the Chi-coms, you know. Did you have anyone in mind?"

"I know Bill Ketcham took a job over there when he retired from the Secret Service, but he's the only one we have so far."

"Well, Bill's a fine man. I think you should contact him."

"That's my next step. I just wanted to see if we had more resources in case this went poorly."

"Actually, why don't you let me call him? Make it more official."

"Official? How so?"

"Mike, he is already one of our assets. The Chamber of Commerce was very cooperative in placing him in their organization."

"Wow. So the Chinese are right."

"What do you mean?"

"Everyone over there really is a spy."

"You didn't hear that from me, Mike."

"I know, Aaron. And thanks."

chapter 25

Inauguration Day, Washington DC – 8:59 AM EST

The pageantry of the Inauguration of an American President had grown to rival the weddings and crownings of European kings and queens of past centuries. As with most inaugural celebrations of modern times, the ceremony was set to take place on the western steps of the Capitol Building.

Preparations had been underway for three weeks with construction of the viewing stage for the oath of office and seating for both the House of Representatives and Senate. The presidential reviewing stand for the Inaugural Parade had been constructed in front of the White House. Everything was ready for the day.

Ronald Hunter faced the street waiting for the precise moment he and his wife, Susan, would be required to step outside to the waiting limousine. The events of the day were planned and timed almost to the second. Precision was the order of the day.

"President Hunter, Mrs. Hunter?" the Secret Service agent said. "It's time."

Hunter smiled and nodded. He took his wife's arm in his and looked at her. "This is what it's been all about. This is our day."

"Let me be the first to congratulate you, dear." She kissed his cheek.

President and Mrs. Hunter walked out the door of their home and down the steps to the limo. It was a crisp, but bright, sunny day in Washington. Being outdoors for the oath of office and his inaugural address would be delightful.

Ronald Hunter beamed with pride. He had it all. He was wealthy but not to the extreme. He had a beautiful wife who possessed charm and grace that would serve her well. And today he would become leader of the free world.

He stopped beside the automobile and looked across the street at the crowd applauding them. *I would prefer the title 'King of the World,' but I don't think the Constitution would approve it.* He smiled and waved to the people. A cheer rose up from the four or five hundred citizens scattered down the street.

He turned to his right and waved. The cheers increased. Then he waved to the left. The crowd loved him. He loved having them honor him.

He assisted Mrs. Hunter as she stooped to enter the car. Then, after one last wave, he entered behind her.

"Pretty good start for the day, don't you think?" Susan said.

"Absolutely, my dear. Absolutely."

NSA Office, White House – 9:10 AM EST

Mike and Steve were spared the rituals of the Inaugural. Their confidence had been lifted knowing a team of trusted American agents would meet the Malaysian airliner when it landed in Hong Kong. However, the two men still faced a pile of loose ends.

"The big thing we're lacking is information on who ordered the strike in the first place." Steve stood at the end of Mike's desk, his hands resting on his hips. The papers before him were cluttered. "Let's go through it all backwards, last and latest to the first. We have to have missed something in here." Every document had a time stamp that established the order in which they had received the information.

"Okay, the plane. That will work itself out in Hong Kong." Mike laid the first and most recent page at the end of his desk.

"*Kouzen*. In custody in Kuala Lumpur. Done."

"Courier at the airport. He'll be met by Bill Ketcham."

"Pings from the backpack in Kuala Lumpur. Again, in Hong Kong."

"Fax from Commissioner Sim about *Kouzen* and his contact with six Americans, apparently rogue agents or freelancers."

"Six Chinese agents killed in Singapore by American weapon—"

"Wait. We missed this. At least I did." Steve flipped to the second page of the fax from Daniel Sim.

"What did we miss?" Mike placed his hands on the papers and leaned across the desktop.

"Here." Steve pointed to the last paragraph of the fax. "The Malaysian police listed a phone call that *Kouzen* received from a number here in Washington."

"Why didn't we see this?"

"Oh no." Steve's face flushed white. "Did you see this?"

"What? Where?" Mike walked around the desk to Steve's side.

"The scribbling that Aaron made."

Mike looked closely at the scratching in the margin of the fax. "PE Hunter." The air left his lungs. "This can't be."

"President-elect Hunter?"

"President-elect Hunter called *Kouzen!*" Mike dropped the paper on the desk.

Steve grabbed the page and looked closer. "What does 'vp' mean? Not *vice* president, I hope."

"No. I saw that when we were following leads on Jalal Udin a few years ago. That's Aaron's abbreviation for 'voiceprint.' They must have confirmed it somehow and we missed it."

"So, the guy who is about to be sworn in as president of the United States is connected with *Kouzen*?" Steve dropped himself into a chair.

"Oh, crap." Mike felt suddenly ill. *This isn't real. This isn't really happening.*

Malaysian Air Flight 425 – 9:15 PM MYT

Yolanda slept quietly in her seat. Robert looked at her. *She is beautiful even when she sleeps.* He chuckled softly. *And no drool.*

The flight was smooth and people around the cabin were making themselves comfortable. The three-and-a-half-hour flight was a perfect time to get some rest. Robert was thinking ahead about the shortened night they would experience traveling east across the Pacific. The speed of the plane and the approach of the rising sun would cut the night in half and make the following day the longest one ever.

I should follow her lead. Robert reclined his seat and pulled the blanket the steward had provided for him over his arms. He closed his eyes.

Memories of the last two weeks flooded his thoughts. Both he and Yolanda had experienced things neither had seen before. She had smiled at their meeting of the baby elephant at Tanjung Aru. The young, pesky pachyderm persisted with inappropriate interest in Yolanda's skirt. She laughed and blushed as she warded off the creature's advances. Robert smiled at the memory.

Someone rushing past him down the aisle firmly struck his shoulder, startling him. Robert was instantly alert. He turned and looked toward the back of the plane. He saw the man who had bumped into him. Two more men were rushing down the aisle on the far side of the center section of seats.

What do they have on their faces? Robert's ears popped. *The cabin pressure is dropping!*

He looked again. The man who had bumped him wore a device he recognized. The SEA MK4 (survival egress system) is issued to helicopter pilots to use if they were to crash in water. The device is designed to provide up to a ten minute air supply from a small tank strapped to the user's arm.

As part of his SEAL training Robert had experienced low air pressure in a hypobaric chamber. He recognized the sensation as the air pressure dropped. He had to move quickly.

Robert watched the man disappear into the galley. The other two men entered the galley area from the aisle on the far side of the plane. He heard what he thought was a brief scream. Again, his ears popped.

He slipped out of his seatbelt and ran after the man who bumped him. He wasn't sure about what was going on, but he knew instinctively that it wasn't good. His fear was confirmed when he saw the man dragging the limp body of a stewardess into one of the toilet stalls. His back was toward Robert giving him the advantage of surprise.

As he closed the toilet door, Robert grabbed the man's shirt collar and jerked him back. In a single movement he snapped the man's neck.

Robert spun around and came face to face with another passenger who had been practically decapitated a second man wearing the small breathing device. Their eyes met. Both men knew they were fighting a common enemy. In an instant, they were warriors on the same side.

A third man wearing an air tank and mouthpiece stepped from a toilet on the far side of the plane. Robert dove at him and killed him with two strikes to the head. He turned to his fellow defender.

"I'm Robert."

The man holding the knife recoiled and shook his head. He didn't understand English. Robert repeated his name in Arabic. The man nodded and replied in Arabic.

"My name is Failak."

"In different circumstances we would most likely be enemies," Robert said.

Failak looked toward the ,front of the plane. "Today my enemy's enemy is my friend." He glanced forward again. "How many of them are on the plane?"

"At least six, counting these three. The others are up front."

"You know they are depressurizing the plane. My ears popped as the pressure changed. You understand?" Failak asked as he held the SEA MK4 device he had removed from the man he killed.

"Yes."

Failak removed another device from the second man Robert had killed and held it out to him.

"Put this on your woman."

Robert was surprised at the kindness of the stranger. He took the device and thanked him.

The plane suddenly lurched to a steep incline throwing both men back against the galley cabinets.

"They're climbing to a higher altitude to force the air out of the cabin!"

"Go back to your seat," Failak said. "We will deal with these murderers later. If we survive."

Robert watched Failak scramble up the steeply banked aisle toward his seat. He then turned and began climbing toward Yolanda, a breathing device clutched in each hand.

The plane banked to an even steeper incline. Robert was climbing from row to row. Passengers awoke with panic on their faces. There was nothing he could do for them. He had to get to Yolanda. *The monsters must have disabled the emergency oxygen!*

After only one minute without oxygen the human brain will suffer damage. After two minutes the damage is survivable. Three minutes without oxygen the brain begins to die. The process is irreversible. He needed to hurry.

He climbed ferociously. His breath was short but he would not stop until he could place a breathing device on Yolanda. Still two rows up. He fought to hold his breath, struggling against the thinning air. Robert could feel himself beginning to blackout.

One final lunge brought him to his seat. Yolanda was beginning to awake, gasping for air. He stretched the strap over her head and forced the mouthpiece into her mouth. Her eyes reflected her terror. She grabbed at him violently, gagging on a scream.

Robert placed the other device in his own mouth and began breathing the bottled air. He looked at the woman he loved. Their eyes locked. She settled back into her seat breathing deeply from the compressed tank. Her eyes filled with tears of confusion and terror. Robert pulled her against him and held her tightly.

People around them cried in their own horror with breathless screams. Slowly the cries diminished. Fewer and fewer sounds could be heard as the plane continued to climb.

The pain in Robert's ears was almost unbearable. Yolanda whimpered and tears streamed her cheeks. But they had air to breathe.

Robert burned with rage. The cockpit was too far away. He couldn't climb that far to kill the beasts who were intentionally murdering hundreds of passengers on the Boeing 777. But he would kill them. Their deaths would be the painful, horrible, punishing deaths that such monsters deserve.

The passengers around him were silent. Slowly the plane leveled. After two minutes at the extremely high altitude the aircraft's nose lowered and began to race toward the earth.

Robert closed his eyes and shook his head. *Did the men in the cockpit kill themselves in the process of suffocating everyone else? What are they trying to do?*

He held Yolanda close to him. She sobbed, but she was breathing. She was alive, at least for now. He could feel the acceleration and hear the wind roaring just outside their window. *Are these idiots going to crash the plane?* The panic passed quickly. Yolanda was with him. He could ask for nothing more. *It'll be over in an instant. We won't suffer.* He was thankful. *We'll just . . . stop.*

OCT Little Rock – 8:20 AM CST

Aaron Stevens called Mike's cell phone. The plans were laid and confirmed. The device would be retrieved in Hong Kong. Kouzen would be held for a few days, and then he would be delivered to the custody of U.S. Marshals in Kuala Lumpur.

"Trapper."

"Hi, Mike. It's Aaron. Everything is set." He let out a long breath as he sat behind his desk.

"Is a twenty-six hour day enough for you?"

Aaron heard Mike laugh softly into his phone. "Only if it's really over when it's over. Is it over yet?"

"Most of it, maybe. At least we'll get the device back."

"Yeah." Aaron stretched, leaning his chair as far back as he dared. "Is DC as crazy as I imagine it being on Inauguration Day?"

"I'm working. I get to miss all that crap. There was one thing that Steve and I found and we weren't able to come to a conclusion about it."

"What's that?"

"The voiceprint."

"The one with President-elect Hunter talking to *Kouzen*?"

"That's it. I was sick to my stomach when I saw it. Is this for real? Are you certain it's *not* a mistake?"

"As certain as can be, Mike. Daniel Sim confirmed it. Actually, they knew before we did. We confirmed it to them. I don't know what we can do, whether it's true or false."

"As long as we get the device back, maybe it will sink in old Foggy Bottom like so much else." Mike was silent for a moment. "I don't know. It just doesn't seem right."

"I know. But we aren't the ones in power. We don't control this."

"So, Daniel and the Malaysian police are aware of all this, and they have *Kouzen* in custody?"

"That's my understanding. I know they tried to stop the plane from leaving but they missed it."

"But we have that resolved, at least for the moment. I'm at a loss. I don't think there is anything we can do to stop or delay the Inauguration of a man linked to a known spy and possibly a killer, is there?"

"I think the only thing that can be done is to run it past Ray Jergins at the Justice Department."

"Yeah, it's either a big deal or it's nothing."

"There doesn't seem to be much we can do until the plane lands. Get some rest and let the guys in Hong Kong handle it. Then we can dig a little deeper, perhaps."

"You're right. Let me know what you hear from Bill after they get the device."

"Will do." Aaron placed his desk phone back in its cradle. *Rest. Good advice.* He closed his eyes.

chapter 26

Police Department, Kuala Lumpur – 9:25 PM MYT

Commissioner Daniel Sim entered the police station with the officers who had accompanied him to the airport. The entire team was frustrated they had missed the plane.

"Remind me to petition the governor about the restrictions on police when it comes to tourists." A chorus of affirming groans echoed from the police agents. Once a suspect was in custody the police had wide expanses of interrogation measures they could use. Getting an individual into custody wasn't always as simple.

Daniel Sim went into the office set aside for him when he was in town. It wasn't as well equipped as his office in Singapore. No cot. None of the "comforts" he had provided himself were provided in Kuala Lumpur. But the chair behind his desk was first rate.

"Commissioner, did you want to interrogate the suspect further tonight?"

Daniel groaned at the suggestion his aide proposed. "No. I don't want to see him. But we need to anyway." Daniel rubbed his face and sat up. "I haven't seen my family in nearly two days, and this scoundrel will only further delay that pleasure."

"We can let him sit it out until morning, sir. No requirement we talk to him tonight."

"No. He's been sitting in that room for the last three hours. Maybe the loneliness has softened him a bit." Daniel forced himself from the chair and followed the officer down the hall to the holding room.

The officer placed his key in the lock and turned it. The lock snapped back, and the door opened.

Commissioner Sim entered the room. His words stuck in his throat.

The room was empty. *Kouzen* was gone.

NSA Office, White House – 9:30 AM EST

Ray Jergins stepped into Mike's office and looked around the room. Even though the move was just down the hall from his old office, boxes were everywhere and nothing was in its proper place.

"This is what makes me glad I'm in Justice. We don't have to move every four years. We just get a new boss." Ray sauntered in and took a chair that wasn't covered with clutter.

"By the time I get everything in place, it will probably be time to move it again." Mike smiled. "But I didn't call you to help me unpack this mess. We've got a bigger, more serious mess to unpack."

"Well, then let's start at the very beginning. Usually the best place."

Mike sat behind his desk and sorted the pages before he spoke. "You know from yesterday's meeting we've been following the USURP device through a feed from Langley."

"And they provided it begrudgingly, I'm sure."

"Like pulling teeth." Mike let out a breath. "That's the part we have fairly well sewn up. We have a team of agents who are going to meet the plane in Hong Kong and recover the box."

"So, there must be something that isn't all 'sewn up?'"

"Yeah." He really didn't want to bring his fears to light, but keeping it buried would undoubtedly cause more problems later. "Last night I learned of the murder of six Chinese agents in Singapore. They were all killed with Springfield 1911s, standard CIA issue. The Chinese agents had been activated that very afternoon, and I believe they were activated because of the attack in the Wahkan Corridor."

"The Chinese knew about the attack?"

"It would seem so. More to the point, someone *else* knew of the attack before the fact. It's a guess, but someone informed the Chinese about the equipment prior to the attack, and plans were put in place for the six agents who were killed to meet a courier and purchase the USURP device."

"How could they possibly know? That's special access protocol, super secret."

"Someone leaked it." Mike's next step was the one that really terrified him.

Ray turned a hard and heavy gaze to Mike. "It was a CIA op, right?"

"Yes."

"Who would do such a thing?"

"That's the million-dollar question. But Ray . . . there's more."

"So now we're moving from 'oops' to 'oh damn,' right?" A blanket of unthinkable fear covered the two men.

"Yeah." Mike turned to his next page of notes. "We have known about a double agent working between the US and Russia, but only as a shadow. No one knows who he is, where he comes from, or what his next move might be. His code name is *Kouzen*."

"Like *Tarzan?*" Ray quipped.

"Sorta. We learned he was being watched in Singapore through Commissioner Sim. The guys at OCT in Little Rock pulled some strings and with the aid of both Russia's and India's secret biometric profiling systems, they were able to identify who *Kouzen* was. He was ID'ed as an American named Mikael Kohen."

"A little heavy on the Russian influence isn't it?"

"Yes, but one-hundred-percent homegrown. He was known to the Chinese as well. And this is where the subterfuge comes in. They had been contacted by an agent they knew as *Táng Di.*"

"Which means . . .?" Ray asked as he motioned his hand, drawing the answer from Mike.

"It means a *father's male cousin.*"

"Of course."

"Then yesterday, or this morning, I don't know. It's night here and day over there. But the Malaysian police followed *Kouzen* and observed a meeting between him and six Americans."

"Same number as the Chinese agents."

"Right. And four of those Americans were identified as former CIA operatives."

"And so the plot thickens." Ray leaned back in his chair.

"So thick I'd prefer to stop right here, but I can't."

"It's all right. I'm sitting down already, Mike."

"Well, just after midnight our time, a call was placed from somewhere here in Washington DC to *Kouzen* in Kuala Lumpur. The Malaysian police were monitoring *Kouzen* in his room when he got the call and they recorded it."

"Great! Voiceprint." Ray tossed his hands in the air. "Who was it? Do we know?"

Mike stopped. Thinking the accusation was one thing, but speaking it into existence made it real, not just a concept. "Ray, it was Ronald Hunter."

Ray's jaw dropped. His face went slack. He bolted forward in his chair, blinking his eyes, and he began stammering. "Y-you m-mean, the president of the United States Ronald Hunter? The one that's going to take the oath of office in what, two and a half hours, *that* Ronald Hunter?"

"That's the one." Mike felt the weight slide off. He sensed the relief of sharing a burden. He took a deep breath. He had done it.

"And you're certain. Who made the confirmation on the voiceprint? Are the absolutely certain it was Hunter?"

"Aaron Stevens in Little Rock ran it through Langley. They weren't able to ID *Kouzen*, but they were very interested in who was recording the president-elect in Malaysia."

"Did the OCT guys let on they were really trying to confirm *Kouzen?*"

"No. They had the presence of mind to blow it off."

"Damn! The president of the United States in bed with selling American secrets to the Chinese! Damn!" Ray's voice was little more than a whisper.

"Not to mention the murder of six agents in Singapore."

"Damn!"

"Ray, you know the law. I don't. What do we do?"

Ray stood. He rubbed his head.

"Today, nothing. There is no way to stop the inauguration of an elected president. He's almost above the law. Hell, he *IS* the damn law!" Ray paced.

Mike watched, wondering what volumes of legal theory spun through Ray's mind. Then Ray stood perfectly still. He looked at Mike with wild eyes.

"Okay. Not today. Nothing today. But right now I need Scotch."

Ray Jergins left Mike's office.

Control Tower, Kuala Lumpur International – 9:46 PM MYT

"Malaysian Four Two Five, contact Lumpur Radar One, over. . ."

The air traffic controller waited patiently. "Has anyone had data drop off your screen?" he asked over his shoulder. The supervisor joined him at his workstation.

"What's wrong?"

"The transponder beacon from MH425 suddenly disappeared from my screen."

"Any distress call?"

"Nope."

"Try again."

"Malaysian Four Two Five, request contact Lumpur Radar One, over . . ."

The two men stared at the screen. Every passing second of silence increased the threat of terrible news.

"Malaysian Four Two Five, request contact Lumpur Radar One, over . . ."

Three more off-duty controllers gravitated toward the non-responsive call to MH425. Chatter in the control room died down. Silence mirrored the plane's response as a dreadful reality set in.

"Malaysian Four Two Five, request contact Lumpur Radar One, over . . ."

The supervisor lifted the phone receptacle at the work station from its cradle. "Radar One General Alert. Radar One General Alert. Non-response notice for Malaysian Four Two Five, maintaining level three five zero. Last hand-off to Ho Chi Minh 120 decimal 9 at twenty-one hundred, one zero hours MYT. Radar One General Alert. Radar One General Alert."

Immediately, teams located three floors below began a review and inquiry routine they had rehearsed a hundred times. Technicians phoned the control tower at Ho Chi Minh International and Hong Kong airport. The audio transcript of the plane's departure from Kuala Lumpur as well as the video record of the transponder location was loaded for review.

"Malaysian Four Two Five, request contact Lumpur Radar One, over . . ."

"Where was it on your screen?" the supervisor asked.

The rattled controller placed his trembling finger on the spot where the transponder marker had vanished. "Here, sir."

"Keep trying. I must go downstairs and file the official report. How many on board?"

"Three hundred forty-six passengers and crew, sir."

"Keep trying." The supervisor left the tower to do the part of his job no one ever wanted to do: file a report of a plane down with passengers.

"Malaysian Four Two Five, request contact Lumpur Radar One, over . . ."

The conversation in the tower was muffled, almost non-existent. Radio communications were spoken softly. The news traveled quickly to other flights. No one reported hearing a distress call. No one reported any visible sign of a plane in distress.

"Malaysian Four Two Five, request contact Lumpur Radar One, over . . ."

As the late-night flights landed in Kuala Lumpur the amount of radio traffic was also reduced. A pause in arrivals and departures finally left the tower quiet except for one voice calling into the darkened night sky.

"Malaysian Four Two Five, request contact Lumpur Radar One, over . . ."

No response came.

OCT Little Rock – 8:50 AM CST

The phone on his desk wrestled Aaron Stevens from a brief, deep sleep. The colonel thrashed, incoherently clawing his way to his desk phone. "Stevens."

"Even *I* can tell you just woke up. I wish I was calling with better news."

"Yeah. Hi, Daniel. What's up?"

"*Kouzen* is gone."

"Gone! How?" He was fully awake, and certain he was not dreaming.

"We don't know. We came back from the airport, and the room was empty. He just vanished."

"Did he have help? I mean, he just can't dematerialize and float through the walls, can he?"

"No one ever has, that I know of."

"That's not news I like to hear. Hell of a deal."

"We have an APB out and every officer in the station is being interviewed. Someone had to cooperate with him. There has to be a payoff somewhere. People cannot float through walls, even in Malaysia."

"I don't feel much better knowing that, Daniel. I'm sure you'll do everything you can to get him back into custody."

"And then some. Next time there will be no opportunity for him to escape even if I have to chain myself to him."

"I had a long talk with Mike Trapper an hour or so ago. He's convinced everything is tied together."

"Mostly loose ends here."

"I know. As soon as the plane lands in Hong Kong we should be able to wrap this up. But we will need *Kouzen* when you get him."

"We have a few minor infractions we need to discuss with him first. You know like false passports, murder, stuff like that. When we're through you can have what's left."

"As long as he can breathe and answer 'yes/no' questions."

"Well, let's both hope he will maintain that ability."

"Talk to you soon, Daniel."

chapter 27

NSA Office, White House – 9:55 AM EST

Mike could feel the exhaustion creep up his neck and cloud his thinking. *Men were not built to live without sleep.* It didn't matter. The work still had to be done. The waiting was the worst. He could do nothing to make time move faster. He couldn't make the plane arrive in Hong Kong before the appointed time. It was driving him nuts.

Steve Granger ran into his office. "Did you see the news? Turn on the TV."

Mike picked up the remote and pressed the power button. Nothing. He pressed it again. Still nothing.

"Rats. I don't think I plugged it in yet." Mike reached behind the flat screen and attached the cable to the receptacle in the wall, then inserted the power cord into the wall outlet.

He pressed the power button again.

". . . departed Kuala Lumpur International Airport at approximately 8:15 in the evening. All indications are that the flight was normal. No distress call was received by any control tower, and no flights report any evidence of an explosion. The plane simply, and suddenly, vanished. Authorities on the ground are reviewing recorded flight data to determine exactly where Malaysian Air Flight 425 may have gone down. In the meantime, reports of the airline's safety history are coming to light that may present a—"

"No! That's not *our* flight 425, is it?" Mike exclaimed.

"From all indications, it is."

"Departure time the same?"

"8:13 p.m., like the man said. The online schedule shows the same departure time."

"And we're absolutely certain that's the flight the device was carried onto? Absolutely sure?"

"From everything we know and worked all night to piece together, it's the same flight."

"Then, it's all lost. Or at least until they find the crash site, right?"

"And that's another problem. Where? What country, or jungle? Or what if it crashed in the ocean somewhere. We have a limited time before the whole thing sinks."

"How long can a triple-seven float? No. Wait. I'm not going there. The folks in Malaysia have experts. We have experts. I'm going to let them figure it all out. I'm tired. I'm going to go home and relax, away from all the inaugural shenanigans."

"Since my new boss is on his way to becoming president, I think I'll do the same. Besides, I'm not on his team until tomorrow."

St. John's Episcopal Church, Washington DC – 10:00 AM EST

President-elect Ronald Hunter stood with his wife in the second row of the historic church. Many presidents-elect had stood in the same spot since Franklin D. Roosevelt began the tradition in 1933.

Different venues were used by other presidents, but St. John's was chosen more than any other.

The congregation sang *"The Church's One Foundation"* with all the gusto of a small country church. Most considered it a duty of tradition. Every senator and representative included on the guest list had work waiting for their return from the ceremonies. Each man and woman also had a party list.

Ronald Hunter endured the tradition. He had rarely attended church. His own moral code was enough, and a code he considered more that most churches required. He knew his presence today was a requirement.

The hymn ended and the crowd took their seats.

Ronald leaned toward Susan and whispered, "I asked him to make it short, you know, to get it over with."

"You are insufferable!" she whispered back with a smile.

That's it. Smiling in church. Lots of smiling. It'll go well with the Bible thumpers. It was a reaction he wanted from her. She responded on cue. Perfectly timed.

The pastor read from the Old Testament about King David and the wealth with which God had blessed his kingdom. The people rejoiced in their new king and the land prospered. "On this day, the United States of America is blessed with new leadership," the pastor said.

He could've just said king.

"Today is the dawning of a new American Era. We will rejoice in God's blessings as our nation rises once again to global leadership."

I am the phoenix rising from the ashes of the past.

"And He will be glorified in the hearts of a grateful nation."

Yes, I will.

"Let us pray."

Let's do just that. I'm here. I am listening.

Roosevelt Room, White House – 10:10 AM EST

Ray Jergins, Department of Justice, and Alex Hodson, FBI, sat in the chairs in the far corner of the conference table. They were facing a challenge neither man could recall ever being encountered in the history of the republic. Presidents had made trouble for themselves, circumvented the intent of the law, and outright lied during their terms in office.

But no president had been implicated in international espionage or murder. The discovery of the accusation had come only hours before the inauguration and no provision could be found in the Constitution to alter the determined course. This was a first.

"Alex, even if we faced a natural disaster, horrible weather, or something totally off the wall like an earthquake in DC, everything would be moved indoors or taken to a private location. There is no way to stop this."

"Even just a brief delay might be enough time to review the evidence and clear the man's name. Are you saying we can't give this concern the due diligence to make the case or clear the charges?"

"That's exactly what I'm saying. A sitting president, and that's what Hunter is going to be in less than two hours, a *sitting* president can only be indicted by Congress. It's a real case of the president being above the law, and the only body empowered to question or correct the fact is the lawmakers themselves."

"So we're wasting our time even fussing over it."

"In a sense, yes." Ray leaned back in his chair. "We don't even know for certain what has been going on for the last two days. It could all be nothing."

"Or it could be the beginning of tyranny."

"Now, there you go, Alex, running off at the mouth like some conspiracy theorist. Granted, it looks bad. And maybe it is bad. But we'll get through it. We got through the last impeachment; we got through Iraq, fumbled through the healthcare issue, and even the mess with email servers. It's what we do. We're the United States of America. We fix things."

"Or blast them off the face of the earth. Remember Hiroshima, Chernobyl, or Yerevan?"

"We only did one of those, Alex."

"Yeah, but it was the first." Alex slumped into his chair and chewed his left thumbnail. "Look at the mess that has followed. Ray, it is at times of uncertainty like this that huge mistakes can happen. We have no idea how Hunter is going to react to this mess."

"No, we don't. We aren't even sure there's an incident for him to react to. The timing on this is the absolute worst."

"Six months ago, news like this would have ruined his campaign."

"And six months from now it could make him look like a savior. We have to come to grips with the fact that there's nothing we can do. Nothing."

Alex threw his hands in the air and turned his eyes away from his old friend. "You're right. Might as well just go get drunk and see what happens tomorrow."

"Well, *that*, I have covered." Ray sprang from his chair and walked to the large credenza against the opposite wall. "I brought this up a little while ago," he said as he retrieved a full bottle of Jack Daniels from the lower cabinet.

The far door opened and Mike stuck his head in.

"You guys seen the news?"

"About the Inauguration? They're all the same. We've been there."

"No. About the plane carrying the USURP device. It's gone down."

Alex leaped to his feet. "Down? Crashed or landed?"

"No one knows. It vanished from radar about half an hour ago. They're working in Kuala Lumpur to find the exact spot it left the radar."

"Isn't it the dead of night over there?"

"Yeah, but even in broad daylight it would be difficult to find a plane crashed in the jungle . . . or the ocean, for that matter."

"One thing is for sure," Alex said walking toward Ray and the Jack Daniels.

"What's that?" Ray asked.
"Now, we have an incident."

Sheriff's Office, Norman, OK – 9:30 AM CST

News of the vanishing of Malaysian flight 425 struck a hard chord in Norman, Oklahoma. Sheriff Perry Hitchens knew his son and daughter-in-law were aboard that airliner. Perry had sent them off on their honeymoon two weeks earlier on the first leg of their journey from Oklahoma City to Dallas.

Yolanda had brightened Perry's life as he had watched Robert fall in love with her. The news came on the day they would begin their trip home. Perry had kept their itinerary on his refrigerator anchored securely by a magnet shaped like a watermelon and another an image of a cluster of grapes.

This was the day. MH425 was their flight. They were on that plane.

Perry's gut was wrenched with grief without really knowing what was happening. He had seen the news. The report was sketchy and uncertain. It frustrated him.

He picked up his phone and dialed a number he hadn't called in almost three years. It rang only once.

"Trapper."

"Mike! Perry Hitchens in Norman."

"Perry, good to hear from you."

"I know you gotta be busy with this inauguration and all, but do you have a minute?"

"It's nuts around here, Perry, but I'll always have time for you. What's up?"

"Robert and Yolanda were on that plane."

The silence on the other end let Perry know his news was a shock to his old friend.

"You know, the one in Malaysia. It was just on the news."

"Yeah. Yeah, I know, Perry. We've been watching that develop. But both Robert and Yolanda?"

"Yup. It's the flight they got for their return trip. They've been over there for the last two weeks on their honeymoon. I talked to Robert just last night." Perry sobbed fighting off his tears.

"No! Oh, Perry, I am so sorry."

"Thanks, Mike. Listen, if you hear anything that would breathe a little hope into this old man, would you call me?"

"Absolutely, Perry. Yes. If anything comes up I'll let you know."

"I don't think I can expect much from the news, this bein' on the other side of the world an' all. But if you do, I would greatly appreciate it."

"I will. Perry, I am very sorry."

"Thanks. I'm gonna sit here and call Robert's cell until he answers or . . . they find them."

"You know that could be a while."

"Yeah, but what else can I do?" Perry's voice weakened with emotion.

"I'll let you know the minute I hear anything."

"Thanks, Mike."

Sheriff Perry Hitchens returned his phone to its cradle and wept.

St. John's Episcopal Church, Washington DC – 10:40 AM EST

The procession to the Capitol Building by the outgoing president and the president-elect has been a tradition since George Washington, with only a few exceptions. The method of transport has ranged from on foot, in carriages, on horseback, to more recently in automobiles.

On this inauguration the presidential limousine affectionately known as the Beast slowly rolled to a stop at the curb in front of St. John's Church. Inside, President Al Makin waited for President-elect Ronald Hunter to emerge from the worship service. The two men did not really care to meet each other, but long established protocol strongly underscored the need for the men to arrive at the Capitol

Stephen T. Gerdel

together. The tradition was a unique and unmistakable symbol of the peaceful transfer of power.

President Makin waited patiently in the limo. Political necessity required him to spend time with the new president. Personally, he never liked the man.

The doors of the church swung wide open, and the president-elect emerged to the cheers of thousands of faithful supporters. Hunter raised his hands and turned waving in every direction. The longer he greeted the throng the louder the cheers grew.

After what felt several minutes too long to Al Makin, Hunter skipped down the steps of the church to the waiting limo. As he arrived at the car the door was opened for him. He again stopped and waved at the crowd. As before, the cheering swelled to new heights. Then he ducked into the car.

"Hi, Al. Man, I don't think I will ever get enough of *that*." Hunter smiled and extended his hand. President Makin returned his smile, leaned forward, and shook his hand.

"What you don't want, Ronald, is for them to get tired of cheering," he replied as he eased back to his seat. "Have you ridden in the Beast before?"

"No. This is nice." Ronald Hunter was very nice, as well, but President Makin knew Hunter's kindness wasn't genuine. The president-elect settled into the luxurious back seat of the limo.

"You'll get used to it," Al Makin said as the limo silently drew away from the curb.

"I think I will do just that. Who's the guy in the right front? Don't we just need a driver?"

"Ronald, they will brief you on the complete capabilities of this automobile next week, but to answer your question, he's the armaments officer."

"The what?"

"He's the guy who operates the defensive and offensive capabilities built into the Beast to keep you alive, should the occasion arise."

"And I'll bet I could launch a nuclear missile too, right?"

President Makin raised the center console between them to display a lighted panel. Hunter's jaw dropped. Then, he smiled.

"You're kidding, right?"

"Everything all right, Mr. President?" the man in the right front seat said over the intercom.

"No problem, William. I'm just showing the new guy some of our toys. Sorry to alarm you."

"Thank you, Mr. President."

"You're *not* kidding, are you?"

"Ronald, being president of the United States of America carries tremendous responsibilities. The first order of control is self-control. International political concerns are subject to your whim. A casual comment can cause markets to tumble and demonstrations turn to riot. You must learn to measure your words like no one else on earth. Every time you speak, your words will be recorded on a thousand devices, and then parsed by tens of thousands of your friends and enemies. Very little kidding can be allowed. You must be the president all the time, every time."

"Then it's good that they love me. Did you hear them at the church? Man, what a trip. What an amazing feeling."

"Yes, it is. May not always be that way."

"Of course it will. I'm not like you, Al. No more fairy tales in my administration. No huckster embellishments about what's really happening for the press. We're going to deal with everything openly and to the point."

"They've heard all that before. You'll need to be focused every time you're in front of a microphone, and that's all the time, Ron."

President-elect Hunter's ebullience dimmed. "Your presidency failed, I mean, everyone knows it. How did you know when it happened?"

"History will tell my story and yours if it's given half a chance. Calling any presidency a success or failure can only be measured by the passing of time. Eventually it all comes out and is made clear."

"But how did you know your administration was in trouble? How will I know?"

The limo came to a stop at the east steps of the Capitol building. President Makin leaned forward in his seat and turned to the president-elect. "You'll know, Ron, when they stop cheering."

The rear doors on both sides of the Beast opened simultaneously, and the roaring cheers of tens of thousands of Americans flooded the inside of the limousine. The two men exited the car and raised their hands over their heads to the enthusiastic throng.

The two men would never speak to each other again.

chapter 28

Robert woke up when something fell into his lap. He could breathe. He could see the moon rising through the window. The plane was flying very low above the water, smooth and controlled.

He blinked the dryness from his eyes and focused on a small radio resting in his lap. He turned to his left to find Failak kneeling in the aisle beside him. The man spoke to Robert in Arabic.

"You must answer. I do not understand them." Failak stood and left.

"Hey! Wake up back there. Did you fall asleep?" a voice said over the radio.

Robert keyed the mike and cleared his dry throat. "Yeah, sorta. What's up?"

"Just wanted to check on how everyone is doing back there."

Robert paused and glanced around the seats near his. All the passengers were still. Too still. Had it not been for the ashen, blood-starved tint of their skin, they would appear to be resting. Robert knew they were dead. "They're all asleep," he said with a coarse voice into the radio.

"Good. We're two hours out, so sit tight and don't to anything kinky."

"Got it." Rage boiled afresh in Robert's blood. These men deserved violent deaths. It would be the least he could do for the mass murder of the passengers and crew.

Yolanda stirred at his side. He needed to explain what had happened. He hoped she would not fall apart. *If she were ever to lose it, something like this would be the cause.* He stroked her cheek, pushing her hair from her face.

If I had waited a minute longer we would be like everyone else on this flying coffin. The thought chilled him.

Yolanda rolled away from him and faced the window. Robert pulled the light blanket over her shoulder. He was thankful they had survived. But there was work to do.

Robert left his seat and headed toward the rear galley.

He needed to find Failak.

NSA Office, The White House – 11:00 AM EST

For more than an hour Mike and Steve switched the channel from the Inauguration to the news of the lost airliner. Nearly two days of effort had vanished with that plane.

"I don't know if there is much else we can do." Steve was lounging in the office chair with his leg propped over the arm. "Isn't the only hope to regain the device dependent on finding the plane?"

"The *only* hope." Mike sighed.

The two men sat in silence. The television was muted. Neither man cared about the speeches from the Inauguration, and none of the news from Malaysia was good news.

Mike reached for his desk phone. "I'm gonna call Aaron." He dialed and waited for an answer. The phone rang a half a dozen times before he heard Aaron's voice.

"Colonel Stevens."

"Hey, Aaron. It's Mike."

He heard a long sigh at the other end of the line. "Yeah."

"Have you seen or heard anything the news hasn't caught on to yet?"

"No. We did get the radar recording from Lumpur Radar. Everything looks normal on the video, and then the plane just vanishes."

"You think they turned off the transponder?" Mike asked as he rocked back in his desk chair. "Or maybe it exploded."

"Other planes in the area would have seen the fireball if it blew up. It looks more like a hijacking to me."

"Has anyone claimed responsibility?"

"No, Mike. Nothing."

"And in the middle of the night it will be impossible to find a crash site."

"That search will begin in about five hours, before sun-up. They'll want to be at the last known position as soon as they can."

"Yeah." Mike thumped the eraser of his pencil on his desk pad. "Is the Internet traffic still in a panic?"

"It's tapered some. We know a couple hundred people have been taken into custody over the last twenty-four hours. But that's just in the States. Haven't heard anything from Europe or Central America."

"Not really a no-news-is-good-news kind of day. It's just frustrating."

"Mike, you're being kind. It's pure crap."

"Right, I'm too kind. I talked to Sheriff Perry Hitchens in Norman, Oklahoma today. His son Robert was on the flight. He and his wife were coming home from a two-week honeymoon."

"Is that the guy we had in Oklahoma City?"

"Same one."

"Too bad. He was a hell of a fighter."

"He was. Okay, let me know if anything pops up."

"Will do, Mike. Bye."

Mike hung up his desk phone. Depression had settled in with the frustration he felt. He looked at Steve who appeared as despondent as one could get.

"What do you want to do?" he asked.

"What I *want* to do is go drink beer. What I *need* to do is spend some time with Sam."

"You're a noble man. Let's get out of here."

Mike and Steve left the office and headed toward their cars.

Malaysian Flight 425 – 11:10 PM MYT

The cabin lights were dim. International flights are programmed for low lights to afford the passengers a restful environment. Everyone on the flight was still except for two men from different sides of the world who had discovered themselves as much needed allies.

Robert and Failak spoke little as they planned their next move. Both men understood their time was limited. Neither knew exactly when the plane might land.

The bodies of the crew members were unceremoniously stuffed into the restrooms on both sides of the aircraft. The fact aggravated Robert, but he had no time to alter the fact. The bodies of the hijackers were a different matter.

"Failak, we must move the bodies of the terrorists to our seats," Robert said in Arabic as the plan unfolded in his mind. "The three of us can go to the lower baggage hold until we land."

"What about the thin air? Will we be able to breathe in the baggage compartment?"

"The baggage area isn't pressurized. But the plane is flying low enough that we won't need additional oxygen."

"Very well. But after we land what will we do?"

"I'm hoping the three up front will call us to come with them so they can search the plane. We will escape through a hatch on the underside of the fuselage."

"You know of this?" Suspicion flooded Failak's face.

"Yes. The hatch is just in front of where the wing attaches to the main body of the plane by the landing gear. We can get away while they are waiting for their friends."

Failak was silent as he considered what Robert had told him. His expression was doubtful.

"Let me ask you a question."

"Please, go ahead."

"Do you know what this device will do? The American soldiers were in possession of it when they blew up our communication outpost in the mountains."

"I have no idea what you are talking about, Failak. I don't know anything about the device."

"The men flying this plane thought it valuable enough to kill all these people. It has to be the reason no one contacted me in Kuala Lumpur."

"All I know is that if we don't escape when this plane lands, they will kill all of us." Robert held Failak's gaze.

Failak nodded. "We will leave the device on the plane and escape. Later we will kill these animals, and we will do it brutally. They will die in terrible agony."

"That's fine with me. These men are monsters."

"You know they are Americans, right?"

Robert faced Failak. "Yes. People can be monsters wherever they come from. These guys qualify in every way. We will kill them together."

Failak smiled faintly. "Killing has never been hard for me, especially to those who deserve death. But certain men are a delight to kill. It is a joy for me to kill men like these."

Robert considered the brutality of Failak's words. In this case, and especially as he thought about how close he and Yolanda had come to death, he agreed. Robert nodded to his new friend.

He locked his eyes on Failak's. "Let's carry one of these men to your seat first."

The Capitol Building, West Steps – 11:45 AM EST

The crowd stretched as far as the eye could see. Tens of thousands were present to commemorate the peaceful transfer of power in the most powerful nation on earth.

Originally, the vice president-elect took the oath in the Senate chamber, but since 1937 the oaths for both the president-elect and vice president-elect have been administered at the same ceremony. The vice president-elect was sworn first.

". . . that I take this obligation freely, without any mental reservation or purpose of evasion; and that I will well and faithfully discharge the duties of the office on which I am about to enter. So help me God."

The cheers from the mass of onlookers swelled into roaring approval as the United States Marine Band performed four *ruffles and flourishes*, followed by *"Hail Columbia."* The atmosphere was jubilant and empowered by a strong sense of national patriotism.

The feeling among the people was that of a new beginning—a new America. The shackles of the past had been loosed. The stilted attitudes of former times, and harder times, faced a fresh view of freedom. Or so it seemed.

Political speeches often fan the emotions of supporters with sweeping promises that are soon forgotten. The cheers and celebration demonstrated by the public was the evidence that change had arrived. The country would soon be great again, and, in the busyness of it all, that hope would be forgotten and everything would remain the same.

Precisely at noon, the chief justice of the Supreme Court motioned to Ronald Hunter to come to the podium. As Hunter stood, the massive crowd raised their voices to a deafening cheer. Ronald Hunter was the symbol of promised change. His presence at the podium was the assurance that the nation's renewal was standing in the starting gate.

Hunter raised his hands high in the air, waving and smiling to the masses before him. *This is it! This is my time to lead America!*

The people responded with hysterical adulation. The scene dragged on and on.

Hunter left the podium and walked to one side of the platform, waving and smiling. The crowd was energized by his attention. He then walked across the platform and greeted the opposite side. They, too, responded with swelling praise.

Finally, the moment had arrived. President-elect Ronald Hunter stepped behind the podium and faced the chief justice. The crowd hushed. Every eye was locked on the two men as they bore witness to the rebirth of the nation.

Silence hovered above the tens of thousands who stood to witness the event. A breeze rustled through the bare branches surrounding the people. The people stood as if frozen in time. This was it.

Ronald Hunter placed his left hand on the George Washington Bible held by the chief justice, and raised his right hand.

"I, Robert James Hunter, do solemnly swear . . . that I will faithfully execute . . . the office of President of the United States . . . and will to the best of my ability . . . preserve, protect, and defend . . . . the Constitution of the United States."

The chief justice grasped Hunter's hand, shaking it firmly. "Congratulations, Mr. President."

"Thank you, Chief Justice Thomas."

President Hunter's words were lost in the celebration. The United States Marine Band played four *ruffles and flourishes* and immediately afterward *"Hail to the Chief."* At the same moment a 21-gun salute was fired using artillery pieces from the Presidential Guns Salute Battery, also known as the Old Guard, located in Taft Park, just north of the Capitol building.

The celebrating did not slacken. Even when President Hunter stepped to the podium to deliver his inaugural address the cheers blanketed the Capitol steps.

"My fellow Americans . . ."

But the tenor of festival only soared to new heights. People danced around the Grant Memorial and the Reflecting Pool to the west of the Capitol building. The cheering was unrelenting, and after several minutes of failing to capture the crowd's attention, he concluded the shortest Inaugural Address in history.

He said, ". . . Thank you!"

The adoring throng went wild, and the band played on.

Malaysian Flight 425 – 12:15 AM MYT

"Sweetheart," Robert whispered. "Yolanda, wake up, honey."

She stirred and absently swatted at the breathing device that Robert had propped against her face.

"You need to wake up, Yolanda."

"What?" Her eyelids fluttered as she struggled to escape the grasp of slumber. "Robert, what are you—"

"Shh. Please be quiet, honey. Please listen to me."

"What is this thing—"

Robert gently placed his hand on her lips. Her eyes were wild with confusion.

"Please listen very carefully." He was close to her face looking her directly in the eye. "Please, listen. You must be very quiet and listen."

Yolanda nodded her head in more of a spasm than a nod. Robert could see terror of the unknown rising in her eyes. It was the same horror he had seen after she had shot the terrorist who was preparing to kill him on their way back to Oklahoma City three years earlier.

As he told her what had happened while she slept, she began to tremble. Her eyes darted to other passengers in seats across the aisle. She gasped, then sobbed, her hand covering her mouth. Robert's tale of the murder of everyone on the plane overwhelmed her. She shook her head violently, denying the very thought of such a horror.

"Everyone?" she whispered.

"Everyone but us, and my new friend." Robert turned and gestured to Failak kneeling in the aisle behind him. "But, sweetheart, the bad guys are in the front of the plane preparing to land somewhere. We need to move quickly and quietly."

She appeared to be in shock. Robert had seen the same horrified unbelief in combat. He knew he would have to walk her through it.

"Ready?"

She nodded, again more spasmodically than in agreement. He helped her undo her seatbelt. She staggered to a stance. When she looked up she faltered as the dead faces of three hundred passengers entered her view.

"Come on. Get past it, honey."

Yolanda shuffled into the aisle and knelt beside Robert.

"Please, wait right here for a moment."

Robert turned his back on her and helped Failak lift the body of one of the hijackers into her seat, and then they placed the body of the last hijacker in Robert's seat. Robert leaned over the two dead men stretching blankets over them, partially obscuring their faces.

He looked at Failak who nodded his approval then turned and headed to the back of the plane.

Robert faced Yolanda. Her face was white with disbelief.

"How did those men die?"

"Failak and I killed them. That's where the breathing devices came from. That's why we're still alive."

She froze for a moment staring at Robert, and then she nodded weakly. "Okay."

"Come on. We need to go."

Robert took her hand and led her to the back of the plane, both hunched in a low position. He could hear her occasional gasps. He knew she was looking into the dead faces of the passengers.

Once in the galley he turned and spoke to her.

"We have a plan, but we will have to wait until we land."

"Where will we wait? Do you mean hide? Robert, where will we hide?"

"We have it all worked out. Please try to remain calm—"

"Robert, everyone is *dead!*"

"Yes, I know. But *we* aren't dead. And for us to remain alive we need to work together. Please stay calm. Can you do that?"

"Yes, I can. As long as you are with me, Robert."

"Good." He held up the small radio for her to see. "We'll be landing in an hour or so. That will give us time to get into the baggage compartment and find our way out after we land. The hijackers will try talking to us on this as the time approaches. Don't be surprised if they talk to me. I know what I'm doing."

Yolanda nodded in agreement.

Failak spoke to Robert in Arabic. "Is she going to be all right?"

"She will be fine, just a little bit of shock," Robert replied.

"Good. She is much too pretty to kill."

Robert spun toward him only to see him smiling. It was a joke; a sick joke, but still a joke.

Robert smiled. "Yes, she is much to pretty to kill." *Afghani humor.* He moved to a small door at the back of the galley and opened it. Inside was a narrow ladder leading to the baggage compartment.

"I'll go down first, and then you can follow me, Yolanda." He then turned to Failak and spoke in Arabic. "Make sure you close this door when you come through."

Failak nodded once.

The plan was set in motion.

chapter 29

Washington DC, East Steps of Capitol – 12:25 PM EST

President Al Makin climbed aboard Marine One. This would be his last flight as president of the United States. He was aware of the shift of power away from him. Authority was his, and then it wasn't. The moment was bittersweet.

He hadn't wanted to be president. He didn't seek the job. The responsibility had been thrust upon him. As he sat in his seat he let out a sigh. *This is it, Al. Time to say goodbye.*

He looked out the window of the magnificent machine. The engines whined and the giant rotors began slowly sweeping overhead. The detail of Marines that had escorted him through the Capitol Building, the most powerful seat of governance on the face of the earth, snapped to attention and saluted. They stood immoveable as the prop wash buffeted them.

Emotion flooded Al Makin. He hadn't expected those feelings. He was caught off guard by the relief, pride, grief, and sadness swarming his thoughts. He fought back the tears and laughed at his sentimental feelings.

Enough of that. My time here was hard, but we did what we could. Memories of his first week in office made him shudder. His entire career floated through his mind, one snapshot at a time. His military service in Europe and the Middle East flickered through his thoughts. Faces of hundreds of men and women he served with marched by in review.

One face slammed his thoughts to a halt. That one man. He knew him. He *knew* who he was.

Al Makin reached for the phone beside his seat. His hand shook, and he fumbled the receiver, nearly dropping it. He dialed a familiar number and heard the abrupt answer.

"Trapper."

"Mike! It's me. I remember who that guy is!"

"Mr. President?"

"Yeah. Like *former* Mr. President. It's me, Al Makin. I remember who that guy really is."

"What guy, sir?"

"That *Kouzen* guy. You know, the one in Singapore."

"You know *Kouzen's* real identity?"

"Yeah, it just hit me. I'm not but a couple of miles from the Capitol, and his face suddenly flashed into my mind. Craziest thing!"

"How do you know who he is?"

"I met him in Germany when I was in the Army. He wanted to get into some special forces thing or other and eventually left. I heard he had gone really deep in counterintelligence, and he sort of dropped out of sight. Hadn't seen or thought of him since. But that picture we saw from Singapore triggered my memory."

"Okay, tell me."

"Mike, his name isn't *Kouzen*, or Dalton, or Kohen, or anything like that. His name is Michael Hunter. He's the president's *first cousin!*"

"What!"

"President Ronald Hunter's first cousin."

"Holy crap! You're absolutely certain about this, right?"

"Mike, I have some old photo albums at our place in West Virginia, from my military days. I *know* I have some pictures of us together."

"Can you send them to me?"

"Absolutely-damn-tively! I'll dig them out tonight, scan them and get them to you as soon as possible."

"Sir, I don't know where this might take us. Are you sure you want to involve yourself?"

"Never been more sure, Mike. The memory hit me like a bolt of lightning. I don't remember when I have ever been this jazzed. I will get the pictures to you. I promise."

"Thank you, sir. Have a good flight. I'll talk with you tomorrow."

"I'll count on it, Mike."

Al Makin hung up the receiver. His heart was pumping rapidly from the excitement. He couldn't wait to get home. *It ain't over, Al. It ain't over.*

NSA Office, White House – 12:30 PM EST

Mike's head was spinning. If Al Makin's memory was correct, an entire new problem was rising. It was no longer simply a loss of some top secret technology, nor was it just the tragedy of a lost commercial airliner. The man who had just assumed the office of the president of the United States of America was deeply connected to a serious crime.

"How do we do that?" he said aloud.

"How do we do what?" Steve responded. He lounged in a chair on the other side of Mike's desk.

Mike startled. "I forgot you were there." He smiled sheepishly.

"Mike . . ." Steve held out his hands in a gesture that said, *You're losing it buddy. I've been here all morning.*

"Sorry. I can't believe what I just heard."

"What's he going to send you?"

"What? Who?"

"Makin. You were just on the phone with Al Makin, right?" Steve's face reflected concern that Mike was cracking up under the stress.

"Yeah . . . right. He's going to send me some pictures from when he was in the Army. In Germany, or something."

"He's sending you pictures."

Should I tell you what President Makin said about Kouzen*? Should you be exposed to this since you're a part of the new administration?*

"Mike?" Steve was leaning forward, alarm etched deep in his expression.

Mike looked at him with surprise. "I don't know that I can tell you this."

"You don't know that you can tell me about pictures from Al Makin's Army days?"

"Not exactly." Mike's gaze shifted to the top of his desk.

"Then *what*, exactly? Come on, Mike. This is *me*. Granger."

Mike let out a long breath. He raised his eyes, looking directly at his friend. "Steve, President Makin remembered something from his time in Germany. It involves *Kouzen*."

"Makin knew him?"

"Yes."

"The president said that picture we got from Daniel Sim of *Kouzen* looked familiar,"Steve said.

"It was probably thirty years ago, but you know how it works. It starts as a glimmer of a memory, and then, out of the blue the whole thing slams you. The hit-by-a-truck thing."

"Yeah, it happens. What did he remember?"

"*Kouzen*. He remembered *Kouzen*. Who he was, and where he met him."

"Okay, I got the part about Germany and the Army. What is it you can't tell me?"

Mike took a deep breath. He knew the information would forever taint Steve's impression of his new boss. It would threaten to limit his ability to serve the new president. *Would Steve risk his own life to protect the president?*

"After I tell you this you might need to rethink what you're going to do for the next four years."

"Mike, work is work. A job's a job. Anything between you and me as friends is bigger than any job, even this one."

"Fine. I agree with you. But this isn't a small thing. I don't want you to react in any way until we can confirm what President Makin has remembered."

"I'm in. No decisions until everything's confirmed. Let's hear it. Come on."

"Kouzen's real name is Michael Hunter. He's President Hunter's first cousin."

Steve's jaw dropped. "No way!" he said in a whisper.

"Remember, nothing until we can confirm it."

"Right. His first cousin?"

"Almost corny. Who uses such an obvious moniker?"

"And in two languages!"

"Maybe more. We need to keep this to ourselves. Nobody needs to know this."

"So, what's next?" Steve rubbed his palms against each other to relieve the tension. It was an old habit.

"We wait."

OCT Little Rock – 11:45 PM CST

The phone on Aaron Stevens's desk rang. "Colonel Stevens."

"Aaron, it's Daniel."

"You been up all last night?"

"And the night before that. Just like you."

"I thought the saying was 'no rest for the wicked.' I'm beginning to wonder what side I'm actually on." He heard Daniel laugh a breathy chuckle, but he sensed nothing funny was happening in Singapore. "What's up?"

"We still don't have *Kouzen* back in custody, but there's an all-points bulletin out for him. Unless he backpacks through the mountains, he won't be getting out of here easily. We did discover the officer who helped him, though."

"That's good, but I wouldn't want to be in his shoes."

"At present, he has no shoes, and with what the interrogators have planned he'll be lucky to have feet by nightfall."

Aaron shuddered. *How can they do that kind of stuff?* "Anything on the airliner?"

"No, other that the fact that there were some Americans on board."

"Not really a surprise. How many?"

"Eight. Some of the video from the airport boarding area shows five or six men that are similar to the men *Kouzen* met with yesterday at the tea salon. We're working on making an identity match."

"That would be bizarre. Who else?"

"A younger couple we haven't found on the video. Their names are Robert and Yolanda Hitchens from Oklahoma. But we can't confirm if they made the flight or not."

Aaron's heart raced to a higher pace. "What? What were their names?"

"Robert Hitchens and Yolanda Hitchens. Their passports show they—"

"Are you sure it's *Robert Hitchens?*"

"Yeah. Is that a problem?"

"No. Daniel, Robert Hitchens is a highly-decorated SEAL. He had a huge role in stopping the invasion in the southwest a few years back. He's a remarkable fighter."

Daniel Sim was silent for a moment. "Well then, let's hope he either missed the plane or has found some way to prevent it from crashing into a mountain."

"That would be a great loss."

"More than three hundred innocent men, women, and children have been lost with them. It is a tremendous loss for many families."

Aaron blushed in the privacy of his office. His words had to have sounded callous and insensitive. "I'm sorry, Daniel. I didn't mean to sound dismissive of the others who lost their lives."

"I understand. It's been a long day."

"Yeah. A couple of them."

The two men sat without speaking for several moments. They were separated by half the planet, yet joined in a matter that would impact everyone on the planet. The bond that linked them strengthened them, and the immensity of the unknown that lay ahead terrified them. They stared into the abyss from opposite sides of the world.

Daniel broke the silence. "Well, call me if something comes to your attention."

"Right. You do the same. Good night, my friend."

Malaysian Flight 425 – 11:25 AM MYT

The cargo hold of the massive jetliner was quieter than Robert had expected. The massive hull-shaped containers absorbed much of the wind noise from the outside of the fuselage. A narrow path down the center of the plane's belly was their only passage.

Robert waited for Failak to descend the ladder before speaking.

"The way for us to get out of here is just in front of the landing gear on the right side of the plane. We don't want to be near the gear area until the plane comes to a stop." He repeated his instructions in Arabic to Failak.

"I want to look around a bit and find the safest and most comfortable place for us to be during the landing. We don't know if the landing spot will be an airport or an open field, so I want to check it out thoroughly."

Yolanda nodded her agreement as did Failak to the translation.

Robert instructed Failak to search out the rear of the cargo hold. He took Yolanda's hand and pulled her after him toward the front of the plane. Walking through the hold was just as difficult as navigating the cabin aisles in the passenger compartment. The gentle swaying of the huge aircraft slipping from cloud to breeze and back could challenge anyone's balance.

He paused. "This is where the wings attach to the fuselage," he said, pointing to the interior structure. She nodded. "Here's the landing gear."

"It's huge!" Yolanda was dwarfed by the massive machinery. Her jaw hung slack.

"Okay, honey. Time to close up that jaw and move on." Robert gently pulled her forward.

Six forty-inch tires were mounted on each truck of the landing gear. Viewed from the ground their size appears normal, what one would expect on a plane. Packed into the belly of the flying behemoth the landing wheels appeared enormous.

They squeezed themselves between the wheels on either side of the cargo hold toward the front of the plane.

"Here's the door." Robert took Yolanda by the shoulders and turned her to face him. "Honey, if anything happens to me after we land, I want you to come here as fast as you can, climb down through that door, and get away from this plane. Do you understand me?"

"Robert, nothing is going to happen to you. God brought us together, and he will keep us safe."

"Right. But nothing is always perfect. We really don't know—"

"*I* know! So don't tell me bad things that may or may not happen."

Robert let out a breath. "Fine. I just want you to know where the door is. Is that okay with you?"

"It's okay. The door is right there." She turned half away from him and folded her arms across her chest. "But we are going down that ladder together."

He bent forward to catch her gaze. "Babe?"

She grinned, quickly glanced at him, and turned away. A tear rolled down her cheek. He wrapped her in his arms.

"Honey—"

"It was all so perfect: our trip, the hotel, the beach. And then, these men. Who are these people? Why are they doing this? They killed all those people—"

"Yolanda, stop. We don't have time to figure this out. We still have to get out of here alive. It isn't over."

She collapsed against him, and sobbed quietly.

Sheriff's Office, Norman, OK – 11:55 PM CST

Sheriff Perry Hitchens picked up his cell phone for the hundredth time and dialed Robert's number. Every time he had almost stopped himself. But every time he tried he hoped for an answer. Every time he had received none.

"Okay, bucko. This time, answer your damn phone. Please."

While Robert had been deployed with the SEALs Perry could contact him almost every day. The covert operations the Navy sent Robert and his team on were brief and usually deadly. Deadly for someone else. Robert's team had maintained a perfect record of never losing a team member in combat.

"That was war! This is your honeymoon. Why can't I reach you?"

The phone buzzed in his ear the monotonous, scratchy sound of his attempt to make contact. The noise itself almost mocked his feeble effort.

Again, there was no answer.

Again, the sheriff turned off his phone and gently laid it on his desk.

"I won't give up, son. I won't give up."

chapter 30

Statuary Hall, U.S. Capitol Building – 1:00 PM EST

The Inaugural Luncheon has been a tradition since the late 1800s. Over the decades it had become elaborate in décor and cuisine. Sometimes the meal had been hosted by outgoing presidents and their wives. But the disgust expressed during the campaign toward the former administration had removed such courtesy from consideration. The Joint Congressional Committee on Inaugural Ceremonies had willingly assumed the role in planning the guest list, the meal, and the events of the occasion. One thing men and women on both sides of the aisle could agree upon—a party.

Statuary Hall was packed with celebrants of both parties, some were rejoicing in victory, while others were overjoyed for their fresh starts. No one wanted to look back. Recent history was considered either too controversial, or pure fiction.

The reins of power were now in the hands of a new team of leaders. President Hunter was a fresh face promising a new tone from the White House. Openness and optimism held the promise of the return of American greatness and world leadership. Every politician in the city was ready for the United States to be on top once again.

President Ronald Hunter entered the Hall, and the participants erupted in applause and cheers. The mood was uplifting. The noise was deafening. President Hunter raised both hands over his head displaying in each hand a two-fingered victory salute. More than one mind flashed to pictures of Richard Nixon at his Inauguration. But it was only momentary. The clamor of celebration rang on.

This is it! This is the time we have all waited for. And I'm the one bringing in the new era! Hunter was nearly carried to euphoria. Whether he turned to the right or the left the cacophonous clamor swelled again and again.

"Congratulations, Mr. President!" echoed from senators and representatives from states across the nation, again and again, "Congratulations!" Every time Hunter lowered his arms for a moment's rest, someone would grab his hand and enthusiastically shake it.

President Hunter knew the exhausting ordeal would pass, but he was also aware that the dawn would come before it subsided. As long as it focused on him, it was fine.

Maamigili, Maldives – 12:40 AM MYT

Robert and Yolanda huddled behind piles of luggage about fifteen feet in front of the landing gear. Failak had remained near the tail section of the plane without offering any explanation for his preference. Robert sensed a little tension from him, but he was not concerned about his choice.

The radio crackled to life in Robert's pocket. He fumbled to pull it out without dropping it.

"Hey, are you awake back there?"

It was the same man who had spoken earlier.

"Are you awake?"

"Yeah. What?" Robert replied in an intentionally coarse voice.

"Gittin' ready to land up here. Thought you might want to tell everyone to fasten their seatbelts and put their trays in an upright position." Laughter filtered through before the mic keyed off.

"Real funny," Robert said softly. Then he spoke into the radio. "We're ready."

"Good. Right after we land we need to make the search for the control device we're supposed to get. You guys start at the back, check all carry-on luggage and everything in the overhead bins. We'll work our way back to you."

"Got it." Robert's reply was curt but the transmission left a question in his mind.

"What is he talking about?" Yolanda asked quietly.

"I have no idea."

"What are they saying?" a voice spoke in Arabic.

Robert turned to face Failak who had come forward when he heard the radio.

"They are preparing to land and then search the plane for something."

"I know what it is they seek."

"You know what they are looking for?" Robert asked.

"I believe I do." Failak's eyes were fixed on Robert's as he told the story of the attack on the communication compound. His face hardened while he related the trek across the mountain ridges pursuing the American soldiers who had made the attack possible. "In the end, my men killed the two American soldiers. We found some very unusual equipment that I took back to the compound to discover what it was used for."

"Did you figure it out? Do you know what it is?"

"No. I called a contact in Islamabad for assistance. While my technician was working on the device, my contact called me back and said an arrangement had been made with a government that opposed American interests. That sounded good to me. I could make some money and help stop the American war in my homeland."

Robert hesitated but understood Failak's alliance to anyone who was against the United States. "Then what happened?"

"I followed my instructions and found myself in Kuala Lumpur. No one approached me as I expected. From the brutal nature we have seen of these men, I can only suppose they killed those who were to meet me and accompany me to the point of sale. I don't know where I was to go after this plane landed in Hong Kong."

"But these guys *are* Americans. Why would they do this?"

"I do not know." Failak never took his eyes off Robert's. "Today, I have learned that good Americans exist. Perhaps these men are *not* some of them."

Robert nodded, holding Failak's gaze. "You might be right, my friend."

Failak started. "Why do you call me friend? What have I done for you to be a friend?"

"Failak, you gave me a breathing mask for my wife. I consider that a good thing."

Failak glanced quickly at Yolanda, then back to Robert. He smiled. "Like I said, she is much too pretty to kill."

The landing gear motor burst into a deafening whine as the doors popped loudly and began their sprawling yawn, freeing the wheel trucks to descend. A two-hundred-mile-per-hour wind roared into the underbelly of the plane. Yolanda buried her face in Robert's chest, and the two men crouched, defending themselves against the onslaught.

Robert glanced out the opening. The red flashing strobe on the belly of the airliner reflected off water only feet below. He could not measure the distance in the dark. Suddenly, he could see rocks, then land, and then the tarmac.

Just as quickly, the plane lurched as the gear wheels made contact with the runway. The three were roughly jostled against each other as the plane settled to the earth. Robert heard the reverse thrusters being applied. Whoever was in the pilot's seat knew what he was doing. Robert only wished he knew what they had planned.

The jet taxied to a stop right on the runway.

"We don't have much time," Robert said to Yolanda, then repeated to Failak in Arabic. "As soon as the engines stop we need to climb down the ladder. When we are all down we need to run as fast and as far as we can, away and under the tail of the plane. Do you understand?"

Yolanda and Failak nodded their agreement. Yolanda trembled with excitement or fear. Robert decided he didn't need to know which one.

The engines began to wind down as the giant turbines slowed. Robert knew when the suction and wash from the turbines was low enough to be safe.

"Let's get out of here. I'll go down first."

He pulled the lever that lowered the ten-foot ladder to a foot off the concrete. His descent was more of a slide than actual climbing. When his feet hit the tarmac, he motioned for Yolanda to come down.

Robert scanned the area. It was barren. The runway was real, but the surrounding buildings of what would someday be an airport were still under construction. He couldn't see another plane near the runway.

Yolanda scurried down the steps of the ladder and within seconds Failak dropped to the ground beside them.

"This way! We don't have much time." Robert grabbed Yolanda's hand and ran toward the tail of the plane. Once past the tail, they ran in the open. Darkness surrounded them. The trio sprinted toward an open structure. No windows or doors to lock behind them. The night was their only protection.

Whatever, or whoever, came with the sunrise, would be a mystery.

White House, NSA Office – 1:25 PM EST

Mike and Steve waited impatiently for Ray Jergins to come to the office. The evidence they were collecting was frightening, both to them and for the country.

Ray entered the office in a slightly less-than-dignified manner.

"How much did you two drink?" Mike asked with a slight smile. He caught Ray's arm to steady him.

"More than we should have for a work day, but not near enough for an Inauguration Day. Country's going to hell in a handbasket. What's up?"

"About an hour ago, President Makin called me. He has pictures of *Kouzen* and him together in the Army."

"*Kouzen* was in the Army? Our army?"

"That's what Makin said."

"Must have been when they were taking anybody and everybody." Ray sat in an office chair beside Mike's desk and was spending too many seconds figuring out how to fold his arms across his chest.

"Are you all right?" Steve asked.

"Sharp as a tack," Ray answered with a slur.

"What President Makin remembered was the disturbing part."

"Mike, nothing could possibly disturb me today. Nothing," Ray answered with a wave of his hand.

"Are you going to remember any of this?" Steve looked at Mike in disbelief. "We're sharing potentially dangerous national security matters with a drunk—"

"Nope," Ray interrupted. "Not to worry. I never forget, and I'm not nearly as drunk as I look. Or as I would like to be, for that matter. Whatcha got?"

Mike took a deep breath. "Ray, *Kouzen* is President Hunter's first cousin."

Ray looked at Mike through blurred eyes without speaking a word.

"Ray!"

He snapped out of his trance and looked at Mike.

"His *first* cousin."

"Yes, Ray."

"And we have a recording of them speaking to each other just last night."

"Just after midnight." Mike thumped his desk for emphasis. "And it was within hours of the murder of six Chinese agents in Singapore."

"The call was placed just after the device went missing," Steve said turning toward Ray.

"And now the entire plane," Mike added.

Ray was silent. Mike assumed volumes of legal documents were filtering through his Scotch-muddled mind. He watched as a lifetime of experience weighed the circumstances, looking for a solution that made sense.

"There's nothing we can do." Ray's face was pallid. His expression was blank.

"There has *got* to be something. This is a national security issue coupled with the theft of military property and murder. We have to do something about this."

"Mike, there is nothing we can do."

"I can't believe that. Isn't this something close to high crimes and misdemeanors? I mean surely the law—"

"Mike! He's the president. He *is* the law."

Mike was stunned. "He's the chief law enforcement officer in the country."

"Yes, he is."

The three men sat in silence.

"Think about it, Mike. He made a phone call. He gave no instructions to anyone. And all the events we know about happened before that call."

"Except the vanishing of the plane."

"Right. But how could he possibly be linked to that? He was in church when the plane was lost. It's all circumstantial."

Mike slumped in his desk chair. He processed all the information he had come across in the last few hours. The links were astronomically huge and equally vague.

"You're right, Ray. There's nothing we can do."

Maamigili, Maldives – 12:40 AM MYT

"This is not a lucky hit. This is a signature kill." Brad Gentry was the leader of the team of hijackers who had taken the plane. "I know this guy."

"Of course, you know him. That's Curtis. Remember, he got on the plane with us?"

"Not him, you idiot." Brad turned and glared with contempt at his teammate. "Neal, I'm talking about the man who killed him."

The three hijackers sat in silence. They had discovered the bodies of their comrades in the seats of three passengers.

"Did you search the overhead compartments?" Brad asked.

"No. Do you think we should?" Neal was a good killer, but a poor strategist.

"If we're going to find the device we'll need to go through every overhead bin." Jace was the third surviving member of the group, and, like Brad, a SEAL.

"My bet is that we'll find it up here," Brad said. "But we might need to go through everything in the baggage compartment." He looked carefully at the contusions left on Curtis' face and neck.

"Why do you say you know who killed Curt?" Jace asked.

"A man can be killed many different ways, Jace." Brad turned Curtis' head slightly to the right. "Look here." He pointed to a dark bruise behind the left ear. "That's what killed him. The first blow to the throat is designed to stun the victim. The second shatters the skull behind the ear and forces a portion of the skull to slide over and separate the brain stem. It's quick, very painful, and indefensible. This is a method of killing a person designs. It's easy for them."

"Who did it?" Jace said looking closely at the dead man.

"I know him. I can see his face. Just can't remember his name."

"Maybe it's in his luggage?" Neal grinned.

"That's the smartest thing you've said all week." Brad almost smiled. "Jace, go over to where we found Wells and check the bin over his seat. Neal, you check these bins here. I'm going to get the passenger list from the cockpit."

"Yes, sir." Neal immediately opened the overhead luggage bin and pulled the contents to the floor.

"Let me know if you find anything," Brad said over his shoulder as he walked to the front of the plane.

chapter 31

Sheriff's Office, Norman, OK – 12:55 PM CST

Sheriff Perry Hitchens sat at his desk. He hadn't left his office since the news of the Malaysian airliner vanishing. Everyone in the station had avoided him, not wanting to interrupt his thoughts or his fears. But they all knew. Robert and Yolanda were on that plane.

Perry looked at his phone. He had worked it out with Robert before they left. The price for worldwide calling privileges were nothing compared to the ability to stay in touch.

If Robert is anywhere near civilization I know I will contact him. But, if he's—No. No ifs.

He gritted his teeth and stared at the keypad of his small phone. His finger shook. Slowly, he negotiated the numbers, carefully pressing each one firmly; pressing each button with hope.

Finally, he entered the last digit. He took a breath, shuddered, and pressed the call button. He waited through the clicks, eager for the first sound of the call actually going through.

Every call he had placed through the morning ended going to voicemail. Perry never left a message. He didn't want to ask Robert to call him back if he was dead. That's when you say goodbye.

This time he heard the sound of a ring. The call was actually going through . . . to somewhere. He had made a connection.

"Hello?"

"Robert!" His booming voice echoed through the station. Every person in the building turned toward the sheriff.

Maamigili, Maldives – 1:25 AM MYT

Robert and Yolanda huddled in the darkness. The moon had set while they were on the plane, and they dared not venture out to look at the stars. For now they were hidden and staying out of sight . . . for now.

Failak sat twenty feet away from Robert and Yolanda. His eyes bore into the darkness, scanning the plane for any signs of movement. The pitch black played tricks on his eyes. Seeing in the dark was much different from seeing in the blinding white of snow-capped peaks. The exact opposite.

"Blinded by darkness or blinded by light, a man sees only what Allah allows him to see," he said softly.

"The eyes of the Lord move to and fro on the face of the earth and brings light to those who seek him," Robert replied in Arabic.

Failak laughed. He smiled at this likable American. "Two poets lost in the dark. Do you think your Lord will bring us some light?"

"I think he will, if we ask."

"Then, by all means, ask. We could wait for Allah all day, and he might get around to us." Failak's faith was seared in skepticism. The banter lightened his heart.

"I've never prayed in Arabic before. I'm not sure how to start."

"I understand Jesus prayed in Arabic all the time, as well as in Greek and Hebrew. Surely, you, a Navy SEAL, an American, you can figure it out." Failak smiled at his tease.

"Well, I'll give it a shot," Robert answered.

"What are you two talking about?" Yolanda interjected. "Not really enjoying being the third wheel of this conversation."

Robert smiled at her. "Failak has challenged me to ask the Lord to help us out a little bit. He says Allah is too busy at the moment."

Yolanda smiled. "Then do your best Robert. In English or Arabic. He knows them both quite well."

Robert lifted his face upward and said, "Lord Jesus—"

The cell phone in his pocket rang.

The threesome stared in shock. Robert fumbled to bring the phone to his ear. "Hello?"

"Robert!" blared from the earpiece.

"Dad? Is that you?"

"Oh, Robert! You're alive. Is Yolanda with you? Did the plane crash? How did you get out? Where the hell are you?"

"Dad, wait! Hold on. No, the plane did not crash. We're fine. But it's not good. It's the middle of the night here, and we have no idea where we are."

"What do you mean, not good?"

"It's a long story to tell right now. We need some help. Can you talk to someone and send in the Marines or something?"

"I can call Mike Trapper. He's in the White House and they are monitoring the search for the plane. Hey! They have the ability to search for your cell phone. Don't turn it off. Maybe they can track you."

"Okay, that would be great. My battery might be getting low so don't waste any time."

"Robert, it has been a terrible day, but I'm so glad to hear your voice."

"Fine, Dad. Remember we're short on battery life here. Please, hurry."

"Will do, son. I will see you soon!"

Robert turned off his phone.

Failak was shocked. He could not speak. His astonishment barely allowed him the strength to breathe. Finally, he spoke in Arabic, "All you did was say his name . . ."

"Failak, I am amazed just like you. This doesn't happen to me every day."

"Perhaps not. But perhaps I must become a Christian." Failak did not laugh. He smiled.

The small radio Robert had carried from the plane suddenly came to life.

"Robert Hitchens! I remember you now. I know who you are and what you have done to my men. I'm coming to get you, Robert."

White House, NSA Office – 2:25 PM EST

The mood in Mike's new office was somber, if not mournful. The knowledge that a heinous crime would remain unsolved frustrated Mike. The fact that a just penalty for a terrible act would never be paid infuriated him.

Ray Jergins was out cold on the couch soft snoring away his earlier celebration.

Steve sat quietly gazing out the window looking at nothing in particular. "The answer for anything should never be nothing."

"What?" Mike asked. "That doesn't make any sense."

"You know what I mean. Everything should have an answer, some kind of conclusion. Nothing should ever be left unanswered or determined unanswerable."

"Steve, you're using more than two-syllable words again. You could end up in therapy because of that."

"Ha ha. Very funny. I mean look at science, or business. Does anyone ever really quit? Aren't they all constantly looking for a better widget, or a faster way of making one? Yes, they are. Constantly. Business demands to be remade all the time—"

"Yeah, buddy. This isn't business, and it isn't science. This is politics. When the people in charge don't want something known, it simply isn't known. And those who try to bring it to light can end up in, well, less-than-desirable-circumstances."

"Those were more than two-syllable words."

The phone in Mike's pocket chirped signaling an incoming call.

"This is Mike Trapper."

"Mike! This is Perry Hitchens. Listen! Mike, they're alive! I talked to Robert just a few moments ago and they're all right. The plane didn't crash!"

"Wait. What did you say?"

"They're alive. I just spoke with Robert. The plane didn't crash."

"You actually talked to him?"

"Yes. Yolanda was with him."

"Where are they?"

"I don't know . . . I mean, they don't know. It's dark and they can't see anything around them."

"Perry, I'm going to put you on speaker." Mike put his phone on his desktop and pushed the speaker button. "Go ahead, Perry. I'm here with Steve Granger." Mike turned to Steve and said, "Wake up Ray. He's going to need to hear this."

Slowly the three men gathered around Mike's phone.

"Okay, Perry, you're speaking with me, Steve Granger, and Ray Jergins from the Justice department. Please, start again and tell us everything."

Perry patiently began his story again. The plane did not crash. Robert was alive. But they didn't know where they were.

"That's when I remembered that machine you guys have that can find particular cell phones."

"Like on the ALI maps," Steve said.

"That's it! ALI maps. We used them to spot the bad guys a few years back."

The Automatic Location Identification (ALI) mapping system had been developed in 1998 to locate people making 911 emergency phone calls. Originally called Enhanced 911, or E911, the technology had advanced to where it could accurately pinpoint the location of a particular cell phone anywhere in the United States.

"But, that system is just for the States, right Ray?"

Ray sat motionless and silent.

"Ray, that system just works in the United States, right?" Mike repeated.

Slowly, very slowly, and only slightly, he moved his head side to side. Ray closed his eyes and softly said, "It is *very* top secret."

"Ray, we used it all over the country to identify groups of invaders. Hundreds of national guard and reserve units everywhere used that system. What do you mean it's top secret?"

Ray continued to shake his head slowly. "Not what it *did*. What it can do *now*." He slowly drew a circle in the air with his finger, around and around. Then, almost in a whisper, he said, "Worldwide."

Mike's jaw dropped. "Then we can find them. We can get the plane and the device back. All those people can be rescued."

"That's what I've been trying to tell you guys," Perry said through the phone. "Crank that machine of yours up and go save Robert and Yolanda."

"Thanks, Perry. Give me Robert's cell number."

Mike wrote down the number. With Steve's assistance, Mike lifted Ray from his chair and dragged him toward the elevator. They had business to do deep in the bowels of the White House complex.

White House North Lawn Reviewing Stand – 2:30 PM EST

President Hunter stepped from the limousine and turned immediately to wave to the crowd. The cheers of approval were thunderous and continued to swell through the mass of citizens across from the viewing stand.

"I love America," he said extending his hand to his wife Susan.

She stepped to his side and raised her hand to the well-wishers. They stood side by side for a full minute drinking in the adoration.

To many, the Hunters were a new version of JFK and Jackie: a new Camelot. To others they were Ron and Nancy made new. The remarkable item throughout the campaign had been his appeal to both sides of the aisle. The candidates on the fringe of the right and the left had remained muted and ignored symbols of everything that had gone wrong in the past. New life was coming to the White House and the nation.

"They really love you, honey," she said smiling up to him. "If only they knew."

He kissed her, and the crowd went wild. She winced slightly under the force of his embrace. "Yes, my dear," he said softly. "But what happens in private remains private, as you well know."

His eyes sparkled above his wide smile. She perfectly reflected his smile with adoring radiance. The couple again faced the people across the street. They cheered madly, incessantly.

"Come, sweetheart." President Hunter took his wife's hand and led her up the steps of the enclosed viewing stand. They were the last to arrive to watch the Inaugural Parade.

To Ronald Hunter the long-standing tradition was a waste of time and money. He endured it for the sake of history, for the nation. He knew it was part of the spectacle that accompanied the presidency. However, in the back of his mind, he had a lot of work to do.

President and Mrs. Hunter stepped to the front and stood before the two large chairs they had selected for their view of the parade. The extremists on Capitol Hill, both liberal and conservative, had complained the chairs looked too much like thrones. But the majority insisted they were merely seats reflecting the honor due to the new presidential family. They would be fine.

The adulation from the onlookers rose again as the Hunters faced them. They waved again showing appreciation to the voters who had placed so much responsibility in their hands. Ruffles and flourishes were sounded and the cacophonous clamor began to subside. The parade was ready to begin.

The one-and-a-half-mile route down Pennsylvania Avenue had been followed by bands, floats, military and civilian participants for nearly two hundred years. Some parades were grander than others, but none more magnificent than this one promised to be. It was a symbol of the nation's rising once again from the ashes. Of course, to some the ashes were the remains of political miscalculations, while others had literally sifted through the burned remains of their businesses and homes.

Susan Hunter sat gingerly in her chair. She did not lean back or drape her long elegant form across the seat. Her back was straight, her smile fixed, and her eyes sparkled in the afternoon sun. She was lovely.

Ronald Hunter gazed approvingly at her elegance and grace. She was perfect for him. She fit his every dream.

He leaned toward her and spoke softly into her ear. "Babe, I think you are going to really enjoy this."

She smiled back at him. "I think you're right. I already am."

chapter 32

The radio transmission left a chill on Robert's spine. The voice was familiar, someone he knew. But not someone he trusted. He reviewed the faces of the Americans he had seen at the pool and at the airport. But none were familiar.

"Robert, are they starting the engines on the plane?" Yolanda asked.

The sound of the giant motors beginning to spin was faint.

"What are they doing?" Failak asked.

"They are destroying the evidence." Robert knew the bodies of more than three hundred people would not be left sitting on a runway to be found at daybreak. "But how are they operating the plane without being inside it?"

"The backpack!" Failak's eyes were aflame with realization of what the device could actually do. "Robert, they found the backpack I was carrying. The one I took from the American Marines in the mountains. That piece of equipment must be able to take control of an airplane. They used it to fly the drone to attack our mountain compound."

"I have no idea what you're talking about Failak."

"The soldiers we killed had the backpack. They used it to fly a drone that fired a missile that destroyed our facility in the mountains."

"You believe the backpack is a remote control for an airliner?"

"How else would they be flying that plane and not have anyone inside it?"

Robert and Failak looked through the darkness. Three men knelt at the edge of the runway, illuminated by the flashing red light on the underbelly of the plane. In front of them sat a rectangular object about the size of the backpack Failak had carried out of the mountains of Afghanistan.

"There. On the tarmac." Failak pointed at the three men painted in the surreal, flashing red light.

"Got it."

Robert strained his eyes to see the men. They were too far away.

As they watched, the engines increased their whine, and the Boeing 777 slowly rotated to face the runway. In moments the plane seemed to square itself, staring down the long concrete path. Then the engines revved to full capacity. The plane lurched forward.

"Where is the plane going?" Yolanda asked.

"It doesn't matter, honey," Robert said somberly. "These guys just killed three hundred innocent people to steal a piece of US Government equipment. It will be like the plane was never here. Everyone will simply vanish."

They watched as the plane gained speed racing down the runway. It rotated, then lifted skyward. When it was airborne the plane banked slightly to the right and leveled off. The lights on the wings and fuselage of the plane turned off, and it disappeared into the night.

"What will happen to all those people?" Yolanda said softly.

Robert watched the plane drift into the darkness. Anger rose in his heart. "They're lost."

White House Lower Basement – 2:45 PM EST

Mike remembered his first ride down this elevator a few years ago. He had felt they were dropping into a bottomless pit when they suddenly braked to a heavy stop. The ride was no different this time.

"I don't know that I could ever get used to that ride," he said when he felt stable on his feet.

"You never do, especially if you're sober." Ray's knees buckled, and Mike and Steve held him upright. "It's okay, boys. I can handle it from here."

The elevator doors rolled back, and the military guard greeted them. The three men exiting the carriage were known personally by the people who worked on this level of the government. It was an exclusive club that had been infiltrated only one time. That one man had helped to cripple the country, and came very close to successfully destroying Mike's family.

The memories of those days sifted quickly through Mike's mind. He pushed them back. *Those were the old days. Focus. We have serious work to do now.*

Ray Jergins walked directly to the command desk for the facility and addressed the man in charge of the electronic assets.

"Mort, we need your help."

Mort wasn't an unpleasant man, but he was a suspicious man. To him, everyone was a security threat. He looked at Ray Jergins without a greeting of any kind. His eyes scanned Mike and Steve, registered a faint recognition and nodded to each of them.

"Sure, Ray. I remember you two. A few years back, right?"

"Yeah, it's been a while." Mike shoved his hands into his pockets and glanced at the floor.

Mort smiled. "Well, that's a good thing. People don't come to see me unless we're almost completely off the rails." He snickered at his own joke, and then he became intensely serious. "What is it?"

"Mort, we need to find a single cell phone somewhere on the other side of the globe."

Mort just stared at him. "Somewhere? Can you be more specific?" While he spoke his eyes shifted to Mike and Steve as if he was checking out their security levels.

Ray drew in a long breath. "At this point we think it's somewhere west of Malaysia."

"Somewhere west of Malaysia. That covers a lot of territory, Ray. Tell me more."

He told the story of Sheriff Hitchens and how he had made contact with his son. He included the information on the stolen device and the danger it posed if in the wrong hands.

"The USURP device."

"You know about that?" Ray asked stepping toward Mort's office chair.

"Hey, secret is what we do. We *know* secrets."

"Right. And I'm drunk." Ray seated himself clumsily in a nearby chair.

"If we are looking for a cell tower somewhere west of Malaysia we really have very few choices. Most of it's ocean." He looked at Mike and Steve. "You know that, right?"

"Oh, yes." Mike nodded. Then he said softly to Steve, "This guy thinks we're idiots."

"Compared to him, we are."

"I heard that," Mort replied without looking back at them again. "I don't think you're idiots. I'm just not sure what clearance you have to be here."

"They're good, Mort. Don't worry."

"Says the drunk." He didn't even pause in his typing. As he gently stroked the keys the vast screen shifted and spun across the globe. It passed over Africa and slowed to a stop over the Indian Ocean. "If we look at the land masses, there isn't much to land an airliner on. We are talking about Malaysian Air MH425, right?"

Ray was startled. "Well, yes. How did—"

"Addition is not a secret science, Ray."

"Addition?"

"Yeah. You know, putting two and two together."

Mike looked at Steve and grinned. "The top secret guru speaks in riddles."

"I heard that too." Mort finished his flurry on the keyboard. "The largest land mass is the southern tip of India. I don't think that would be a good choice for hijackers. The most likely place one could land a plane undetected and still have cell phone connection is at this unfinished airport in the Maldives."

"How did you know that?" Steve asked. "I mean, that was quick."

Mort looked at Steve, then at Ray. Ray shrugged his shoulders and waved his hand giving Mort permission to reveal the information.

"We've been using it for several years. After the father and son who were building the airport went broke and construction stopped, we decided we could slip all sorts of stuff in under the radar, especially in the dead of night. Which it is over there right now. It's a perfect spot. You can sneak in, and then call your mom and tell her you'll be late for dinner."

"Okay, what's next?" Ray asked.

"I need a phone number."

Maamigili, Maldives – 2:00 AM MYT

Darkness was their best friend and their worst nightmare. Robert knew their pursuers would be difficult to see. He also knew those looking for them would have difficulty seeing them in the pre-dawn darkness.

He spoke to Failak in Arabic. "We don't know if they have night vision equipment or not. We must keep a low profile at all times."

Failak nodded his response. Their speech was not covered by darkness. Even the softest whispers could give their location away.

Robert and Failak scanned the tarmac between their hiding spot and where the plane had been. Nothing moved. The light was too dim to highlight anything on the ground.

"There!" Robert whispered. He pointed toward the place the men had knelt to fly the plane into the night. They faintly saw three large forms spread out across the tarmac.

The threesome hugged the pavement beneath them.

The radio in Robert's hand suddenly chirped. No one spoke to him through the small unit, but the signal was loud enough to reveal the direction of their hideout.

"Turn it off!" Yolanda demanded in an urgent, but hushed voice. "They can hear that, can't they?"

He was already fumbling in the darkness for the off switch.

The radio chirped again. Then, a voice spoke.

"We're coming for you, Robert."

Robert found the switch too late. The scratchy sound of the transmission echoed through the unfinished building. He heard a shout and the sound of footsteps on the concrete runway.

"We have to move *now!*"

Robert grabbed Yolanda's hand and pulled her to her feet. They pressed their backs against the interior wall of the building. Failak followed his lead. Between them was the open span of a window without glass.

Robert motioned with his arm to move, keeping the walls between them and the plane. *Maybe, just maybe the use of night vision wasn't a part of their planning.* They ducked and ran toward the far side of the large, unfinished room.

He heard shouts. Had they been seen? The footsteps behind them were quicker. The pursuers were coming closer!

Failak reached the far side of the building before Robert and Yolanda. He leaned against the interior wall. When Robert stopped on the opposing side of another window, Failak nodded at the ground on the other side of the wall. It was twenty feet below them.

"You go down," Failak said. "I will lower your woman to you."

Robert quickly slipped over the edge and dangled the full length of his body. The drop was still more than twelve feet to the dirt. He dropped.

The sensation of falling was hidden by the dark around him. But the jolt of hitting the ground jarred every joint. He stood slowly, checking every limb for any injury. He was fine.

"Okay, lower her down."

Failak knelt beside the opening and held his arm up for Yolanda to grab.

She hesitated, looking from Failak's urgent gaze to the darkness where she hoped her husband would be. "Robert?" she called faintly.

"Take his arm, babe. I will catch you."

Yolanda got on her knees beside Failak. He grabbed her wrist with a vice-like grip and pulled her to the edge. She cried out.

"Shhh!" he insisted.

Yolanda slipped over the edge, suspended in Failak's strong hold.

"Ready?" he asked in Arabic.

"Ready."

A small squeal escaped from her as she fell into Robert's arms.

"Are you all right?" he whispered.

"Yes, I think so," she replied rubbing her arm.

Overhead, Failak spoke to Robert. "Now, you go. I will catch up with you later."

Failak's silhouette vanished into the shadows.

"Failak!" Robert called softly. "Failak!" No response.

He was gone.

White House Lower Basement – 3:05 PM EST

"There he is." Mort leaned back from his screen. The last twenty minutes had been dedicated to pinging a specific cell phone at an unknown location on the other side of the planet. It had worked. "Do you want to call him?"

"No!" Mike replied urgently. "We don't know their situation. Are they in harm's way? Are they being pursued? Just mark the location and have it ready for an Evac team."

"Consider it done." Mort tapped his keyboard and locked the screen shot showing the precise coordinates of the cell phone.

Mike's phone began to buzz.

"It's the pictures from President Makin." Mike opened the first picture. The image showed President Ronald Hunter standing with a man Mike could easily identify as the suspect *Kouzen*. "That's him. No doubt about it."

He held the phone for Steve to see the image. Steve looked at the picture and back at Mike. "No doubt."

"Whatcha got?" Ray asked returning to Mort's workstation.

Mike held up his phone. "The pictures from President Makin."

Ray took Mike's phone. "Damn. Hasn't changed very much, has he?"

"What about an evacuation effort?"

"Officially, we don't have any assets available to rescue American citizens in trouble. Fortunately, we do have a couple of teams on alert pending the discovery of the USURP device."

"Wouldn't you know it? Save the equipment; to hell with the taxpayers," Steve added with a huff.

"Don't blame the soldiers. It's standing protocol. Do you know how many innocent American citizens are being held in Iran right now?"

"No." Steve had seen the effects of bad protocol and poor rules of engagement when he was in Iraq. He also knew who had been the source. "It doesn't matter how many. It's still too many."

"And the Evac team?" Mike asked again.

"Right. We'll need to contact both Langley and the joint chiefs."

"That means August White needs to be brought in on this, right?"

"I'm afraid so, Mike."

"I don't know what it is, Ray, but that guy just rubs me raw. I don't feel I can trust him. Know what I mean?"

"I know. But he's on our side. We have to trust him."

chapter 33

August White waited patiently to catch President Hunter's eye. The phone call he had received made him nervous. He needed to talk to the president.

The marching band from Springfield, Missouri, drew the president's attention with its display of flags and props. The new president and his wife were riveted on the performance.

August White impatiently stood beside David Carapella.

"Would you please tell President Hunter this is important? I need to speak with—"

"Not during a performance. I have explicit instructions to not disturb him during a performance, even that of a marching band from Missouri."

The inaugural parade contained a performing group from every state in the union. It was not unusual for the new president's home state to receive additional honors for more than one entry, and this parade was not an exception. Five entries from Virginia made their way past the reviewing stand to the delight of the president and his wife.

Finally, the band concluded their presentation and marched away. Carapella stepped beside the president and spoke softly in his ear. Hunter glanced back to see August White waiting. He said something to his wife, stood and walked toward White.

"Augie, good to see you. What a day, right? Man, did you see those kids? They were fantastic. We didn't do stuff like that when I was in high school. Wow. They were good." Hunter was beaming. August wasn't.

"Mr. President, there is an urgent issue we need to discuss."

"Today? Oh, not now, Augie. This is a celebration!"

"No, sir. You need to know this now."

The color drained slightly from Hunter's face. A faint cringe wrinkled his brow, and he drew very close to White.

"All right. Give it to me head-on," he said placing his hand on August White's shoulder. The president's eyes bore steadily into White's. "What is it?"

"The plane." White's voice was low. "They made it to the Maldives and recovered the device, as planned. But someone survived."

"How the hell could that—"

"No one knows. This is all coming from Mike Trapper at NSA. I don't know exactly what's happening, but somehow *he* knows, and there is a scramble for a recovery operation."

"Recovery? What do you mean?"

"We had two teams on alert to recover the device. It's protocol since Benghazi. Somehow Trapper found out where the device was. The two teams have been activated."

"Will the recovery teams get there before the plane takes off again?"

"No, maybe. I think the plane is already gone. I've got to call Gentry."

"So, it's a problem because of the witness, the guy who survived."

"That's what I think."

"Then get in contact with your team and have them *finish* their job." The jubilation had drained from the president's expression.

August kept his face turned away from the crowd and those in the reviewing stand. Hunter followed his cue but his agitated gestures had drawn attention.

"Okay, take a breath, Ron. People are watching you."

"You're right." President Hunter smiled broadly and turned just enough toward the street that anyone looking would see him happy. "I got it. I just don't want one lucky stiff to mess up this whole plan we have with Dmitri. We have to make the deal work."

Hunter turned toward the next float moving past the stand. He smiled, pointed at the float and waved with his left hand. His right hand tightly gripped August's shoulder. "Don't mess this up, Augie. Don't mess this up."

August's face didn't reflect the pain that lingered in his right shoulder as the president returned to his oversized seat.

I didn't mess anything up, Ronnie. But it is one lucky son of a bitch on the plane that just might do exactly that.

White House, NSA Office – 3:25 PM EST

Mike and Steve watched the news reports about the lost Malaysian airliner. Mike was conflicted between his concern for the passengers and the need for tight security. Bringing August White into the circle of those seeing the intelligence was a risk, but it was necessary.

"Are you thinking talking to White was a mistake?" Steve asked.

"Probably. I don't know what else we could do. We have to have the troops go in for evacuation of the passengers and regain control of the device. He was the only way."

Mike flipped the channel to CNN to watch the inaugural parade coverage. The first shot on the screen was of the reviewing stand. President Hunter's seat was empty.

"Huh. Where's the president?"

"What?"

"The president. He's not in his seat."

Steve moved next to Mike and looked over his shoulder.

"Wait. Is that him over by the exit?"

"Where?"

"Just to the right. There are two men standing by the door. Do you see them?"

"Yeah, but that could be anything." Steve sauntered back to his seat.

"Anything can always be something, Steve." Mike leaned back in his chair and looked at his friend. "But it just isn't a normal day. This whole thing isn't normal. The plane vanishing. Perry Hitchens calling to tell us he talked to his son who is on the lost plane. We ping Robert's phone on the other side of the planet and find out he's in the Maldives, thousands of miles from where he's supposed to be, and the president is not watching his parade. On a day like today, it seems that everything is something important."

"You mean like the president being out of his seat?"

"Could be. What's so important that could draw him away?"

"Maybe he's just getting an update on stuff, who knows?"

"Steve, ole buddy, Hunter is up to his neck in this deal. I'm just not—"

Mike stopped mid-sentence. The CNN camera slowly zoomed in on the reviewing stand. Not just the stand, but on Hunter's empty seat.

"Look. Look what they're doing. The director is probably wondering where the president has gone."

"Wait. What?" Steve sprang from his seat and again looked over Mike's shoulder.

The camera shot paused on the two throne-like chairs for President and Mrs. Hunter. She was seated and applauding the parade, smiling broadly. Then the camera slowly panned to the right, toward the entrance into the stand, toward the two men standing by the entrance. At that moment, one of the men turned and flashed a championship smile.

"Holy crap! It's Hunter and White!"

"Where?" The picture was from a distance, but there was no question in either Steve's or Mike's minds that the president was talking to August White.

"Well, there goes the security on all this."

"Mike, you don't think the president would release sensitive information, do you? I mean, even by accident?"

"No. What bothers me is that now the president knows that we told White about Robert Hitchens surviving that flight. Everyone else thinks the plane crashed somewhere. What if there aren't supposed to be any survivors?"

Steve's stare froze with Mike's words. "The six American guys Commissioner Sim told us about."

"Right. Not to mention the device, and the guy carrying it. Who is he? Why was he on that particular flight? Did he survive the flight like Robert did?"

"Did the plane disappear *because* the device was on it?"

"We need to talk to Robert Hitchens." Mike turned to his desk and began searching for the number.

White House North Lawn – 3:40 PM EST

August White knew the plan had to be carried out completely. Some of it was bound to be messy, unfortunately. In his mind that was simply what life was, messy.

Too bad all those people just had to fly on that plane. People make dumb choices. Some of those choices can get you killed.

He pulled his satellite phone from the breast pocket of his suit coat. He stood out in the open, in broad daylight, right in front of the White House to make a call that could put him and his boss in prison. He thought it was hilarious.

Right under their noses. Once we get this cleaned up, the party can really begin.

August White had the number on autodial. He pushed it.

Maamigili, Maldives – 2:00 AM MYT

Brad Gentry moved slowly across the tarmac toward the unfinished building that sprawled beside the runway. If the building were ever finished this would be the ramp area where passenger planes would leave their travelers. As it was, the area was solid concrete blanketed in darkness.

He moved slowly to silence his footsteps. His breath was shallow. The pounding of his heart threatened to muffle a distant sound that would reveal the location of those he pursued.

He knew Robert Hitchens. They had been in the Navy together. Both men were SEALs. Both men were among the best with the skills they possessed. Brad Gentry was not certain he could beat Robert's speed. Then again, if anyone could it might be him.

His two surviving teammates, Jace and Neal, were spread out to his right across the concrete slab. He could barely make out their forms in the darkness. Fifty yards separated them, but in the shadows, it could have been a mile.

The last sounds he had heard had come from the cavernous concrete shell he assumed would someday be a concourse of the airport. Those faint sounds had sent Gentry and his men on their present course. Somewhere in the murky night ahead of them, their targets were hiding.

The satellite phone in his pocket vibrated. *Damn! Who the hell—*

Gentry knelt on one knee and cupped his hand over the mouthpiece to muffle his voice.

"What?" Rage fomented just under the surface.

"Gentry, it's August White in DC."

"What in the name of God are you doing?"

"I needed an update. What's happening with the passenger who survived?"

If White had been standing in front of him he would have killed him on the spot.

"Not now!" Gentry whispered into the phone. "We're searching for them right now."

"Them? Don't you mean *him*?"

Gentry gritted his teeth, stifling the urge to scream at White.

"No. There were three of them. Don't ask me how, but they killed Curtis, Jeff, and Wells and left the bodies in their seats. One of them is a Navy SEAL."

"Three of them? Well, that's not good. Just take care of it. That's why you got the job. Now finish it!"

The line clicked off.

Gentry growled out a deep breath and slowly rose from his knee to a crouched position. He moved forward.

*   *   *   *   *

Robert and Yolanda had made their way along the backside of the concrete concourse on the far side away from the runway. The terrain was what one might expect at a construction site. Piles of earth and sand had been dumped indiscriminately atop bricks, discarded reinforcement rods, and rough chunks of concrete. Someday it would all be buried and topped with green sod.

Robert's perspective of where the plane had been was only in his head. He wasn't certain how far they had moved in the last ninety minutes. Every sound around them was threatening. Any sound from the empty building or the runway on the other side was dangerous.

Yolanda gripped his hand and remained silent the entire time. He knew she was terrified. Her actions mimicked his every move.

He heard a voice. It was muffled, distant, and angry. *Are they arguing?*

Robert took advantage of the distraction and moved quickly through the rubble pulling Yolanda behind him. He could make a reckoning from the voice he had heard and decided his best move was to get around and to the right side of the man talking.

They moved, stopped, listened, and moved again.

His cell phone rang.

No, no, no. Not now!

Stephen T. Gerdel

*   *   *   *   *

Neal held the far -right position of the three-man advance toward the concourse. He had heard nothing, seen nothing. He was closest to the building of the three men. He hated the night.

Neal had been a part of hundreds of night patrols during his time in Iraq. Door-to-door searches in both day and night left him as good as a poster boy for PTSD. Since returning from the fight he had learned he was good for nothing except the fight. As the war had wound down he found work with special teams performing military tactics outside of generals' and government oversight.

This assignment was supposed to be a catwalk. Ride in the plane, kill all the people, collect the equipment, and dump the plane. Easy.

This isn't easy. I hate dark.

A cell phone rang in the distance to his left. Neal gasped and turned toward the sound. His radio sputtered to life.

"Okay, I've got a fix on them. Neal, come toward me. Jace, wait for Neal and come toward me. Now move!"

Neal recognized Gentry's voice and turned to move in his direction.

Darkness exploded in front of him. The ten-inch blade of a knife was thrust into his throat, the very tip of which pressed against spine.

A shadowy form wrenched the knife from his neck and moved away. Neal slowly fell into permanent darkness.

*   *   *   *   *

Failak moved quickly toward the man in the middle. His stealth had given him the advantage. While the horrible men who had murdered hundreds on the plane searched for Robert and Yolanda, Failak had worked the darkness, using it to position himself for his attack.

He had moved swiftly and without mercy. He was trained to attack brutally. All of his life he had been told the stories of jihad going back centuries in his people's quest to bring the light of Allah to the world.

The old stories of what the Europeans had called the Crusades were some of his favorites as a boy. The pasty white men had covered their bodies with metal, providing themselves only small openings through which to see. He would laugh imagining the sight.

The warriors for jihad were much faster and could attack a single rider from several directions, never from the front. They would inflict wounds in the steel-covered man's side and back until he would crash to the ground, weak from the loss of blood.

Failak had trained for years to be fast and merciless. The first man he killed this night was surprised and found himself dead before he knew what had struck him.

He now ran toward the second man. This attack would also be brutal and final. Death was his companion tonight, and Failak was Death's servant.

He could make out the form of his next victim.

Why is he just standing there? Does he not see I am coming at him?

The man stood still, watching Failak's approach. He raised his right hand almost as a sign of greeting.

Failak did not slacken his pace. He was close enough to see the man's eyes. They widened, and his mouth began to open. In one ferocious sweep Failak's blade separated the man's head from his body. Failak heard the thump of the head as it struck the concrete and a second ruffling sound as the body sank to the tarmac.

Failak moved away quickly into the shadows.

chapter 34

Carrier Strike Group Five, Indian Ocean – 4:00 AM MYT

The giant Sikorsky SH-60B Sea Hawk slowly lifted from the flight deck of the USS Ronald Reagan loaded with eleven battle-hardened Navy SEALs. Every man knew they were on a mission to save one of their own.

The side hatch slammed shut. Overhead the giant props swept limply across the carrier deck, ever stiffening as their speed increased.

"Razor Hawk 60, this is Flight. You are cleared for liftoff. Over."

"Roger that, Flight. Razor Hawk 60 is dustup."

The massive machine rose from the flight deck with a pounding, thunderous roar amid the screaming of the twin turbine engines. The chopper seemed to bob in the air suspended above the deck. The motion of the aircraft carrier added eeriness to the pre-dawn liftoff.

"Cleared the deck. Bring him home safely, boys. Flight out."

Razor Hawk 60 rotated, veering left and out over the open sea. The engines screamed to full throttle rising only a couple hundred feet above the level of the deck. Coordinates had been entered into the navigational system from Navy Rescue in Washington DC. The plan was simple. Make the flight, collect the package, and head home.

Three miles to the east a second chopper lifted from the deck of the USS Gerald R. Ford, the newly commissioned super-carrier on its maiden tour with Carrier Strike Group Five. The Black Hawk HH-60W carried heavier armaments than the Sea Hawk and fewer Marines. Their mission was to ensure the success of Razor Hawk 60.

The Marines on the Black Hawk were prepared to fast-rope and engage any hostile fire. The ship itself was armed to battle a significant ground force with the same targeting system that had been used in the Wahkan Corridor.

The seemingly small force of two choppers and eighteen warriors was more than capable of meeting the objective. Success is never a guarantee, but preparation and heavy munitions turned the odds in their favor.

The two helicopters swept above the black of night, waves endlessly undulating below them. They were an hour from their destination.

OCT Little Rock – 4:05 PM CST

Colonel Stevens and Keith Dillon hunched over the tabled screen in the grid room. Ninety minutes earlier Keith had seen a most unexpected flash on the screen. It was identical to the signal that had led them to follow the backpack from high in the Hindu Kush Mountains.

"You're sure you saw something," Stevens asked for the tenth time.

"Positive. We can look at the tape . . . again, and confirm it if you like."

Stevens let out a long breath. "No. Don't need to do that . . . again. Why do you think it was the same beacon?"

"Same register, same frequency. You know, they're almost like fingerprints."

Keith's eyes were glued to the screen seeking a flicker of light, any signal that might lead them back to the USURP device.

"Why do you think that plane could have made it to the Maldives? I don't think a single agency is searching this far west."

"That's why we get the big bucks and all the dames. We think differently from most other folks. Pretty sure I have a diagnosis to prove it."

"A diagnosis? I can vouch for you as definitely certifiable."

The two men remained bent over the table. The satellite feed was not very reliable or current. Most of the attention was focused on the eastern Indian Ocean and the waters around Malaysia. The plane had vanished from radar less than nine hours earlier, and the search boundaries had been extended several times. Each expansion demanded more men and equipment, more eyes looking for signs of wreckage, looking for bodies.

Keith stood erect and stretched his back. His long, lanky frame was more suited for reaching that bending.

"Do you think we should go back and look at the HOP data from Langley?" Since the mid 1990s satellites had been photographing planet earth. High Observation Photos, or HOP, eventually gave rise to many of the digitized mapping systems available on the Internet for anyone to see.

But HOP data is thoroughly screened before it is made available to the public through Google Earth, Bing Maps, or many other mapping services. The pictures can provide easily overlooked intelligence especially when confusion is leading the program.

Stevens sat back from the table and rubbed his eyes. "Do we have access?"

"We can procure the last twelve hours of photos of just about any place on the globe. All we have to do is ask. I mean, you have to ask." Keith smiled limply.

"And you have someplace in mind?"

"Of course."

"May I ask what you would like to see?"

"Sir, we've been looking at occasional live feed of the Maldives for the last hour. How about we start there and see what we can find."

"My command is for your wish."

"Golly, colonel, that was almost funny."

Stevens's phone rang before he could pick it up to make his call to Langley.

"Colonel Stevens."

"Hey, Aaron. Daniel Sim."

"Hi, Daniel. Any good news?"

"None. Our entire agency is grieved by the fact that the mysterious criminal known as *Kouzen* has slipped through our grasp."

"Well, that stinks. Sorry, Daniel. I guess it's a day we score one for the bad guys."

"More like two. Malaysian Air MH425 is a total bust. No sign of any wreckage anywhere."

"We haven't given up on that one quite yet. I'll let you know what we find, if we find it."

"Thanks, Aaron." He hung up.

"What stinks?" Keith asked.

"*Kouzen* slipped through their net."

"Ouch. That does stink."

"But we still have work to do. I'll call Langley."

Maamigili, Maldives – 4:30 AM MYT

The cold hard fact that he was alone finally sank into Brad Gentry's angry mind. He had waited for his teammates to join him. They never did. Frustration and impatience finally overwhelmed him, and he went looking. He had found the pieces.

He knelt in the dark. The first glimmers of dawn had begun to tint the eastern horizon. Soon he would be able to see. He would also be able to be seen. The tarmac offered no hiding place.

How did Robert sneak around me to kill Jace and Neal? The thought haunted him. He had dismissed the courier as any potential threat. *No Afghani rag-headed rebel could possibly master those two guys. But how did Robert do it?*

The thought hit him from a blind spot. The knife. One of his men on the plane, Curtis, had been throat slit from ear to ear. The knife. *It was the courier! And he's still out there.*

Gentry was suddenly alert to a new threat. Now he was outnumbered. No one had his back. No one was coming to help.

Maintaining a low profile, he scurried across the ramp toward the center of the unfinished terminal. Daylight was coming. He had limited time to find Robert and kill him. That's what he had to do. He had to kill Robert Hitchens.

OCT Little Rock – 4:25 PM CST

The files arrived from Langley. Immediately Keith loaded the satellite shots into the system and began to single out the timestamps that drew their interests.

"The time difference isn't exactly twelve hours, is it?" Stevens asked.

"Twelve hours and fifty minutes, exactly."

"What was the time when you saw that signal?"

Keith stood up and gazed off into the distance as he did the mental math. "Our time, it was twelve twenty-fiveish. PM. Give or take. That would make it one thirty-five in the middle of the night . . .ish."

Colonel Stevens scanned through the digital files until he arrived at one thirty-five a.m. in the Maldives.

"Okay. Here's the approximate time you saw the signal you believe is from the device."

"How far can we zoom in?" Keith knew. It was rhetorical.

"You're kidding me, right?"

Keith grinned. "Just wanted your input." Keith tapped the keyboard entering the coordinates that matched those of the signal. The view blurred and zoomed to an altitude of two thousand feet.

"Looks like a runway."

"Nothing there, is there?"

"Nope." Keith stood and scratched his head. "I did say *ish*, right?"

"That you did. What is the time on the next picture?"

"Going forward or back?"

"I'm going to guess *back*."

"Good choice, colonel. It's fifteen minutes."

They repeated the process, entering the coordinates, then zooming in. What appeared made them both smile and take a breath.

In the precise same spot that was empty fifteen minutes later, sat a full sized Malaysian Air Boeing 777.

Maamigili, Maldives – 4:45 AM MYT

Robert and Yolanda sat close together against a concrete wall. The grey mist of morning hung around them like a foreboding shroud. Sunlight had touched the highest atmosphere dispensing a colorless sheen on the darkness.

"Do you know where he has gone?" Yolanda shivered under the early morning chill. She had left her beautiful shawl on the plane.

"I'm not sure what's going on, honey. I don't know where those three men went, and I wish I knew what has happened to Failak."

"But he's okay, don't you think?"

"I hope." Robert and Yolanda had escaped the three men who had pursued them after the plane took off. But in their hurry to find a hiding place they had lost track of where the men were. "Listen. I want you to stay right here. I don't want you to move. I'm going to look around for a minute."

"No, Robert! Don't leave me alone."

"You won't be alone. I'll be very close. Just stay here."

"You come right back, do you hear me?" Her voice was too loud.

"Shh. I'll be right back."

Robert slipped into the murky darkness. Yolanda watched until he vanished in the shadows. She wrapped her arms around her shoulders to warm herself. *He had better come right back here. I will wait, but he'd better—"*

She heard a scraping sound to her left. Her breath was short. She strained her eyes into the gloomy haze. Her ears wrestled the silence, listening for any revealing sound. Nothing. The silence became more frightening with every second Robert was gone.

She forced herself to think of their time on the beach at Shangri-La. She thought about their last sunset. She smiled. She could feel the tension easing from her. Just the thought of Robert comforted her.

Yolanda blushed as she remembered being angry with his halting response about her new dress. She smiled and softly laughed at the memory of the look on his face when she slammed the door. She had been mean to him. She snickered.

Her plans for their first evening at home began to shape in her mind. She would treat him like royalty. He would think he was the luckiest man on—

"Hello there, sweetie pie." The barrel of a gun pressed against her neck.

NSA Office, White House – 5:30 PM EST

Mike waited as the phone at Mid West OCT continued to ring. *That's not like Aaron. Wonder what's up?*

"Stevens."

"Aaron, this is Trapper in DC."

"I was just going to call you. We found the plane."

"You found it? Where?"

"We didn't exactly find it, we found where it *was*."

"The Maldives?"

Aaron paused. "You knew that?"

"More suspected it. We didn't have any proof other than a ping of a cell phone. What did you see?"

"We picked up a signal exactly like the ones we received from the Wahkan Corridor. You know, when someone handles the device and their body heat sets it off?"

"Right. We saw those on the tapes from Langley."

"That put us on the trail for some physical evidence. We ordered the HOP data for the last twelve hours. That's when we found the plane. But the picture taken fifteen minutes later showed a blank runway."

"It was gone?"

"Yup. I think they used the USURP device to dump the evidence somewhere in the ocean."

Mike wasn't surprised. In his mind the plan was morbidly brilliant. Steal the equipment, and then use it to fly the plane and its victims into a watery tomb.

"You there, Mike?"

"Yeah, sorry. One problem. We know there is at least one surviving passenger who got off the plane."

"You're kidding. Who was it?"

"Robert Hitchens and we think his new wife. You remember, she was the woman who witnessed the attack of the Dallas police station a few years ago."

"From what I read in the reports, Hitchens isn't someone you'd want to tick off."

"He's a tough warrior."

"So, you think he is alive?"

"Yes. The pentagon just activated two rapid response teams from aircraft carriers in the Indian Ocean. Can you send me the HOP data?"

"Sure. You have the clearance, right?"

"As of noon, I got a raise, so, yeah."

"They're on their way."

chapter 35

"Hitchens!" Gentry wrestled a struggling Yolanda from the shadows into the light of early dawn. He knew he would be seen. He wanted Robert to see who he was holding and the way his hand groped her.

Yolanda fought with every step. "You let go of me, you miserable son-of-a—"

"Now, now. That's no way to talk to your hubby's old Navy buddy." He pulled her harder against himself, increasing his grip on her breast. "Hitchens! Look here old friend, old pal. I got your little lady right here, just not for you this time. Come on out you big, brave, Navy man."

"Don't do it, Robert! He has a gun!"

"You little—" Gentry angrily grabbed her face with the hand holding the weapon. He pushed the metal hard against her face, causing her to cry out.

"Gentry!" Robert yelled as he stepped from behind a concrete wall twenty feet away. "What are you doing? What's your point?"

"Well. . ." Gentry smiled. "Been a while, hasn't it, Robert?"

"What do you think you're doing, Brad?"

"So, now it's *Brad*," Gentry spat in a mocking tone. "I don't suppose you remember the last time we met? Don't imagine you remember what you did?"

"I remember. But that has absolutely nothing to do with her. Let go of her."

"Oh, no, sailor boy. Oh, no. You have messed up my entire operation here. I'm going to finish my business, and while you are bleeding to death, I have some real interesting things to do with little missy here."

Yolanda fought against his grip even harder, biting his hand that gripped the gun.

"Damn you, girl. You just made your day a little more difficult."

"Gentry, let her go. This is between you and me. Let's finish it right here, right now, just the two of us."

Gentry laughed coarsely. "Oh, you mean like a fair fight where we each go into our corners and come out swinging? No way in hell am I gonna do that. I have a schedule to meet. A job to finish."

"There is no need for that, Gentry—"

"Need? Who said anything about *need*? I'm going to shoot you so you can't move, and the only thing you'll be able to do is bleed. While you watch, your little sweetheart and I are gonna have some fun."

Gentry raised his pistol toward Robert.

At that moment a screaming rage broke from the shadows behind Gentry. He turned half around to see Failak charging him with his ten-inch knife. As he swung back toward Robert to fire, Yolanda slammed her head back against his face. The shot went wide.

Failak charged faster toward Gentry.

Gentry's face was bloody. Yolanda threw her head against his face again and fought to knock him off balance.

Gentry fired at Failak. *Bang! Bang! Bang!* The shots went wild.

Robert charged from the other direction.

Gentry spun toward him and fired hitting Robert in the left shoulder.

He swung around to face Failak. *Bang! Bang!*

Both shots struck Failak in the chest at almost point-blank range. He staggered and fell against Yolanda and Gentry. He smiled at her, and then slid to the ground.

In an instant Robert struck from behind. His impact threw Robert, Gentry, and Yolanda sprawling across the tarmac, the concrete ripping the skin on their hands and knees.

Robert was up first. Gentry pointed the gun at him and pulled the trigger. The gun clicked. He faced Robert with blood streaming down his face, fully enraged. Gentry threw the empty pistol, sending it skittering across the pavement. And with a mighty growl, he charged.

Robert's skills were rusty and limited by the wound in his shoulder. But he was very fast. His first move deflected Gentry's charge, causing him to stumble forward and again fall to the tarmac.

However diminished Robert's ability may have been, Gentry's were more so. It was something Gentry didn't realize until he smashed into the runway the second time.

He got up, covered in his own blood and filled with unreasonable rage.

"Think you're pretty fast, do ya?" Gentry sneered, wiping his face with his sleeve.

Robert had positioned himself between Gentry and Yolanda. He wasn't going to move, and Gentry wasn't going to get past him.

Again, Gentry charged, driven by jealous madness. His grasp never came close to Robert.

Robert's first jab was to Gentry's throat, crushing his windpipe. The impact of Robert's fist stunned Gentry and left him gasping for air. But only for a moment. The second strike was to the temporal mandible joint. The force of the blow separated the jaw bone from its socket, and sent the jagged edge of the bone into the brain stem. His signature kill.

Gentry dropped to the pavement and didn't move again.

Robert fell to one knee and gripped his bleeding shoulder. Yolanda ran to his side. The shot had opened the axillary artery and nicked the cephalic vein. The bleeding was heavy. Yolanda ripped her belt from her waist, wrapped it around Robert's arm and pulled as hard as she could.

The bleeding slowed and then stopped. She fell against him exhausted. He held her with his strong arm. "I love you, babe."

She sobbed.

In the distance they heard the drumming approach of two giant helicopters.

Robert looked toward the sound and saw the Sikorsky and the Black Hawk emerge from the twilight.

Help had arrived.

NSA Office, White House – 5:40 PM EST

The HOP data was the final piece. The grainy picture provided proof that Malaysian Air MH425 had landed at an unused airport in the Maldives. It was reasonable to assume the device was the instrument used to remotely fly the plane to a watery grave hundreds of miles out in the sea.

"How do we deal with this?" Mike asked. "This bit of information would confirm the existence of a top secret piece of equipment. We can't do that."

"Not even for the families of the people who died on that plane?"

"I don't know, Steve. Ultimately, it's not my call."

"You mean it belongs to President Hunter."

"Afraid so. Think about it. If the existence of the USURP device becomes public knowledge, questions would arise about how it was lost. Where was it lost? Who took it? Why? Who was going to purchase it? And the worst of all, who was trying to sell it?"

"And then *Kouzen* comes into the picture, and someone discovers his true identity. That links everything back to President Hunter."

"Yup."

"Mike, it will never see the light of day."

"True. But the other side is that *someone* didn't make the sale and have a payday. And someone else is going to be pissed they didn't get the promised package. It doesn't look like smooth sailing for the new administration."

"So, it stops here?"

"We'll see."

Maamigili, Maldives – 4:45 AM MYT

Robert and Yolanda were surrounded by SEALs and Marines moments after the choppers landed. The medic tended to Robert's wounds while the others took fingerprints and pictures of the dead men on the tarmac.

"Mr. Hitchens, there's one still alive over here." The Marine was standing over Failak who was lying in a pool of blood.

"Quick, I'm fine. Get over to that man and see if you can help him," Robert said to the medic. Yolanda helped Robert to his feet, and they moved to Failak's side.

The medic examined the wounds on Failak's body. He spoke softly to Robert. "Too much damage, too much blood lost. Too far away from anything that would really help. Sorry."

Robert knelt beside his strange friend. They spoke in Arabic.

"You Americans always give me trouble," Failak said softly. He coughed.

"Thank you, my brother." Robert held his hand and bent close to him. "You saved our lives. I can never repay you."

"I told you she was much too pretty to kill." Failak smiled and laughed at his joke. He coughed again, this time spitting up a little blood.

"You are a brave warrior, Failak."

"Thank you, Robert. Either a brave fighter, or a dead fool."

"Brave is my description."

Failak struggled and pulled at the clothing around his waist.

"No, you need to rest," Robert insisted.

"I am almost gone. No need for rest now when I'm mostly dead." He continued pulling at his clothing.

"What is it? Can I help you?"

"There is a belt . . . money in belt." He coughed violently. It was clear his lungs were filling with blood. "You . . . you take the money."

"No, I can't. It doesn't belong to me."

"It does . . . . now. Take it." The coughing was violent, wracking his already broken body.

Robert looked at the medic. "Can you make him comfortable?"

The medic dropped to a knee and injected morphine into Failak's side.

Failak let out a long deep breath and relaxed. The pain was gone.

"Listen," he said to Robert. "You don't need the money. You are rich American, right?" The next spasm ripped through his body violently. "Take the money to my village in Tajikistan. Make schools, hospital."

"I will, Failak. We will do that with the money."

Failak was quiet. His breathing was labored.

Robert thought it was over until Failak grabbed his sleeve. He bent close again.

"I was waiting for Allah to come and get me, but he hasn't showed up yet." His voice was barely a whisper.

Robert laughed softly. "He'll be here soon."

"Yes, but if he doesn't show up before I leave, the next time you talk to your Jesus, would you mind mentioning me to him?" He wheezed a labored laugh.

Robert could not believe he was watching a dying man make jokes about whether Allah would show up. Robert wiped the tears from his eyes. He looked again at Failak.

He lay still. No breathing. No coughing. No more jokes.

He was dead.

chapter 36

Mike walked the short distance from his office as the National Security Advisor to the president to the Oval Office. In his right hand he gripped his complete file of the events of the last two days.

President Hunter had called him in for a briefing, the first of the new presidency. He had made it clear he preferred having the reports read to him rather than reading the account himself. He had told Mike, "I'm a hands-on sort of guy. We'll be talking a lot, so get used to it."

Mike was used to it. For the last six years he had talked daily with presidents, on the campaign trail and while in office. He was quite used to it.

He pushed open the door to the Oval Office and was greeted by President Hunter and August White. The men were standing close to each other in front of the Resolute Desk. Their discussion ended abruptly when Mike entered.

"Mike, good to see you," the president said walking toward him. His hand was extended and a warm smile lightened his face.

"Thank you, Mr. President. I'm honored to be of assistance." He shook the president's hand and acknowledged his companion. "Mr. White."

"Evening, Mike."

"I appreciate your staying around to brief me on the events regarding the USURP device. I know you have a family waiting for you and I want to respect that."

"Thank you, Mr. President. They all understand the flexibility in hours my job demands. We've been through things like this before."

"I'm sure you have. So, fill me in," the president said as he ushered Mike to one of the couches in front of the Desk.

"It seems everything has turned out well as far as the device goes, but there have been many lives lost through this entire string of events." Mike sat.

"How do you mean 'turned out well'?" White asked, still standing by the Desk.

President Hunter's face darkened as he lowered himself to the couch facing Mike.

"We have the device back in our possession."

Both the president and August White flinched ever so slightly. Mike noticed.

"I thought it was lost? Taken by rogues in the field." White said.

"It was. However, OCT in Little Rock was able to track the device through markers that would set off a locator beacon when it was handled. They were activated by body heat."

"And to where did they track it?" Hunter's face was matter-of-fact. Mike knew he already knew the answer to his own question.

"Malaysia. Specifically, a small airport on the north side of Kuala Lumpur. We suspect that location was selected due to the lower level of security. All flights from the U.S. and European nations are routed to Singapore where security is extremely high."

"So was this airport in Kuala Lumpur easier to smuggle the device through?"

"That's what it seems. Those flights usually carry diplomatic couriers, families, and business people back and forth to Hong Kong and other major Asian cities."

Stephen T. Gerdel

"What about the courier who carried the device? Was he Chinese?"

"No, Mr. President. He was an Afghan soldier who found the device in the Wahkan Corridor where our two Marines were shot."

"One survived, right?"

"Yes, Mr. President. The sergeant was airlifted to Bagram Field in Afghanistan."

"What happened in Kuala Lumpur that tipped us off?" White asked.

"There were a couple of things, but not just in Kuala Lumpur. The evening before the device arrived in Kuala Lumpur, six Chinese agents were murdered in Singapore. They all died from bullets fired from Springfield 1911s, standard CIA handguns."

"But anyone can buy one of those, right?"

"Yes, Mr. President. They are very expensive and many are owned by private citizens."

"So, you believe there could be some American connection?" White asked.

"Possibly. We were able to follow the device as the courier boarded Malaysian Air MH425 yesterday afternoon. Well, we were in the middle of the night here. It was about four-fifteen a.m. here."

"The one that crashed." White's statement seemed more a leading statement than an inquiry.

"That's what everyone believed at first." Mike watched the two men for signs of discomfort, even the slightest twinge of question. He saw a tiny response in both men. "All the search efforts conducted by several countries, including our own military, have failed to find a crash site on land or in the water. At this point, the plane is missing."

"It didn't crash at all, then?"

"No, it didn't, Mr. White. To this point no evidence has been found that it did. In fact, the evidence we have discovered is quite to the contrary."

The pause was brief, but it was well noted.

"Here. Let me show you what we have discovered." Mike sensed the unease within both White and the president. "We have three pieces of evidence that helped us conclude the plane did not crash. First, we were able to ping the cell phone of an American who was on that flight."

"There was an American on MH425?" White asked.

"Actually, there were eight Americans on the plane."

"Whose cell phone did you ping?"

"Mr. President, it belonged to a retired Navy SEAL named Robert Hitchens."

"That name sounds familiar," White said as he moved to the couch beside the president.

"You may have read about him in the incident report from Oklahoma City almost four years ago. That was the first piece of information that directed us away from the Far East."

"Go on," the president urged.

"Secondly, OCT picked up the locator beacon that is activated when someone picks up the device. It was being carried by a person at the exact location of the cell phone ping."

"Do you think this Hitchens fellow is the one who stole the device?" White's question was just a shade too eager. Mike felt he was attempting to direct the conversation.

"No. I think he's the reason we found it."

"Mike, you mentioned a third piece of evidence."

"Yes, Mr. President. The technicians at OCT conducted a search of HOP data that—"

"HOP data?"

"Yes, Mr. President. HOP stands for High Observation Photography that routinely takes snapshots of several places around the world. They aren't very good quality, but just good enough."

"So, they have an actual picture, or something?" White was visibly agitated.

"Yes." Mike pulled out the picture of the Malaysian airliner on the runway.

"Is that MH425?" the president asked looking from the photo to Mike through his eyebrows.

"We believe it is."

308 Stephen T. Gerdel

"But that's just a grainy picture of an airplane. It could be anywhere."

"You're right, Mr. White. But if you notice the coordinates here in the upper right corner, they are the precise location of both the cell phone ping of the passenger who was on that plane, and the beacon set off on the device."

"Where did all this happen?" the president asked sitting back on the couch.

"Maamigili, Maldives. There is an unfinished airport we have used for years for clandestine operations. No radar, no security. Hardly anyone knows it's even there."

The reaction, the flush in the faces in the two men across from him, was unmistakable. Mike knew they were disappointed the device had been recovered.

"Is that it, Mike?" President Hunter asked softly.

"Mostly. We still have the problem of the broker, the guy who set this whole deal up." It was Mike's turn to sit back on the couch.

"You know who that person is?" White was almost perspiring.

"Yes. For months agents in Singapore and the States have been on the trail of a man we believe to be American, but who has dealt as a double agent for both the United States and the Russian Federation. Recently, he had come to be known by the name *Kouzen*. He had other names in different languages, but they all meant the same thing, a first cousin."

The president was tense. He would not make eye contact with Mike.

"With the aid of the India Bureau, Singapore, and believe it or not, President Makin, we were able to identify him as an American citizen. He was originally in the military, graduated up the line into Special Forces, and then struck out on his own. We believe he is the one who set up the original deal with the Chinese. Then he arranged for the Chinese agents who were to collect the device, to be killed and replaced by six Americans—you might call them privately contracted special agents."

The president and White were silent and kept their eyes on the picture of the airliner on the ground in the Maldives.

"Somewhere along the line, the decision was made, or a higher price was offered by the Russians. The job given to the six rough Americans seems to have been to eliminate the Chinese and intercept the device."

"And the crashed airliner?" President Hunter asked, raising his eyes to meet Mike's.

"We believe the Americans used the device to remotely send the plane back into the air on an unknown course, with all passengers aboard."

"Wouldn't the passengers fight or struggle with the hijackers?" White asked.

"I can't be certain, but if you follow the radar information before the plane vanished, you'll see the plane quickly climbed to a very high altitude. High enough to de-pressurize the cabin. The passengers were probably all dead before the plane disappeared from radar."

President Hunter cleared his throat and looked at Mike. "You mentioned President Makin helped you somehow. How was that?"

"After we received confirmation of *Kouzen's* identity we were able to obtain photographs of him, particularly from India. Looking at those photos, President Makin recognized him as a member of his Army unit in Germany, years before. He provided us an old picture where he was standing beside our suspect, *Kouzen*."

"And you know who this elusive spy really is?"

"Yes, Mr. President, we do."

Mike looked directly into the president's eyes. Hunter flinched slightly. That was the second everything came into perfect focus for Mike.

Hunter knew. He knew it all.

Sheriff's Office, Norman OK – 5:20 PM CST

Perry Hitchens had never left his office. He had delegated his responsibilities to others who were more than willing to step in and help. The fear of losing Robert and Yolanda had brought him to near collapse. Everyone in the office had shown concern for their sheriff and the burden he bore.

The phone on his desk rang. It was the line he used for personal calls. Everyone in the station turned toward Sheriff Hitchens.

"Hello." The sheriff's voice was weary, breathy.

"Dad. It's Robert."

The sound of his son's voice was the final stroke. The sheriff collapsed in sobs, sobs of relief and thankfulness. The frayed ends of a father's emotions finally let go.

"Dad?"

"Yes, Robert. I hear you. I'm sorry. I've just been so worried."

"Dad, we're fine. I wanted you to know we made it."

"But, the plane. It crashed, right?"

"We can talk about that later. For now, please get some rest and know we're on our way home."

"But where are you? How will you get here?"

"Don't worry, Dad. A couple dozen Marines showed up to get us home."

"Marines?"

"Yeah, and some SEALs. We're with friends. We're good."

"Okay, if you say so."

"Love you, Dad. See you soon."

The line went dead, but the heart of an old warrior breathed new life into his soul.

Maamigili, Maldives – 5:35 AM MYT

Robert turned off his phone and put his arm around Yolanda. She slipped her arm around his waist. They watched as the Marines gently placed Failak in a body bag for transport.

"Do you think we can do it?" Yolanda asked.

"I don't see how we can't. I mean, he saved our lives by giving his own. It was his dying wish."

Four Marines lifted the black, zipped bag and gently carried it to the Black Hawk. Failak's body would be treated according to

Islamic tradition and transported to his home village for burial. Robert and Yolanda would travel with him.

Yolanda held Failak's money belt in her right hand. She had taken it at his insistence. Together, they vowed the money intended for an evil purpose would be used for a good purpose.

They walked together arm in arm. The procession was solemn, noble. Even the soldiers who had no way of knowing Failak showed respect. They had heard only small parts of what this enemy warrior had done to save the American couple.

He was a hero.

Inaugural Ball – National Air & Space Museum – 8:00 PM EST

Mike's presence at the Inaugural Ball was a requirement. He couldn't skip. As a member of the White House Risk Assessment team and National Security Advisor to the president his presence was mandatory.

He stood at the side of the dance floor with Elli on his right. She looked amazing in her formal. As a mother of four, her daily attire was most likely either jeans or sweats. Tonight, she glowed with elegance.

"I'm not gonna get you out on that dance floor, am I?" she asked him out of the side of her mouth.

"Probably not."

"How about if I just go crazily orgasmic right here? Would that help?"

"You'd probably make a real name for yourself. But, it won't help."

"And if I made a list of torrid sexy promises to entice you?"

"Nope. I'm solid as a rock, right here."

Elli sighed. She loved him. Even the stubborn parts. But she was persistent. She turned toward him.

"Mike! Mike! Mike! Mike! Mi—"

"No! And there is nothing you can do to get me out there." He looked straight ahead. He squirmed a little

"Please, can we dance just once? Please?"

"No." Mike stood at parade rest, his hands folded in front.

"Mike, look at me. Look at this dress." He did.

"I know, honey. You are beautiful. You're always beautiful. Even in jeans."

"But I don't feel beautiful in jeans."

"You look great out of them, that's for sure," Mike said with a bit of a swagger.

She swatted him and stomped her foot. "You lunk. But tonight, I *feel* beautiful, and, Mike, you're ignoring me."

"Elli, no. I'm not ignoring you." He turned toward her. "You know I hate to dance. I'm no good at it. Now *please* stop this before you embarrass yourself." He turned back toward the dancing, folding his hands in front.

Elli grunted and dropped her forehead against his arm in resignation.

President Hunter stepped to Mike's side, close to his side.

"Good evening Mike, Mrs. Trapper."

Elli looked up surprised to see the president. She blushed and quickly repositioned herself to watch those on the dance floor.

"Good evening, Mr. President."

"Beautiful night, wouldn't you say, Mike?"

"Yes, Mr. President. And it's a beautiful event in your honor."

"I wish I could say I had something to do with it."

Mike remained silent.

Finally, the president spoke again.

"You know, regardless of what evidence you find, you won't be able to touch me."

"Yes, Mr. President. I know that."

"I just wanted you to know. And I'll be watching. I'm keeping my eye on you, Mike."

"Yes, sir, Mr. President. I'm pleased to be at your service."

He turned toward Elli. "Sweetheart, may I have this dance?"

He swept her onto the dance floor while the band played on.

Epilogue

Trapper Home – Two Weeks Later

The doorbell rang. It wasn't a bell in any sense. It was the same scratchy buzz that had annoyed Mike since they moved in ten years earlier. Someday he'd fix it.

Mike opened the front door of his home to greet Robert and Yolanda Hitchens. Mike had known Robert as a young boy when Perry Hitchens was deployed with him in Iraq. He had only spoken to Yolanda by phone in the early days of the invasion of the southwest. The meeting was something of a homecoming.

"Robert, so happy you could come. And Yolanda, good to finally meet you."

She hugged Mike. "You saved my life, you know."

"All in a day's work, my dear. All in a day's work."

He escorted his guests into the hallway. Elli greeted them as she came from the kitchen and ushered them through the house to the patio. It was an unusual day in February, one of those unexpected gifts of near summer weather that occasionally help the populace endure the remainder of winter.

Steve and Samantha Granger were waiting on the patio. Steve stood and greeted Robert and Yolanda. Sam remained seated. She was due. Or in her words, "Long overdue."

"Are you rested and healed up from your adventure?" Mike asked as he pulled four cold beers from the cooler.

"No thank you, for me," Yolanda replied.

"The more for us, then."

"My shoulder is still a little stiff, but I'll be back and ready to go soon." Robert rotated his shoulder as he spoke. The bullet had passed through, but the torn muscle and vessels had required surgery. He still hurt.

"He's pretty tough," Yolanda chided. "But I have him wrapped around my little finger."

Everyone laughed.

"She really does."

"How are you feeling, Sam? Is your baby due soon?" Yolanda asked the too obvious question, embarrassing herself. She laughed and blushed.

"Officially it's two days away. For me, this little fella is two weeks late!"

"Lest we bore the gentlemen, why don't we move the girl talk indoors? I have some finishing touches on dinner to make." Elli stood, helped Sam from her comfortable position with minimal complaint, and the three girls stepped inside.

The men sat quietly admiring their women.

Mike broke the quiet.

"Robert, I need to tell you something about your time in the Maldives."

"I figured some explanation would be in order. Let's get it out of the way now."

"Good. You know any mention of the device that Failak carried onto the plane is classified. You cannot speak of it."

"I figured as much. Dad was a little hard to convince. Thank you for calling him."

"He's an old friend. I owe him much more than that."

"You also need to know that the president was involved in a limited way. The men you and Failak killed were working for his cousin. He knows your name and has a file on you. I doubt that anything will come of it, but you need to know."

Mike paused. The knowledge of being presided over by a corrupt president was chilling. He let it sink in.

"You mean, there is nothing that can be done to him even if the evidence gives proof?" Robert asked.

"No. The only way a president can be removed from office is through a vote of impeachment by Congress. In order for that to happen, the existence of a top secret piece of equipment would need to be made public. That's not going to happen."

"I can see that." Robert's eyes dropped to the ground between his feet.

"The other matter that is of grave concern is that we would have to admit that rogue American agents were responsible for the deaths of hundreds of people from many countries. The plane is lost and will probably never be found. Any further information about MH425 would bring serious damage to the president's ability to conduct foreign affairs."

"So, it's pretty sealed shut then?"

"Pretty much, Robert. At least, I can't see another way around all the issues involved." Mike hated bringing such news. "Personally, I'd rather see him fry."

"It fits the 'high crimes and misdemeanors' the Constitution describes," Steve added, "but there is zero will in Congress to embrace another cataclysmic event."

"Does anyone in Congress know about this?"

"Some. Everyone involved with national security knows. Others suspect."

"But they won't do anything."

"No."

The mood was depressing. They had come to a stalemate on the matter. The president and some of those around him were guilty of a horrible crime, but they were also the highest legal officials in the land. Nothing would ever be revealed.

"The inmates are running the asylum," Mike said as he sat up straight, "but here, the beer is cold."

They all raised their glasses in a toast.

Glossary of Terms

HH-60W Black Hawk: Modified version of the UH-60M for the U.S. Air Force as a Combat Rescue Helicopter to replace HH-60G Pave Hawks with greater fuel capacity and more internal cabin space, dubbed the "60-Whiskey".

CHAMP (Counter-Electronics High-Powered Microwave Advanced Missile Projectile) is an operational system that can take down any enemy data centers and infrastructure without blowing anyone up.

The Mahdi ("guided one") is the prophesied redeemer of Islam who will rule before the Day of Judgment (literally, *the Day of Resurrection*) and will rid the world of evil. According to Islamic tradition, the Mahdi's tenure will coincide with the Second Coming of Jesus Christ (Isa) who is to assist the Mahdi against the Antichrist.

Mahdi Islamic State Caliphate (MISC) is a mythical religious war brought on by zealous adherence to ancient tradition. No such state exists at the writing of this text.

Daesh - A derogatory acronym taken from the name "ad-Dawlah al-Islāmīyah fil 'Irāq wa ash-Shām" that is banned by ISIS leaders. It is commonly applied as meaning "bigots who impose their views on others."

Uninterruptible Staging Unit and Remote Piloting System (USURP) is a real system actually called the Boeing Honeywell Uninterruptible Autopilot System. The system is designed and in place to take remote control of airliners in distress. The acronym for the real system just wasn't as much fun.

NOAA – National Oceanic and Atmospheric Agency. Monitors global weather patterns.

VizLab - An operational system used for measuring ground temperatures from space.

Klick – One kilometer measurement.

NSA – National Security Administration

Laser-augmented Airborne Telescopic Unit (LAAT) is a functional system for munitions targeting.

BRITE Star II Turret and Targeting System is a fictional combination of two currently operating systems.

0331 – Zero-three-three-one is the USMC designation for a machine gunner.

Paint it – A term referring to marking a target.

Bravo zulu – Military jargon meaning "good job."

Dust up – Military jargon referring to a helicopter taking off.

Sikorsky SH-60B Sea Hawk – Workhorse helicopter for the U.S. Navy and Many other nations for the last thirty years.

USS Ronald Reagan – U.S. super-carrier assigned to the South Seas with Carrier Strike Group Five command vessel.

USS Gerald R. Ford – The newest U.S. super-carrier on its maiden voyage with Carrier Strike Group Five.

High Observation Photos (HOP) – Totally fictional (I think) data system I created when I needed physical evidence of the plane's location. So, I made it up. It's fiction, right?

www.ingramcontent.com/pod-product-compliance
Lightning Source LLC
Chambersburg PA
CBHW062112170626
46813CB00002B/422